Enticing the Devil

Wright Bastards, Volume 2

Amy Sandas

Published by Amy Sandas, 2022.

ENTICING THE DEVIL

First edition. June 14, 2022.

Copyright © 2022 Amy Sandas.

ISBN: 979-8201275587

Written by Amy Sandas.

This one is for Deena who has inspired me a thousand different times in a thousands different ways. I will always be grateful for our rainy Tuesdays!

Chapter One

August 1820
Redthorne Manor
Buckinghamshire, England

Lady Anne Humphries leaned closer to her subject. Concentration tugged at her brow as she studied the intricate petal formation that gave the bee balm flower its distinctive look.

It was not yet noon and most of the other guests attending the Earl and Countess of Harte's country house party were still keeping London hours, which suited her perfectly. She'd come out to the estate's extensive garden in search of solitude and had found a lovely spot tucked into a quiet little corner where even the gardeners passed by without noticing her presence.

It was there that she'd discovered a butterfly garden with red and purple bee balm, several varieties of coneflower, geraniums, and lush buddleia bushes. After spreading her shawl across the grass to protect her pale blue frock, she'd arranged herself to begin rendering the vibrant summer blooms in watercolor.

Painting was one of the few things—perhaps the only thing—in her life that brought her true contentment. Growing up an only child with a mother who'd died in childbirth, a father who'd visited his child once or twice a year, and an army of servants who'd treated her with a sort of distant kindness, she'd often suffered from bouts of melancholia. At times in her youth, she'd wondered if she even truly existed if there was no one around to *know* her. The act of studying

1

a subject—discovering what made it unique and beautiful—in order to render its image on canvas always seemed like a sort of communion. For a person who lived so much of her life in relative solitude and internal reflection, painting became a way for Anne to feel connected to something beyond herself.

She had no idea how much time had passed while she'd been engrossed in her beloved pastime when her concentration was abruptly interrupted by a low baritone voice.

"I thought I made my position clear to you last evening."

The man's tone was rough and forbidding, causing Lady Anne to freeze mid-brushstroke. It sounded like he spoke from beyond the stone wall behind her which separated this section of the garden from a walking path beyond. The speaker could have no idea she was there, but for a split second, she thought the man was addressing her.

"There's no need to feign false propriety with me." The reply came in a woman's voice, pouty and suggestive. "I've noticed you looking at me. Trust me, I know what men like you want."

Lady Anne held her breath through the heavy pause that followed those words.

"Men like me?"

There was a painfully harsh edge in the man's tone. He sounded quite angry.

His companion didn't seem to notice as she practically purred her response. "Mm-hmm. Men who possess a more *earthy* nature than the insipid gentlemen of London. Men with needs that are less *civilized.*"

Anne's cheeks burned at the shockingly intimate nature of the conversation. In a near panic, she began to collect her art supplies, tucking her paints and brushes into the custom wooden box before setting aside her painting to carefully yet quickly dismantle her small easel—all while trying to move in utter silence.

The only thing that could make her unwitting eavesdropping worse was if the two people on the other side of the wall somehow discovered her presence.

As she stood to swipe up her shawl, movement drew her attention down the stone path toward the house where a man was striding intently into the garden.

Lady Anne recognized him instantly.

She'd met Lord Mayhew during her debut season three years ago. Eldest son of a duke, he'd been at the top of her father's list of prospective suitors and had been one of the few Anne hadn't found objectionable in some way. Mild-mannered and openly kind, if a bit shy and socially tentative, he'd always had a polite word for her when they'd happened to encounter each other throughout the season. Unfortunately, nothing had ever developed between them as he'd had his eye on the lovely and popular Miss Breckenridge from the very first ball. The couple had married soon after the close of the season.

As Lord Mayhew drew closer, Lady Anne couldn't help but notice the strain in his usually good-natured features. The man was clearly upset about something.

Something on which she seriously did not have time to speculate considering the man behind the wall was once again speaking in a voice that had gone dangerously low.

"I won't say this again, my lady, so listen well. I don't now—nor will I ever—have the slightest desire to bed you."

The woman laughed, a distinctive twinkling sound that was suddenly, distressingly familiar. "We don't need a bed, Mr. Thomas. And you can't fool me with your hostile glares and forbidding scowls. I know you want me. *All* men want me."

Goodness gracious!

Lady Anne suddenly knew exactly whose private conversation she'd been inadvertently listening in on. Just as the stark realization hit her, she heard something that disturbed her even more. A short grunt of surprise followed by the unmistakable sound of what could only be a very passionate kiss!

Frozen in shock, she stared with encroaching horror as Lord Mayhew continued straight toward the gate that would take him to the footpath where he would undoubtedly get a shocking view of his beloved wife kissing another man.

Her insides twisted with the implications of what was about to happen. The poor man would be utterly devastated. His love and devotion to his wife were well known. Even if they weren't, Lord Mayhew would be honor-bound to challenge the other man.

Though she wasn't an active player by any sense of the word, she suddenly found herself dead center in a potential scandal with dreadful consequences. Her mind flew through her options in rapid succession. She had to act fast or not at all.

Quickly gathering her supplies, she stepped from her secluded little spot to the garden path. As she did so, her paint box slid from her grip. It opened when it hit the ground, spilling her paints and brushes all over the stone walkway. The incident caused quite a clatter, immediately drawing Lord Mayhew's attention. As she'd intended.

As she also anticipated, the lord promptly altered direction to come to her aid.

"Lady Anne, allow me to help you," he said as he neared with a polite, though clearly distracted, smile.

"Thank you, Lord Mayhew," she answered. If her tone was a bit louder than necessary, the kind lord gave no indication of it. "I'm frightfully clumsy, I'm afraid."

"Not at all," he replied as he crouched beside her to start collecting the strewn objects. "I don't suppose you happened to see Lady Mayhew pass by?"

His question had her stiffening as her tongue tied into a knot. It wouldn't be an outright lie to say she hadn't seen his wife since she'd only heard the woman, but she couldn't quite bring herself to say the words.

Then she didn't have to as the lady herself came sweeping toward them. "My darling, whatever are you doing out here?" she asked with a wide smile and hands outstretched. The seductive purrs the lady had employed only moments ago had been replaced by a cajoling, almost patronizing tone that prickled roughly over Anne's tightly strung nerves.

Rising, Lord Mayhew took the lady's slim, ringed fingers in his. "I saw a flash of your gown from an upstairs window as I headed down for breakfast. I thought you were planning to sleep in this morning."

"Oh, I was, but the garden was just too inviting. I couldn't resist." As she answered, Lady Mayhew slipped her arm through her husband's and began to lead him back toward the house.

They'd gotten a few steps away before the gentleman came to a halt and glanced back at Anne where she still knelt on the ground gathering her things.

"Allow me a moment to assist—" he began, but his wife interrupted.

"The lady appears to have everything in hand, don't you, dear?"

There was a sharp note in the woman's sugared words that did not escape Anne's notice. Clearing her throat, she quickly replied, "Yes, of course. Thank you for your kindness, my lord, but I can manage the rest."

"If you're certain?"

"Quite," Anne replied with a smile of assurance.

As the married couple continued back toward the house, the ill feeling in Anne's stomach only grew worse.

Had she done the right thing? Perhaps it would have been better for Lord Mayhew to discover his wife's faithlessness. But just the brief imagining of such a scene filled her with dread and compassion for a man who didn't deserve such a painful betrayal.

Still, she probably should have just stayed out of it. Now she felt complicit in the woman's disloyal behavior and that didn't sit well with her at all.

With a heavy sigh, she closed her paint box then tucked it beneath her arm along with the rest of her supplies and started to rise from where she'd been kneeling beside the path. But as her gaze lifted, she caught sight of a pair of worn boots and brown trousers standing right in front of her. She gasped and would have fallen back on her rear if the man who'd approached her so silently hadn't taken a quick, firm grip of her shoulders to unceremoniously haul her the rest of the way to her feet.

"Thank you," she muttered automatically, feeling distinctly unsettled by the man's sudden appearance and abrupt handling of her person.

"Yours, I believe," he said thickly in a voice she now recognized as he extended one of her paintbrushes in his large, calloused hand.

Her heart raced as her gaze traveled from his very masculine fingers up the length of an obviously strong arm clad in a simple coat of dark brown that also spanned frightening wide shoulders to a face framed by longish waves of black hair. Broad, rugged features were shaped into an expression of undeniable irritation as the man glowered down at her.

Mr. Beynon Thomas.

Lady Anne had heard of him—there weren't many people in London who hadn't—though she'd never actually met the man. His introduction to society at the start of the most recent season had been the scandal of the year. Not his introduction per se, but the fact that he'd been introduced as the Earl of Wright's illegitimate half brother. Apparently, the prior earl had produced quite a few illegitimate children. Mr. Roderick Bentley, who owned a popular gambling hell, had been known as the earl's by-blow all his life. But no one had been aware there were others until recently. The most surprising part was that the current earl was making a very obvious point of acknowledging his siblings despite the damage to his family name.

The earl didn't seem very concerned about public opinion when it came to his half siblings, which Lady Anne understood to number four in total, though she hadn't heard much about the other two. But that didn't stop the gossipmongers from going absolutely wild with the information. Especially once Mr. Thomas made an appearance in the London social scene.

Most bastard children, even when acknowledged and supported by family, were subjected to rejection from a significant portion of society. And Mr. Thomas surely faced his share of such prejudice and judgement. Not only was he a lord's by-blow, but he was also an outsider—a Welshman who was wildly rumored to be a farmer. That in itself caused a bit of an uproar when he started making appearances at a few select London parties.

But more than those things, it was Mr. Thomas's manner that had become the juiciest topic of conversation. Apparently, he tended to be rather brusque and surly. The gossips liked to speculate on the reason for his somewhat malevolent nature, and anyone who managed to keep the ton twittering in private boudoirs was destined to become popular in a social scene that adored spectacle in any form.

Whenever the gruff and unpolished Mr. Thomas made an appearance at an event, it was sure to be talked about for days afterward. No hostess could resist such an incentive to include him on their guest list. Even so, he accepted invitations very sparingly, which, of course, made him all the more desirable.

Forcing herself to meet his dark gaze now, Lady Anne understood why some people called him the Welsh Devil in dark whispers. The man exuded animosity. In his large stature and intimidating bearing. And in the rigidity of his somber features.

Though the anger she'd heard in his voice as he'd spoken to Lady Mayhew was still evident in the tension of his firm lips and the heavy scowl marring his brow, it was his stare that unsettled her most. His black-eyed gaze was deep and penetrating. It felt as though he peered straight into the pit of her soul.

A chill swept down her spine. And for a sharp, breathless moment, Anne was lost.

Her mind went utterly blank. Her nerves sparked. And her belly twisted in the oddest manner.

As he waited for her response, he cast a glance over her shoulder to the stone wall stretching behind her, then to the spot of grass that had been flattened where she'd sat for so long. His dark brows lowered even further.

Heat flooded her body. He knew she'd overheard every bit of his rendezvous with Lady Mayhew.

His focus returned to her. If possible, his eyes appeared even blacker. His glare, heavier. "Do you intend to take it or not?"

Anne blinked. Then glanced down to the paintbrush still held in his fingers.

"Oh. Yes." Quickly swiping the brush from his hand, she stuffed it into the deep pocket of her skirt. "Thank you," she added in an embarrassingly breathless murmur, but Mr. Thomas was already walking away with a long, purposeful stride.

Disoriented and disturbed by the encounter, Anne could only stare at his broad back until he turned and disappeared around a row of tall hedges.

Chapter Two

B eynon glanced over the drawing room occupants with a swift tightening of the muscles banding his chest. The Earl and Countess of Harte's guests, numbering more than two dozen, gathered in little groups to chat and gossip and flirt. The gentlemen had just rejoined the ladies following their after-dinner port and a few introductions were taking place, but for the most part, it appeared as though everyone was already acquainted.

As the August heat had begun to make London unbearable, residents of town had escaped en masse to the open spaces and fresh air of country estates for extended visits. Going along had sounded like a welcome reprieve. But it was only the first full day of the summer house party and Beynon was already regretting his decision to attend.

He should have just gone back to Wales for the summer.

No. He'd committed to a lengthy visit with his newly discovered siblings. He wouldn't go back on his word. His little sister, Caillie, would give him hell if he dared even suggest it.

But he'd come to England to become better acquainted with his brothers and sister, not to engage in pointless socializing. Caillie, though in attendance at the party, was unfortunately too young at only thirteen to participate in the evening activities. A shame because, between her and his older brothers, she was by far his favorite.

He turned a dark glance to the corner of the room where the current Earl of Wright, his oldest brother, Colin, sat with his wife. Ainsworth had been Caillie's guardian up until two years ago when Colin had brought them both from their home in the Scottish Lowlands to stay with him in London. It was difficult to understand how two people as different as Colin and Ainsworth could get on so well together, but they'd apparently found ground common enough to marry and appeared happy for it.

His other brother, Roderick Bentley, stood not far away talking with their host, Lord Harte. Their wives, who were sisters, sat on a nearby sofa chatting with a large group of ladies. Beynon's scowling gaze slid over the gathering of pastel frocks, fancy coiffures, and bright, smiling faces. The obvious wealth and frivolity pricked at his nerves. He couldn't imagine any of the young women present—or the gentlemen, for that matter—lasting a moment in the world he was from. And yet, his brothers seemed to think he should use the party to seek out a bride.

Beynon's snort of derision was curbed only by the fact that, at that moment, his focus happened to fall upon the pale-haired woman from the garden. He instantly stiffened. He hadn't noticed her at dinner—no doubt she'd been seated some distance from him at the enormous table—but as he looked at her now, he couldn't help but feel a swift return of his vexation from that morning.

It had been bad enough that his morning walk had concluded in a frustrating encounter with a female who refused to acknowledge his rejection. But that some insipid young debutante had overheard the whole thing chafed at the bit of dignity he'd managed to retain since joining London's social scene.

He'd initially been grateful for the eavesdropping blonde's clumsiness since it succeeded in freeing him from Lady Mayhew's grasp. But when he'd helped the young woman to her feet, her wide eyes had darted over his person like those of a frightened rabbit.

Fascination and fear had swirled in her blue eyes and he'd *felt* her discomfort like a gut punch.

In the last months, he'd learned the women of the ton tended to see him in one of two ways. They were either scandalized and repulsed by his refusal to conform to the expected appearances and behaviors of polite society, or, like Lady Mayhew, they were fiercely attracted to his rougher qualities and sought to use him as a means of escaping from their boring, genteel lives.

It was all so damned ridiculous.

The attention. The wariness. The sly glances and the gossip and the constant scrutiny.

When he'd eventually decided to acknowledge his position as one of the Earl of Wright's bastards, he'd agreed to accept everything that went with it. If he'd known how much of a spectacle he'd become in the eyes of the ton, he might have chosen differently.

Before he could look away, the young woman from the garden happened to glance up. As her eyes met his, he muttered a gruff oath and quickly redirected his gaze, hoping she'd think his attention had fallen to her only momentarily. But after another quick scan of the room, he couldn't help glancing back. Thankfully, she was no longer looking his way. But neither had she reengaged in the conversation around her. The blush pinkening her cheeks was obvious even from his position across the room.

Wonderful.

He redirected his focus once again. And this time caught the unfortunate gaze of his brother.

Roderick lifted the corner of his mouth in a half grin. Then he leaned down to whisper something in his wife's ear before making his way to Beynon's side.

Beynon considered walking away, but he'd realized some time ago that avoidance never worked with this man. It was better to face

Roderick and whatever observation the man wished to share head on. And this brother always had *something* to share.

"Good evening, Thomas," Roderick greeted as he gestured to a footman, who quickly approached with a tray of champagne. "You look like you'd benefit from a drink."

Beynon eyed the bubbling wine with suspicion. "Isn't there anything stronger?"

Roderick gave a short chuckle. "Later. For now, we engage in the game of social nicety as we display our sparkling wit and polished manners."

"And if I've neither wit nor manners?"

"Then you get to stand in shadowed corners as you glare and glower at all the happy people gathered about you."

"I wasn't glowering," Beynon protested then wished he'd kept his mouth shut. Roderick had an uncanny knack for drawing him into arguments in which he had no real wish to participate. And he suspected the man did it on purpose.

"But you were glaring," his brother noted triumphantly, "and rather intently, I might add, at poor Lady Anne."

Lady Anne. The name suited her. Traditional, meek, and dull.

Beynon's attention angled back toward the group of women, where a redhead was currently regaling the group with some tale that appeared to require rather animated gestures.

Lady Anne was listening politely, her posture perfect, her hands folded in her lap, her chin lowered just a bit. Her face was rather narrow, which suited her straight patrician nose and the pert shape of her mouth, and although her eyebrows were a bit too dark for her fair coloring, all of her features together formed to an expression of quietly enduring temperance.

Traditional, meek, and dull.

As soon as he confirmed the assessment, the redhead came to the conclusion of her story. While the others around her laughed, Lady

Anne offered a faint smile that transformed her face in the oddest way. As if a fairy lamp had just been lit in a hazy dawn, her rather ordinary features took on a quietly ethereal quality.

"See? Just like that," Roderick noted in amusement before his tone turned earnest. "I wouldn't stare at the lady with such intensity for too long, brother. People will make certain assumptions about your interest."

Beynon immediately shifted his focus back to Roderick. "There is no interest."

"Of course there isn't," Roderick agreed as he sipped from his champagne glass.

Frowning in frustration, Beynon knew the only way out of the conversation was to be blunt. "*If* I were to develop interest in a young woman, it sure as hell wouldn't be one such as her."

Now Roderick frowned as he turned an assessing gaze back toward the lady in question. "Why not? What's wrong with Lady Anne?"

Beynon nearly growled his annoyance at being forced to voice such a thing out loud, but he knew he'd never get Roderick off his back if he didn't. "Look at her. I doubt she's ever done anything more physically exerting than a country dance."

Roderick glanced back to him with lifted brows at that. "Just what kind of physical activity would you have her do?"

Realizing how his words had sounded, Beynon decided to shoot down his brother's teasing before it could go further. "You forget where I come from. I'm no pampered English lord. The woman I eventually take to wife will have to be prepared for a simple and arduous life of rural domestication. Do you really think any of the ladies present would find that appealing?"

His brother had nothing to say to that, but he continued to meet Beynon's gaze with a sharp look in his eyes. Then, after a long pause, he finally replied, "I see your point. I apologize."

"Not necessary." Beynon tried to wave off the man's earnest regret. Such sentiments were almost as distressing as the matchmaking.

"It is," Roderick insisted. "But I promise there'll be no further expectations of your stay. We all really just want you to enjoy yourself, Beynon, with the obvious hope you'll continue coming to visit."

Now it was Beynon's turn for regret. He hadn't meant for the conversation to end up on such sensitive ground. His acceptance of this new family Wright was trying to create had been a shaky one. He'd initially rejected the idea altogether until young Caillie had hunted him down and given him a good lecture. Only eleven years old at the time, his sister had possessed the insight and perspective he'd needed. But that didn't mean his transition from simple Welsh farmer to bastard son of an English earl had been an easy one.

Hoping to shift the tone a bit, he responded gruffly, "You know, the roads go north, as well."

Roderick's eyes flickered, then he laughed and clapped Beynon on the back. "Is that an invitation? What a damned good idea. A visit to Wales might be just the thing young Owen needs."

Max Owen was their youngest half brother at twenty-one years old. They'd only just managed to track the boy down a couple weeks ago after more than two years of searching. Though Owen seemed to welcome the news of being a bastard son of the prior Earl of Wright and gave no resistance to getting to know his brothers and sister, he'd made it very clear he enjoyed his life as the leader of a prolific criminal gang in one of London's roughest neighborhoods just as it was.

"The lad is proving to be rather stubborn, isn't he?" Beynon noted.

"No more than you, I'd say."

Beynon grunted, neither agreeing nor disagreeing with that last comment. In his opinion, his own prior reluctance and that of his youngest brother were entirely different situations. Beynon's loyalty had been to the family in which he'd been raised. Owen's loyalty was to a gang of dangerous hoodlums.

"Regardless," he grumbled, "I'm afraid there wouldn't be enough room for the lot of you at Gwaynynog."

"We'll just visit you in rounds," Roderick quickly assured with a wide grin. "You could have a different set of Londoners every month."

Beynon gave a loud objective groan, not even bothering to hide his abject dismay at the thought. It seemed to be exactly the reaction Roderick had been goading for as the older man gave a hearty chuckle.

"No need to worry, brother. Emma and I won't be taking any cross-country trips until the boys are both a bit older."

Roderick and his wife had two sons, an infant barely a couple months old and a two-year-old, currently upstairs with their nurse. The couple rarely went anywhere without the boys in tow.

"Wright, on the other hand," his brother continued with a grin, "might be a different story. You *have* been regaling Cailleach with stories of your home. If I were to casually suggest a visit to our young sister, there's little chance she'd let up on the idea until the carriages were packed and headed north."

Though he suspected Caillie—Roderick was the only one to call her by her full name— would love his home, there's no way Colin or Ainsworth would allow the girl to travel so far without them, and Beynon just couldn't imagine his very proper and lordly eldest brother finding any enjoyment in rural Denbighshire. But as he gave Roderick his fiercest glower, the man's grin only widened further, reminding Beynon of just how much this brother enjoyed tormenting him for his own amusement.

He decided to give the man a taste of his own medicine.

"We should wait until our sister is at least fourteen," he replied thoughtfully, "old enough to barter her hand to a local farmer for a nice fatted pig."

Roderick's humor fled in an instant. His expression turned as ferocious as Beynon had ever seen it. "The hell you say."

Beynon held a straight face as long as he could manage before he noted thickly, "You really think I'd consider such a thing?"

Though he was well aware of the prejudices and speculation about his background that had been flying through the gossip mills, he'd truly hoped his brothers didn't buy into any of it.

Shame flickered in Roderick's blue eyes. "Of course not."

"Glad to hear it," Beynon said with a stiff scowl before he glanced away again as though it were the end of it. "I'd accept no less than a bull in his prime for our sister."

Then he had to turn and vigorously pound on Roderick's back as the other man choked on his champagne, which in and of itself was nearly as satisfying as catching his brother off guard for once.

Chapter Three

While Roderick struggled to regain his composure, Beynon noticed a stirring across the room. Everyone seemed to be convening around their hostess, Lady Harte, who'd risen to her feet with a very large punch bowl cradled in her hands.

"What on earth?" he muttered in confusion.

Roderick tilted his head to follow Beynon's gaze. "Ah. The games."

"Games?"

His brother's reply was a bit too casual. "I didn't tell you about the games?"

Beynon's brow drew downward in answer.

"It was something Lady Harte came up with during last year's summer party. It was such a success among the guests, she decided to bring it back again this summer."

"Bring what back?" Beynon pressed as one of the ladies gathered around their hostess stepped forward to draw a small slip of paper from the bowl.

"A series of competitions spread out over several days at the end of which the winners receive a small purse."

"And what does that have to do with a punch bowl?"

"The games are played in pairs. Married couples partner up, of course, but the unattached members of the party are paired up randomly. The names of each unmarried gentleman are placed in the bowl. The ladies blindly draw and whichever name a lady chooses from the bowl becomes her partner."

"*Every* gentleman?"

Roderick's mouth twitched a bit, sparking a suspicion the man knew exactly how Beynon was feeling just then. "Only a rare few guests are allowed to pass on participation. You're not one of them, I'm afraid."

"You failed to tell me about this on purpose," he accused sharply.

"Now, why would I do that?" His brother was all innocence.

Beynon wasn't even slightly fooled by the act. "Because I'd never have accepted the invitation if I'd known I'd be obligated to play some ridiculous game."

"Don't be so dismissive. It's rousing good fun, actually," Roderick replied with a clap on Beynon's back and a subtle shove forward. "You do like to have fun, don't you, brother? Come on, let's see who you're partnered with."

LADY ANNE HESITATED at the edge of the twittering crowd. If she could have excused herself from the games, she would have. At last year's party, she'd been partnered with Lord Reiner, an older gentleman who enjoyed his wine a bit overmuch. He'd stumbled through half of the competitions and didn't bother learning the rules to the rest. It had been an extremely disappointing experience.

She'd have preferred to avoid repeating such unpleasantness and had briefly considered sending her regrets when she received her invitation to the house party. But Lady Harte was one of her best friends and she knew how badly Lily wanted this country gathering to become an annual success.

So, when it came round to her turn to draw a name from the bowl, she stepped forward with a smile for her friend and plucked the first slip of paper her fingers happened to touch.

It took her another moment of staring at the arrangement of letters to accept it wasn't some trick of the light and they'd somehow read out differently if she gave it another couple seconds. But the name remained unchanged. And undeniable.

Mr. Beynon Thomas.

With a tight sigh, she glanced upward to see the man approaching with his brother, Mr. Roderick Bentley. Mr. Thomas's angry countenance was no surprise as she'd already determined the man apparently always carried that dark, forbidding expression.

"Who've you drawn?" Lily asked as she held her hand out for the paper.

As had happened for each pick before hers, the name would have to be read aloud and the partnership recorded by Lily's sister, Emma Bentley, in order to make it official.

Anne handed Lily the name but couldn't bring herself to glance back toward Mr. Thomas as their hostess read the name with a pleased smile.

There were a few quiet gasps and murmurs from some of the ladies nearby, which Anne intently ignored. What she couldn't ignore, however, was Mr. Bentley as he stepped up beside her.

"Hello, Lady Anne."

She turned to her friend's charming brother-in-law and gave a quick smile. "Good evening, Mr. Bentley."

There was a time not long ago when Mr. Bentley, as the owner of a scandalous gambling club, would have been an extremely inappropriate acquaintance for an unmarried young lady. But the man's marriage to Emma Chadwick and his close association with the Earls of Wright and Harte had shifted society's tide a bit in that regard. There was also the fact that after three years out, Anne simply didn't care quite so much about that the ton deemed appropriate. Not that she'd ever do anything outright scandalous, but there were certain freedoms a young lady could claim once everyone decided she wasn't worth such intent concerns.

"Allow me the privilege of introducing you to your game partner," Bentley noted with a grin that seemed just a bit more delighted than the situation warranted. Stepping to the side, he gestured to the man beside him. "Lady Anne, I'd like you to meet my brother, Mr. Beynon Thomas."

Doing her best to avoid looking directly into the Welshman's hard, dark eyes, Lady Anne gave a nod in greeting and murmured, "A pleasure to meet you, sir."

Mr. Thomas responded with a proper bow and gruffly uttered, "Lady Anne."

Thankfully, the last unattached lady and gentleman were matched up and Lady Harte once again addressed her guests. "The schedule of games will be posted tomorrow morning in the breakfast room. The first event shall take place tomorrow afternoon. Good luck, everyone."

As the small crowd began to disperse once again, Mr. Bentley flashed a smile. "If you'll excuse me, it looks like my wife needs my assistance." Without waiting for a response, the man turned and walked away, leaving Anne and Mr. Thomas to stand in stiff and awkward silence as they both seemed intent on looking anywhere but at each other.

Unfortunately, peripheral vision was more than competent when it came to Mr. Thomas.

Anne was quite tall by common standards at five feet, ten inches, but she noticed with a dose of unexpected discomfort that if she wished to meet her partner's gaze, at this proximity, she'd have to tip her head back. It was not an experience she had very often, but it meant Mr. Thomas stood at least a few inches over six feet.

The man was undeniably large. And not at all in a portly way. His bulk appeared to be comprised of solid muscle. The combination of such obvious strength and exceptional height made her feel distinctly disadvantaged when standing so close to him.

Disadvantaged and vulnerable. And oddly...trembly.

As soon as she realized how intently she was considering his physical form, she forced herself to thaw her frozen tongue and make a little small talk. But as soon as she lifted her focus to his face, the dark displeasure in his broad features gave her a bit of a start.

The muscles along her spine tensed and she quickly lowered her gaze.

He'd worn the same fierce expression that morning in the garden. The man did not like her at all. Having never before inspired such animosity in anyone in her life, Anne was at a total loss on how to respond. Especially when she wasn't sure what she'd done to earn such enmity.

They'd only had that one interaction in the garden. Unless he thought she'd eavesdropped in his encounter with Lady Mayhew on purpose?

"Lady Anne." His rough baritone immediately brought her eyes back up to see him offering another bow of his head.

Then he turned and walked away.

Not just away. The man left the drawing room altogether. Leaving her standing rather conspicuously in the center of the room.

As she took a breath to steady herself after such a direct cut, Lily stepped up beside her.

"I'm sure he didn't mean anything by it," the kind woman whispered gently. "He's just not accustomed to—"

"What? Employing basic manners?" The interruption came from Bethany Pinkman, another of Anne's good friends. The three of them had gravitated toward each other during their debut season. Though each of them possessed very different personalities, they somehow managed to complement each other. "The man may be *devastatingly* attractive, but that cannot excuse such boorish behavior toward our dear friend."

"Now, Bethany..." Lily began, but the other woman wasn't finished.

"Can't we pair our dear Anne up with someone else? *Anyone* other than the Welsh Devil himself?"

"Hush!" Lily firmly admonished, "You shouldn't call him that."

"Perhaps he shouldn't behave in a way that supports such a moniker," Bethany retorted. "Did you know he did not ask a single young lady to dance all season, though he attended no less than five balls? His manner is practically hostile whenever anyone attempts to engage him in a bit of light conversation and he seems to make a point of glowering intently at any female who dares to come within a few steps of him."

Lily shook her head, a small frown marring her brow. "That is a blatant exaggeration, Bethany."

"Is it?" the other woman asked with obvious surprise. "You saw how he just treated our dear Anne, yet you'd defend him?"

"I believe Mr. Thomas is misunderstood," Lily noted. She had always been one to give people the benefit of any doubt. "I've had a few conversations with him and found him to be kind and well-spoken."

"That's hard to imagine," Bethany retorted and Anne was tempted to agree.

"The truth is," Lily continued with firm conviction, "Mr. Thomas is not the menacing figure everyone so enjoys making him out to be. And I happen to think he will make Anne a perfect partner."

"I suspect this is one time your eternal optimism will fail you," Bethany insisted.

"It's all right," Anne interjected. "Truly. There's no need to make an issue out of it. I'll be fine."

"He's really not what everyone says," Lily insisted. "Give him a chance."

Anne smiled. "Of course. Please, think no more of it." It was far more embarrassing to have her friends worry over such an inconsequential thing than it was to be slighted by the man in the first place. Her pride might have been bruised a bit by his attitude and sudden dismissal, but it was taking a far more brutal beating at the insinuation that she couldn't handle a little adversity. She was her father's daughter, after all. Adversity had been her nursemaid.

She could certainly handle a grouchy partner for the handful of days assigned to the games.

Gratefully, the issue was dropped as Bethany leaned toward Lily to whisper conspiratorially, "Since it's just the three of us, how about you give us a few tips on what to expect this year?"

Lily widened her eyes in shock then had to press her lips together to hide her mischievous grin. "Not a chance. That would be cheating."

"And Lady Harte is far too noble to consider such a thing."

The last was declared loyally by Lily's husband as the tall, dark-haired gentleman came up beside his wife. Though he remained back a step from their trio, his intense presence immediately altered the atmosphere of their conversation.

As she had many times before, Lady Anne wondered at the unexpected union between her open-hearted friend and the enigmatic lord. There had been a time when Anne had been convinced Lord Harte would never have been capable of making Lily happy, but her friend had been utterly infatuated with the earl from the first moment she'd seen him. And, as Lily tilted her head to flash a smile at her husband, Anne had to admit the couple was undeniably and very deeply in love.

"I apologize, ladies, but I must steal my wife away for a moment."

Though the lord's words were contrite, his tone was anything but.

Bethany's lashes fluttered. "Of course, my lord. She's all yours."

Lord Harte bowed as Lily promised to chat with them both more later, then the couple walked away. Though they didn't touch—not even with a hand on his arm—the connection between them was clear to see and had grown even stronger since their wedding.

Bethany sighed dramatically, drawing Anne's quick glance.

Seeing her friend's questioning expression, the lady gave a short laugh. "Don't mistake me, dear Anne, I love my husband deeply." She paused to lean closer. "But there's just something about men who emanate such"—she narrowed her eyes as she seemed to search for the right word—"wickedness that honestly makes my toes curl."

Anne shook her head in a way she often did when in earnest conversation with this particular friend. "I haven't the slightest idea what you're talking about."

Bethany flashed a condescending smile as she patted Anne's hand. "I know. You're still such an innocent," she lamented. "But I hope you figure it out soon, darling." Her gray eyes brightened as something seemed to occur to her. "You know, I might have to consider agreeing with Lily's assessment, after all. Mr. Thomas, with all his broody intensity, could prove to be exactly what you've been so desperately lacking these last few years."

And with that oddly cryptic and slightly insulting statement, her friend walked away and once again Anne was left standing alone in the middle of the room.

Chapter Four

The next morning, Anne was one of the first guests to the breakfast room. Lily's elderly great-aunt—a wonderfully eccentric Frenchwoman—sat reading a newspaper at one end of the table while the Countess of Wright stood at the buffet with a girl who appeared to be around twelve or thirteen years of age. The countess glanced up as Anne crossed into the room and smiled widely in greeting. "Good morning, Lady Anne."

Anne had been introduced to the auburn-haired Scotswoman shortly after the woman's unexpected marriage to the Earl of Wright two years ago.

"Lady Wright," Anne replied politely, "it's nice to see you again."

"And you," the countess said in a slight burr as she set her hand on the shoulder of the girl beside her. "Please allow me to introduce Miss Cailleach Claybourne. Although the lass won't be participating in any of the games, I suspect she'll be an avid spectator."

As the girl gave a proper curtsey, Anne smiled. "Pleased to meet you, Miss Claybourne."

"You as well," the girl replied with an accent similar to Lady Wright's. "You're Lady Anne Humphries, then?"

"I am."

The girl smiled widely. "So, you're to partner my brother in the games."

Anne's eyes widened. "Your brother?"

"Aye. Mr. Thomas."

Suddenly realizing this girl was another of the prior earl's illegitimate children, Anne blinked in surprise, unsure exactly how to respond. She wouldn't have expected a fact most would consider shameful or scandalous to be acknowledged with such casual self-assurance.

Lady Wright gave a short laugh as she shook her head. "You've shocked the poor lady, lass. I've warned you about being so forthright all the time."

The girl just shrugged. "People will find out eventually. I see no point hiding who I am." Then she directed a focused gaze back to Anne. "I've decided to champion you and Beynon for the competition."

Anne blinked again. "Well, thank you, Miss Claybourne. I appreciate the vote of confidence."

"Have you taken a look at the event scheduled for today?"

"Not yet."

"You should," the girl asserted before she narrowed her gaze and glanced at Anne's feet. "I hope you brought some sturdy shoes."

"Caillie luv," Lady Wright interjected with a smile though her tone was a bit firm, "why dinnae you allow Lady Anne to have a wee bit of breakfast before you interrogate her about strategy."

"Right. Sorry," the girl noted, only slightly admonished. "Do come find me if you'd like to discuss the games further."

"I'll be sure to do so," Anne replied. The girl, though bold for one so young, seemed a good ally to have and Anne wasn't about to shrug off any support she could get for the lengthy competition ahead.

Especially considering she wasn't sure just how supportive her partner would prove to be. A shadow hovered over her mood as she recalled Mr. Thomas's abrupt departure the night before.

She'd tried—she really had—to consider all the reasons he might have had to treat her so rudely, but she just kept coming round to the likelihood that he was simply unhappy with having her as his partner. That or he was simply an unconscionable grouch.

Lady Wright and her charge stepped away to claim seats at the table as Anne began to fill her own plate at the buffet. A few minutes later, two young gentlemen entered the room and went directly to the game schedule, where they commenced a little good-natured ribbing. A young woman and her mother arrived next then a married couple as the room slowly began to fill with guests. Some came for the food, but nearly everyone took a moment to review information Lily had posted about the day's competitions.

Anne did her best to focus on her breakfast, but more than once, she found herself glancing impatiently toward the schedule posted across the room. She'd never have known it about herself if not for her experience during the games last year, but apparently, she had a rather strong—though previously dormant—competitive streak.

Lord Humphries had set very specific expectations for his daughter's education and upbringing. Seeking any opportunity to gain her father's favor, Anne had excelled in reading, history, arithmetic, and any other subjects deemed appropriate for the female mind. She'd mastered the skills required in order to present herself as an accomplished gentlewoman. Dance, embroidery, the managing of household accounts and staff, the proper planning of a menu. She knew to stay current on the latest fashions and trends in home decorating. She'd memorized Debrett's guide to the peerage and knew the proper behavior for any number of social situations.

Focusing so intently on fulfilling her father's strict curriculum hadn't left much room for fun and games—even if she'd had someone with whom she could have engaged in such activities. So, it had come as a bit of a surprise during last year's competition when Anne had discovered the excitement and motivation in competing against others in various tasks of mental and physical skill. Even without an active partner, the experience had been exhilarating and rather eye-opening. But also, highly disappointing. Apparently, she didn't like to lose and she'd done a lot of that last year.

And now, here she was once again with a less than enthusiastic partner.

Since backing out of the competition would be a terrible disappointment to Lily, Anne had no choice but to forge ahead.

When she noticed a brief lull in the constant flow of guests, she rose to her feet and started toward the game posters tacked up in the corner of the room. Passing by the doorway, she happened to glance up just as the large and imposing figure of Mr. Thomas crossed the threshold.

Without any conscious directive, her steps stuttered to an awkward halt. As her eyes met his, an odd disquiet swept through her. His perpetually broody countenance darkened even more as he caught sight of her, yet she somehow managed to stand tall and proud before decisively turning her gaze to continue across the room.

By the time she reached the board where the latest information on the games would be posted each morning, she had to take a moment to subtly force a steady breath into her lungs as she pressed her hand to her abdomen.

She might have discounted the odd trembling in her center as a lingering reaction to the man's rudeness the night before, but the truth was, she'd felt the same internal disquiet that morning in the garden when she'd met his solemn stare.

The man simply unsettled her.

And now they were to be partners for the next several days, though Mr. Thomas had made it clear he would have preferred anyone else. Rejection was not entirely new to Anne. She'd just gone through her third season, after all, without an offer for her hand. She'd already spent far too many nights wondering what it was about her that young men seemed to find objectionable and had no intention of wasting another moment on the futile question.

With another deep breath, she lowered her hand back to her side and focused on the information before her.

Listed at the top of the board were all of the partnerships. Ten teams in all, equally comprised of married couples and randomly matched pairs. Her gaze was automatically drawn to her own name near the bottom of the list.

Lady Anne Humphries and Mr. Beynon Thomas

Forcefully ignoring the discomfiting twist in her belly, she scanned quickly over the rules and the scoring process. Since the games were designed for entertainment and diversion, a great deal depended on the honor system in terms of following expected guidelines and procedures for the various activities.

Points would be awarded to only the three top scoring teams for each event. Five points for first place, three points for second, and one point for third. Each evening, points would be tallied, and the leader board would be adjusted accordingly. The partnership with the most points at the end of the week would be declared winner. In the event of a tie for first place, a final contest would determine the outcome between the two leads.

The game schedule revealed that a few events were being repeated from last year but there were also several new ones. Anne noted a couple in which she felt as though she had the appropriate skills to compete confidently, though others were definitely outside her realm of experience. Such situations were exactly where a partner might come in handy assuming they'd be bringing their own unique aptitude to the pairing.

If your partner was willing to participate.

She assumed Mr. Thomas was still in the room. No doubt he was eating a hearty breakfast, utterly uninterested in the games schedule or his partner. Would he even bother showing up to the first event?

Resentment of a kind she hadn't felt since she'd been a young girl who'd still craved the attention of a cold, neglectful father burned through her veins. Before she could douse the subtle ire, someone came up behind her. Heavy steps came to a halt and a weighted presence seemed to hover over her.

Stiffening, she didn't bother to glance over her shoulder to confirm who'd joined her. She already knew it by the sudden quiver in her belly and the prickling across her nape. She pressed her lips together and forced steady breaths through her nose.

Since he'd made the choice to approach her, she felt no compulsion to offer a greeting.

Unfortunately, the decision led to an odd length of silence since, apparently, he wasn't inclined to speak either.

Well, this was going to go well.

The sarcastic thought caused a quick tug in her chest as Anne released a slow breath then turned in preparation to walk away. Before she could take that first step, Mr. Thomas roughly cleared his throat.

"Good morning."

Anne stilled. *Now* he chose to address her.

She replied without turning to face him. "Good morning, Mr. Thomas."

There was another stretch of awkward silence. Then he made a short sound in his throat before noting with obvious reluctance, "I should apologize for my rudeness last night."

The Welsh accent rolling along his weighty baritone caused another strange dip in her belly, which she did her very best to ignore.

When he said nothing more, her rising tension caused her to note somewhat caustically, "Indeed."

"If I could withdraw from the competition, I would," he replied in a gruffly lowered tone.

So, instead of an apology, he decided to add further insult to injury. Was she really such an undesirable partner?

Finally turning to face him, she was once again surprised by his significant size. Lifting her chin, she noted the thick column of his throat, then the hard line of his jaw—freshly shaven—and his firmly pressed lips. He was closer than she'd expected, which caused a swift disturbance through her system. With a quick blink, she lifted her gaze the rest of the way to meet his darkly glowering stare.

"Withdraw, then," she replied, her tone cool despite the flames licking along her nerves. "I shan't try to stop you."

His thick brows drew together in a fierce scowl and the muscles of his jawline tensed, hardening to stone. She could almost hear his back teeth grinding together.

Had he expected her to beg for his participation?

Not a chance.

"Perhaps you could try to convince another gentleman to switch partners," she suggested, "so you can pair up with someone more to your liking." The man glared down at her with frustration evident in every hard-edged line. But he didn't speak. "Otherwise, I'm afraid you're quite stuck with me, sir."

He visibly swallowed, drawing her attention to the muscles of his throat, which was right about at her eye level. When he responded, she found herself watching the play of his Adam's apple as it lifted and fell with his words.

"I've no interest in participating in a bunch of silly parlor games."

"Parlor games?" Anne repeated, wondering if he'd even bothered to glance at the schedule he'd been standing in front of for the last several minutes.

When her eyes flew back up to his, she noted a distinct glimmer of disdain in his gaze. Was he expecting quaint little rounds of Kiss the Nun and Bullet Pudding?

Drawing herself up a bit to dispel the unusual sense of smallness she experienced when face-to-face with the man, she offered a tense smile. "There's nothing I can do if you choose to forfeit your position in the competition, Mr. Thomas. However, if you intend to stay in the games, I hope you come to the first event a bit more prepared than you are now."

After dipping her chin in a quick nod, she stepped past him and strode from the room. As a set down, her parting words hadn't exactly been cutting, but at least this time, *she'd* been the one to walk away. A small victory.

Chapter Five

B eynon had never been very good at admitting a mistake, so he was well aware his apology to Lady Anne had fallen short of the mark. But it was the best she was likely to get from him.

He'd struggled with a difficult temper all his life. It had gotten him into more than a few scrapes as a lad, but as he'd matured, he'd worked hard to correct that failing. Unfortunately, there were still those rare occasions when his emotions got the best of him and he'd speak or react without thinking. He realized his frustration in being roped into some frivolous competition—even if they weren't exactly parlor games—might have colored his interactions with Lady Anne. But the idea of putting himself on display for entertainment when he was already the focus of so many unwanted whispers and distasteful gossip quite frankly irritated the hell out of him.

The only other option, however, was not an option at all. Requesting a change in partner would only cause further insult. And as his sister, Caillie, made clear to him, she expected him to be on his best behavior for Lady Anne. Apparently, the girl had taken a liking to his partner. He suspected it was a case of championing the underdog, since Caillie's lecture included comments on how the lady had endured three failed seasons despite being as kind and gracious as a princess and certainly didn't deserve any poor treatment from him.

Beynon was just a bit concerned with how the girl had gotten so much information while not even being a full participant at the party. But he'd reluctantly agreed to his sister's demands, acknowledging to himself anyway that anything other than cooperation would bring even more attention his way. The best way to get through this wretched ordeal was to lend himself to the competitions in a capacity that would not draw additional gossip.

At the appointed hour, he left the house and headed for the south lawn where the competitors and spectators—those guests who'd somehow managed to escape from participating—were to gather for the first event. After breakfast, he'd changed into clothing more suited to the planned activity, and as he joined the others, he realized he'd not been the only one. Woolen trousers, simple frocks, and sturdy boots had replaced the more sophisticated attire that had prevailed through the previous day.

Many of the guests were already standing in pairs with their partners while others had gathered in small groups. There was an air of excitement and anticipation as they all chatted gaily about the race ahead. Beynon spotted Colin and Ainsworth standing with Caillie off to one side. Preferring not to receive another lecture from his young sister, he simply nodded a greeting while continuing on.

He didn't realize he'd been subconsciously scanning for a tall, lithesome woman with pale hair and a gaze that somehow managed to be direct and modest at the same time until he spotted her.

His partner stood in conversation with their hostess, Lady Harte, and the story-telling redhead from the night before whose arm was linked through that of a slim gentleman wearing a somewhat distracted expression. Lady Anne's graceful neck was slightly bowed as she lowered her chin to listen intently to the woman beside her. Beynon could just barely make out the gentle curve to her lips suggesting a smile.

He scowled at how the subtle change in her expression again seemed to brighten her whole appearance.

After another moment, the redhead and her companion stepped away. It was then that Lady Anne looked up and caught his heavy stare. Her smile slid away and her posture tensed as she seemed to realize he was coming toward her. Even when Lady Harte said something, she didn't glance away and the steady awareness in her eyes made him think of a rabbit watching the approach of a wolf.

Beynon had met Lady Harte several times throughout the season since her sister, Emma, was married to Roderick. In their few conversations, he'd found her to be a gentle, compassionate sort. He could see why she and the equally mild Lady Anne would be friends.

He gave a bow first to his hostess then to his partner. "Good morning, Lady Harte. Lady Anne."

They both acknowledged his greeting but only Lady Harte gave him a smile. "Hello, Mr. Thomas. Are you all set to begin our games?"

"I believe so, my lady."

Rising to her toes, Lady Harte glanced out over the gathered crowd to say, "I suppose it's time to welcome everyone and get things started. Best of luck," she added in a tone of genuine encouragement before stepping around them to weave her way through her guests.

Beynon cleared his throat and turned to his partner.

Her expression was somewhat placid and enduring, but as the sun reflected in her steady gaze, he noted how the blue of her eyes was really just a ring around out the outer edge which blended into a soft green near the center. The strange coloring was unsettling and brought to mind Y Tylwyth Teg, the fair folk of childhood stories.

She blinked. The swift fall of her lashes alerted him to the fact he was staring.

Clearing his throat, he glanced over to where Lady Harte had been joined by her husband and was welcoming the competitors to the first event of the games. The spectators had already begun making their way along a path that would take them to watch the race from the finish line.

As Lady Harte went into a brief overview of the rules and expectations for the race that was about to commence, Beynon glanced about, directing his attention toward anything other than the lady beside him. Unfortunately, his sweeping gaze happened to locate Lady Mayhew as she stood beside her husband, her arm looped through his, appearing for all the world as a sweetly devoted wife. No one observing the woman now would believe she'd forced her tongue down Beynon's throat just the day before.

He recommitted himself to maintaining a clear distance from that one.

As the lady beside him made a short sound, he angled a quick glance to see her staring rather intently forward.

"Since you're here," she said, "I hope that means you've acquired a better understanding of what this competition entails?"

The lady's tone was properly polite and there wasn't anything particularly challenging in her words, but Beynon instantly squared his shoulders. "As you said, I'm here."

Her gaze flicked up to briefly meet his before her attention shifted to something behind him. "They're lining up."

Without another word, she stepped past him and headed to where couples had started to take their places at the starting line. He caught up to his partner quickly, despite her rather long strides, and got his first glimpse of the sloping hill they'd be racing down.

It was far steeper than he'd imagined. Long grass concealed the details of the terrain, which he imagined would be rough and bumpy. The spectators had taken up position at the bottom of the hill where the earth eased back to level ground. A significant distance beyond that, the Earl of Harte's private lake glistened in the sunlight.

Downhill races could be dangerous and it appeared this one was not likely to be an exception. If your feet couldn't keep up with the increasing momentum of your body, there was a strong likelihood you'd end up tumbling arse over crown down the hill. Gratefully, he was accustomed to physical tests of all sorts and was confident in his ability to manage the terrain while not being overcome by the significant pull of gravity.

As a footman stepped up with a length of ribbon in his gloved hands, Beynon recalled a significant detail about the race he'd momentarily forgotten.

Lady Anne lifted her finely arched eyebrows in question then sighed and stepped closer to his side. "Your hand, Mr. Thomas."

She held herself stiffly as her fingertips slid across his wrist to delve against his palm. The lady tensed subtly and briefly before her hand settled into a surprisingly firm grip around his much larger one. Once their hands were clasped together, the footman wound the ribbon around their wrists, properly securing them to each other.

Dammit. Things just got a lot more difficult.

Though Lady Anne's form and step were certainly graceful, they were far more suited to a ballroom floor than the sort of test they were about to face. He'd have to adjust his stride to match hers or risk throwing them both headfirst down the hill.

He had no more time to consider all the implications of being expected to safely descend a reckless slope while tied to a woman possessing less than half his bulk and strength when a shot was fired, signaling the start of the race. Lady Anne immediately stepped forward and came to an abrupt halt as Beynon failed to move with her.

"Come on," she urged beneath her breath as she tried again. "You do realize this is a race?"

Beynon glanced at the other couples. Most were easing their way with small, careful steps. One pair, however, had started out too vigorously and was already sprawled on the ground. Another couple tumbled to the grass even as he watched.

Focusing on keeping a measured pace and shortened strides, he grasped the lady's hand securely in his and started forward. The ground was as uneven as he'd anticipated but at least he didn't see any rocks or boulders that could cause significant injury in a fall.

The small crowd below was cheering on their favorite teams and shrieks of laughter could be heard from the other competitors as the way grew slightly steeper. Leaning back and digging his heels into the soft ground, he managed to keep them to a slow pace despite how the woman beside him seemed intent upon leaping carelessly forward.

"We're falling behind, Mr. Thomas. We must go faster," she implored.

"Any faster and we'll end up rolling down the damn hill," he retorted.

Her response was a very unladylike snort of frustration just as the couple next to them tried and failed to keep their feet. The gentleman was pitched to the side in his fall, directly in Beynon's path. Only a quick leap to the side kept him from tripping over the poor fellow.

He gave his partner a look of triumph as his warning was instantly justified. But the low pull of her dark blonde brows and the firm set of her jaw told him she hadn't been swayed.

"We're going to lose," she muttered into the wind.

"But we'll make it to the finish line on our feet."

Despite his words, the lady kept trying to quicken their pace. Her determination managed to pull Beynon off-balance more than once, but he dug in harder and leaned his weight back even more.

There were only five couples left as they reached the final slope to the finish. Two couples were ahead of them and two were a significant distance behind. If they maintained their steady progress, they'd easily take third place.

Just as they reached a sudden dip in the landscape, the lady's grip tightened around his. "We can win this," she muttered fiercely as she thrust her full weight forward. He had no idea if she'd simply not noticed how much steeper the terrain had gotten or if she'd intentionally decided to use that to her advantage, but he wasn't at all prepared for the sudden increase in their downward momentum.

Her lunge forward pulled him with her, sending his shoulders forward over his feet. As soon as that happened, it was over. His lower half couldn't keep up with his upper half. All he could do was pull her roughly against him and wrap his free arm around her back to cup her head as he twisted to take the brunt of the fall. But they didn't stop once they hit the ground. Their impetus was too great.

The world spun and the scent of earth filled his nostrils as they rolled through the rough grass, finally coming to an abrupt stop at the bottom of the hill.

Beynon didn't move right away as he took a moment to breathe and assess his status. No injuries beyond a few minor bruises perhaps. His relief was brief, however, as the woman half sprawled atop him with her face tucked into his shoulder—due to the heavy hand he still cupped over the back of her head—issued a short, muffled sound and tried to rise.

He lifted his hand and she instantly planted her palm to his chest as leverage to sit up. Her expression was tense and a deep flush colored her cheeks, but she didn't appear to be in pain. Then she looked up to gaze past his sprawled form and those elegant brows of hers pulled downward in a fierce little scowl.

Having heard the celebratory shouts, he had a strong suspicion what had triggered the dissatisfied expression.

Lifting to brace himself on his elbow, he watched as the lady started tugging at the ribbon still wound around their wrists. It had gotten tangled during their roll down the hill and she was having trouble releasing the knot.

With a grunt, he sat up the rest of the way and reached over to help her.

Since their sides were pressed against each other from knee to shoulder, he felt the ripple of tension slide through her body when his fingers brushed hers.

"We could've won," she said stubbornly as they struggled to work together to untie the knot.

He made a harsh sound of disagreement. "I believe the tumble we just took proves otherwise."

"If you'd allowed me to set a quicker pace from the start," she argued, "we'd have beat them all."

Beynon looked up from their task and found himself staring into a gaze made turbulent with emotion. The blue and green actually appeared to swirl around each other as gold sparks ignited in their depths.

Had he thought her meek?

"Or we'd have broken a few bones," he suggested gruffly.

With a huff, she rose to her feet in a swift and graceful motion. The tug on their bound hands released the loosened knot and the ribbon drifted to the grass beside him.

"I guess we shall never know," she replied stiffly.

Then she turned and, with grass-stained skirts and tendrils of pale blonde hair falling in disarray around her face and shoulders, stalked gracefully toward the crowd gathering around the winners.

Beynon watched her with a deeply furrowed brow until he heard someone approach him from behind.

"Good showing, brother," Roderick said with a wide grin as he held a hand out to help Beynon rise.

Though he could have gained his feet just fine on his own, Beynon grudgingly accepted his brother's assistance.

"Emma and I were out early," he laughed. "My fault entirely. I was too eager to win, I suppose."

"You'd have been well-matched to my partner, then," Beynon grumbled in reply.

Roderick laughed. "Does the gentle Lady Anne possess a competitive spirit?"

Beynon just grunted in response as he bent to brush the grass and dirt from his trousers. He feared his brother's words might be a gross understatement.

Chapter Six

D inner that evening was filled with rousing conversation as everyone laughed over the afternoon's successes and failures.

Anne hadn't spoken to Mr. Thomas since she'd left him sitting on the ground at the bottom of the hill. Of course, she'd noticed the moment he'd entered the drawing room, but she'd very purposely made sure to be deeply engaged in conversation with Bethany. It was an easy thing to do since her friend always seemed to have a great deal to say, something Anne appreciated when she didn't wish to talk herself.

Since his gaze only briefly swept past her, she realized it wouldn't have mattered if she'd been blatantly waiting for him. The man clearly wasn't inclined to acknowledge her with a quick greeting let alone a full conversation. It didn't matter that he didn't approach anyone else either and seemed quite intent on keeping to himself. She was his partner. That fact should count for something.

He was honestly the most infuriating man she'd ever met. Ill-tempered, rude, arrogant in a way she'd never encountered before, Mr. Thomas was proving to be a sore test to her patience. And she was obligated to spend the next several days in close company with him.

By the time dinner was finished and the ladies adjourned to the drawing room while leaving the gentlemen to their port and tobacco, Anne was anxious to get away from Mr. Thomas's brooding presence. Unfortunately, she wasn't exactly fit for socializing with her friends right then, either. So, when Lily gently beckoned her to take a seat beside her on the sofa, Anne smiled and gave a small shake of her head in favor of strolling around the room instead.

Unfortunately, the men did not dally long and soon they began filtering into the drawing room in groups of two and three.

Anne continued along her path around the perimeter of the room, doing her best not to glance toward the doorway or take note of how eagerly some of the gentlemen sought out their partners. Many of them were married couples, but not all of them. And at least the other unmarried gentlemen made some effort at showing a bit of solidarity with the lady they'd been paired with. Her gentleman being the only exception, of course.

She shouldn't be surprised. Hadn't her three failed seasons taught her anything?

Despite coming from a good family, possessing a sizeable dowry, and mastering the skills her father had insisted would secure an exemplary match, she'd received exactly zero offers of marriage. She was intelligent and kind and well-mannered and passably attractive. She was also extremely loyal to those who'd bothered to become well acquainted enough with her to be considered a friend, though that number was admittedly very small. And not a single whisper of scandal could be remotely attached to her name. Yet, in three whole years, no gentleman had attempted even a tentative courtship.

She had, however, gotten quite accustomed to men's glances sweeping right past her, polite but distracted dinner conversation, and dancing partners being chosen from all around while she remained unclaimed. In essence, being out in society had succeeded only in reviving the painful and fruitless hope of her childhood, when she'd done everything expected of her and had still failed to earn her father's regard.

At least, she'd managed to cultivate a couple lovely friendships over the last few years. And true friends were far more valuable than some reluctant husband.

Realizing that her internal agitation had lengthened and quickened her strides, she'd already begun to slow her steps as she neared the doorway connecting the drawing room to the dining room. Even so, she barely managed to avoid colliding with a gentleman stepping across the threshold.

It had to be Mr. Thomas, of course.

Reacting far more quickly than she was capable of doing, the man stepped back just as she swept by him, resulting in just the swish of her skirts against his boots instead of more devastating contact.

It all happened quickly enough that no one else in the room seemed to notice.

But Anne's heart had leapt right into her throat before dropping back down to thud against her ribs. She intentionally didn't glance back but she did slow to a more sedate pace. The low sound he'd made as she'd passed him stayed with her—settling low in her belly—as she left him and the other guests behind and walked confidently from the room.

She continued across the main hall to a narrow passage that led toward the water closet.

In the small, private quarters, she dabbed a bit of water from the bowl on the washstand to cool her heated cheeks and took a moment to calm her reckless heartbeat.

She'd have to return. But not yet.

Anne Humphries was no coward, but neither was she a woman to put herself on display while in such an emotionally flustered state. And though she would have liked to blame her current distress on her unfortunate partner, in truth, it had been her own internal thoughts which had gotten her so worked up. Mr. Thomas had simply served as yet another indicator that she simply wasn't the type of woman men tended to seek out for companionship—of even the most casual nature.

It was something she had to accept since she abhorred the idea of spending the rest of her years pining over the lack of a husband. No man—imagined or real—was worth that kind of self-limiting misery. She did not need a man at her side to enjoy her life.

She'd spent her entire existence to date trying to fulfill her father's expectations and then society's. She'd perfected the comportment and attitudes she'd been told were desirable and had mastered every skill required of a female in her position. And for what, exactly?

Peering at her reflection in the oval mirror set above the washstand, she saw the answer in her own disenchanted gaze.

It had all been for nothing.

Well, she was done with that.

In a way, spinsterhood offered something she'd never had before. Liberation. A chance to live as *she* wished—to explore herself, her interests, her abilities. Surely, she had more to offer the world than pretty manners and an array of common accomplishments. She just had to figure out what. Anne took several deep breaths, acknowledging that the task might be easier to declare than it was to accomplish. But she was nothing if not determined. Her new life started now.

With a final, firm nod at her reflection, she turned and left the water closet and headed back toward the party.

Unfortunately, all of her reclaimed poise nearly fled in a rush as she stepped into the drawing room and her gaze was immediately draw to where Mr. Thomas stood alone in a far corner of the room. His deep, black gaze cut right through the distraction of the other gathered guests to strike her with a curious force. For a split second, it felt like he'd been waiting for her to reappear. Impatiently.

But then he glanced away, shifting his attention with an expression of tortured boredom.

For the rest of the evening, she made a sincere effort to enjoy the general air of revelry and anticipation present amongst the rest of the guests. But as soon as a few people began to make their excuses, Anne also murmured a few quick good nights and made her way up to her bedroom, where her maid was waiting.

Without an appropriate female relative to fill the role of chaperone, Anne's father had hired a woman to fulfill the duty her first season, after which he determined the expense unnecessary. Apparently, the idea that Anne might actually engage in anything that could resemble scandalous behavior was inconceivable to her frugal father. And the staid Lord Humphries certainly wouldn't deign to attend any of the frivolous social events in support of his only child. Such things were for the realm of women, not serious men such as he.

As an alternative, Anne had been forced to prevail upon her friends, asking to accompany them to the various parties and events. Bethany and Lily had never made her feel like a burden or an extra wheel, but by her third season, Anne had started attending social events alone, despite the possible perception of impropriety.

Perhaps not surprisingly, no one even seemed to notice her breach in etiquette.

Once she was alone and all the candles had been snuffed, Anne sat in the window seat overlooking the garden and recalled the mantra she'd often repeated as a child.

Alone does not have to mean lonely.

Then she added something new: *And I am capable of more.*

THE ENTIRE HOUSE WAS bustling with activity the next morning as everyone came down early in order to be ready for the first competition of the day.

Archery.

There was still a morning haze in the sky when the guests gathered on the south lawn. A row of targets had been set up at three different distances from the five tables where the archers were to take aim. One partner would have three shots at the closer target and the other partner would take the one farther away. Based on the results of the first two rounds, the couple could choose between them who would take on the third and farthest target. The targets themselves consisted of three colored rings with three points being awarded for each hit in the center ring, two points for the next one out, and one point for the outermost ring.

Anne was one of the first to arrive at the scene of the competition, having walked from the house with Lily and Lord Harte. As more people made their way to the small archery range, Lily and her husband stepped away to greet their other guests and offer words of encouragement for the coming event.

Anne was soon after joined by a couple of the other unattached ladies who were just as quickly swept off by their partners to discuss who would shoot first between them. Lily's sister, Emma, and her husband, Mr. Bentley, also stopped to chat for a bit before moving on.

All the while, Anne kept glancing about for a sign of her partner. With his height and breadth, the man shouldn't have been hard to spot amongst the small clusters of guests sprinkled over the expansive lawn, yet she didn't catch a single glimpse of him.

She considered the possibility that after the debacle of yesterday's opening event, he might have decided to withdraw after all. The thought threatened to trigger a rush of annoyance, but she held it down. If she ended up having to continue through the games on her own, she'd find a way to manage.

At least archery happened to be one of the very few physical activities her father had deemed appropriate for young ladies, so Anne wasn't without some skill with a bow and arrow. There had been a couple years in her adolescence when she'd been quite committed to mastering the skill, sometimes spending hours a day practicing. It wasn't as if she had a whole lot else to fill her time.

Since it had been a few years since she'd picked up a bow and arrow, she only hoped she'd retained enough skill not to embarrass herself.

Five tables were set up several paces from each other. A footman was on hand at each table to assist with the archery equipment. As there were ten teams and they could only go five at a time, the event was likely to last through much of the morning. The first five contestants, which included Bethany along with two other women and two gentlemen, were already getting set up.

As Anne made her way toward the side where the other competitors were waiting their turn, she gave one last glance around for Mr. Thomas. She saw him almost immediately, off to one side in the shade of a nearby oak, and realized it was possible he'd been standing there the whole time, his position blocked from her view by the thick trunk of the tree.

His hands were tucked casually in the pockets of his coat as he leaned one shoulder against the tree and watched the first round of archers preparing their shots. The casual stance made him look almost relaxed and, for a moment, he looked rather dashing. But then he shifted his focus and the full force of his dark gaze landed quite abruptly on her. Her nape tingled and toes curled. Just like last night, it felt as though he'd been waiting for her to appear.

Don't be ridiculous, she admonished herself.

He wasn't waiting for her. He just happened to have a very intense stare. One to which she was apparently rather sensitive. It would be best for her to get over that little issue.

Shaking off her momentary disquiet, Anne crossed the lawn to her partner. Though she'd have been fine keeping herself at a distance from the man who clearly wanted even less to do with her than she did with him, they needed to decide who would shoot first.

She didn't realize just how removed his position was from the rest of the gathered participants until she reached his side and turned in place to look back toward the game. Even though there were well over two dozen people within sight, she suddenly felt quite alone with the brooding Welshman.

"Have you experience with a bow?" she blurted in her sudden discomfort.

There was a pause during which she forced herself not to glance at him. Best to keep her eyes trained forward.

"Some," he finally replied. "And you?"

"Some," she answered.

Why did it always seem so terribly difficult to converse with him?

Anne wasn't a social butterfly by any means, and though she was somewhat reserved by nature, she wasn't shy, either. She was well practiced in the art of small talk and knew the basics on how to set a person at ease, as anyone trained to be a good hostess would. She'd also encountered men with far more ill-tempered manners. Her father being a prime example.

So why couldn't she seem to manage a proper bit of communication with Mr. Thomas?

Because he unsettles you, came her instant internal answer.

Yes, but why? she pressed.

There was no satisfactory answer forthcoming.

"Would you prefer to go first or second?" she asked, hating how stiff her tone had gotten.

"I've no preference."

And then, because the first round was finishing and Anne felt a sharp need to get away from the large, dark man beside her, she volunteered, "Then I'll go first."

She walked away without waiting for his response, knowing he wouldn't bother to argue.

A few minutes later, she took her place at one of the tables and found herself standing next to the Earl of Wright. The young Miss Claybourne was there, offering her half brother a bit of encouragement before she turned to Anne with a smile.

"Good luck, Lady Anne. I'll be cheering you on."

"Thank you," she replied as the girl skipped away to join Lady Wright among the spectators.

Glancing to the earl, Anne marveled at how different he was from Mr. Thomas. Fair where Thomas was dark. Trim and athletic rather than broad and solid. Lord Wright was everything an earl should be—refined, proper, handsome, and though he sometimes seemed a bit standoffish, he was understatedly kind.

It was difficult to believe he and Mr. Thomas were brothers. But then she realized those elements were not the only differences between the siblings. Mr. Roderick Bentley was as different from the earl in looks as Mr. Thomas. But Bentley was a charismatic sort. A man who could charm just about anyone. And it seemed their young sister might share that trait. Mr. Thomas...did not.

Did the Welshman realize how different he was from his half siblings? She risked a quick glance in his direction. Was that why he still stood by himself beneath the oak?

The thought caused a pang of distress before the footman assigned to her table handed her the bow and then an arrow.

As the call was made to take aim, she forced any distracting considerations clear of her mind as she created a mental block between herself and everyone around her. The archery gear felt surprisingly comfortable in her hands despite the years since she'd last taken aim. She fell right back into the old patterns as though they were second nature.

First, she steadied her breath. Gazing intently at the target, she envisioned the point of her arrow flying straight and true to the center. When she released the drawn string on an even exhale, there was a moment of suspended anticipation, then a flash of pride as the arrow hit slightly off to one side but within the center circle.

Keeping her gaze on the target, she held out her hand for the next arrow. In fluid motions, she notched it and pulled the string back.

Steady breath. Focused gaze.

Then a moment of disappointment. The second arrow missed the bullseye by a tiny margin.

With a press of her lips, Anne accepted the third and final arrow of this round.

This one lodged into the target right beside the first. Dead center.

With a smile of satisfaction, Anne handed off her bow to the footman.

"Very well done, Lady Anne."

She nodded toward the earl in acknowledgment. "Thank you, my lord."

"The best of the day so far, I'd think."

Anne blinked. Really? Then she glanced toward the other targets. A few people hadn't finished all three attempts yet, but she only saw two other arrows that had made it into the center circle, each of them by different competitors. She was a bit surprised there were so few.

She watched the last of the arrows fly and noted only one more bullseye.

As the round ended and the footman collected the targets for scoring and to get them out of the way for the next round, Lily and Bethany both came up to Anne to offer their congratulations.

"I had no idea you could shoot like that," Lily exclaimed with a wide smile.

"It was wonderful to watch."

For Bethany to offer such effusive praise was saying something.

Anne was a bit surprised. She hadn't really thought herself particularly skilled at archery, but then, she'd always practiced alone and had never had anyone to compare herself to.

She remained with her friends as the second round began, but she couldn't help glancing toward Mr. Thomas every now and then where he remained beneath the tree. At least he was no longer alone since his young sister had joined him along with Lord and Lady Wright.

When it came to their turn, Mr. Thomas and Lady Wright approached the same tables from which Anne and the earl had shot. Anne found herself relaxing a bit as she noted the ease with which her partner handled the bow and notched the arrow. He was clearly no stranger to archery. Neither was Lady Wright. Her first two arrows landed in the center while a third hit the outermost ring. Even with the one rogue arrow, it was clear the woman was quite adept.

Not that Mr. Thomas was a poor shot by any means. Two of his arrows found the second ring while his third landed right at the edge of the center circle but was enough inside to count as a bullseye.

There was a brief break as the points from the first two rounds were tallied to determine the five highest scoring teams that would advance to the final round. Most people gravitated toward refreshments which had been arranged on a long table off to one side to await the final round. But when she noticed Mr. Thomas wasn't amongst them, Anne lingered behind.

Though she hadn't closely watched the very first archers, from what she *had* observed, she suspected she and Mr. Thomas would be advanced. And that meant they'd have to discuss who would shoot.

It took her a moment to spot her partner through the shifting crowd, but when she did, it was to find him heading straight for her with a dark countenance and ground-eating strides.

Her father used to approach her in such a manner when he was upset over some perceived ineptitude she'd unwittingly displayed. But it had been many years since her father had concerned himself so closely with her activities and she'd long ago released any desire to appease a man who saw her as nothing more than an extension of his estate.

Anne was not so easily intimidated these days. And Mr. Thomas was not her cold, judgmental father.

Squaring her shoulders, she waited with a calm that was only skin deep and hoped he'd never discover how his intensely focused attention always seemed to trigger a strange swirl in her belly and a rise of heat through her blood.

When he came to a stop in front of her and she had to tilt her head back to meet his gaze, she forcefully ignored how it made her feel small and feminine in a way she'd only ever experienced in his company.

"Mr. Thomas," she greeted simply.

He gave a nod. Then, "You'll want to participate in the final round, I imagine."

The way he phrased the statement caused her to hesitate. She frowned. "I certainly don't have to. But if you'd rather not..."

"You're clearly the better shot," he noted gruffly as he glanced over her head.

She turned to see what he was looking at, but there was nothing at all of interest behind her. She was inclined to agree with his assessment, but her father would say such hubris was decidedly unladylike and unattractive.

"My targets were much closer. It would be hard to say—"

"You're better," he interrupted firmly.

She fell silent, unsure if his curtness was simply an aspect of his nature if or if he were actually put out by her skill. Before she could determine if it was one over the other, he gave a short bow of his head and walked away.

Chapter Seven

The final archery round proceeded rather quickly. The five archers took their shots in rapid succession as the spectators and other competitors watched on in obvious excitement.

The moment her third and final arrow met the center of the target beside her first two, Anne knew she'd won. Since she and Mr. Thomas had the highest points going into the final round, even if each of her competitors got three bullseyes as well, they wouldn't have been able to overtake first place. With a small smile, she'd lowered her bow and glanced to where she'd last seen her partner.

He was no longer there. A quick glance over the crowd confirmed what she already suspected; he hadn't bothered to stay to the end of the event.

Before the fact could burrow too deeply into her mind, Lady Wright stepped around her table with a wide grin.

"Verra well done, Lady Anne," she said with a grin. "I find I dinnae mind losing when it's to someone with such skill."

Anne glanced to the countess's target. "I see you made three in the center as well, my lady."

"Aye, which means I can blame the loss on my husband. And I surely intend to," she added with a wink. "But you're quite magnificent with a bow and you should acknowledge that. I've never seen anyone aim and shoot with such fluid grace. It's fascinating."

The final scores were tallied quickly and resulted in a first place for Lady Anne Humphries and Mr. Thomas, with the Earl and

Countess of Wright claiming a very close second and third being earned by a local squire Mr. Gallagher and his partner, Lady Muriel Ratcliffe.

Lady Wright's comments weren't even the most effusive Anne received as others came forward to offer their congratulations. Though the atypical amount of attention made her feel rather uncomfortable, she couldn't deny how much she enjoyed taking the win.

Eventually, everyone began to make their way back toward the house. Anne walked beside Bethany and Mr. Pinkman, only half listening as the couple teased each other for their poor showing at the morning event. Unfortunately, it took her longer than it should have to realize when their light quips became low, intimate murmurs, but as soon as she did, she slowed her pace to put some space between them and allow the couple some moments of privacy.

Of course, then she lost the distraction they provided and she found herself searching about for broad, muscled shoulders and black hair worn a bit too long. As soon as she realized what she was doing, she gave herself a mental shake and kept her focus trained on the ground two steps ahead of her.

Lily had arranged for lunch to be served picnic style in the estate's extensive flower gardens. Guests would have a choice between enjoying their meals on blankets spread over the soft grass or at one of the tables set up beneath several tents which had been erected in the garden's lush little arbors.

As soon as Anne stepped through the back gate and made her way along the path toward the main area where everything was arranged, she realized her mistake in taking her time. It appeared that everyone had already claimed their spots.

Lily and her husband were lounging on a picnic blanket with Mr. and Mrs. Bentley and their two very young boys while the Pinkmans had joined two other couples seated at one of the tables.

Anne glanced about for anyone else she knew well enough to join, but there didn't appear to be any space left. Just as an uncomfortable dread seeped into her bones, the young Miss Claybourne skipped up to her.

"Lady Anne, do come sit with us. I've been saving you a seat."

Looking up to where the girl gestured toward a blanket spread beneath the branches of a lovely draping willow tree, Anne felt a quick flash of relief. The blanket was occupied by Lord and Lady Wright, who glanced up with a smile and a wave.

"Thank you, Miss Claybourne, I'd love to join you."

--------⟨⟩--------

BEYNON MADE HIS WAY through the garden, keeping an eye out for Caillie. His wily sister had caught him as he'd tried to leave the archery field unnoticed. She'd chided him for leaving before the congratulatory scene that would inevitably follow his partner's triumph and had only let him go when he promised to join her for lunch.

He'd hoped to skip the quaint little garden luncheon, but he'd given in to his bold sister's bribery because the need to escape the covetous gaze of Lady Mayhew had been much more urgent.

The faithless woman was proving to be a serious problem.

He'd never been pursued so intently before. And so bloody obviously. Her husband might have been participating in the final archery round, but there were plenty of others about to take note of her overt glances and suggestive smiles. Since Beynon had failed to dissuade the woman with harsh honesty, he didn't know what else to do but avoid her as much as possible.

He quickly spotted Caillie waving to him from beneath a willow. With his attention focused on ensuring he didn't pass too closely to Lady Mayhew, he failed to take note of who else had been included in Caillie's party until he was upon them.

That Colin and Ainsworth were there was no surprise. He didn't, however, expect to see Lady Anne sitting straight and tall with her long legs tucked properly to one side beneath the skirts of her pale pink dress. How such a tall woman could look so effortlessly elegant while seated on the ground was a bit unnerving. But it wasn't nearly as unsettling as the graceful line of her neck or the faint little whisps of pale golden hair that brushed her nape.

Furrowing his brow to dislodge the troublesome focus of his thoughts, he looked up to see Colin staring at him rather oddly. It was a look that would have been much more at home on Roderick's irreverent face.

"Are you going to have a seat, Beynon?" Ainsworth asked bluntly. "Or do you intend to loom over us throughout the meal?"

Resisting the urge to clear his throat, he stepped forward to lower himself to the open spot still available on the blanket, which happened to be beside his reluctant partner. It did not escape his notice how tense Lady Anne's slim frame became at his nearness.

She exhibited a similar reaction whenever she saw him. A barely perceptible flinch followed by a slight drawing back of the shoulders and a quick lowering of her chin. As if she somehow felt she needed to brace herself against him.

And every time he saw her do it, a sharp barb of irritation burrowed a bit deeper inside him. He knew his frown was darkening, but he couldn't seem to help it. It was on the tip of his tongue to tell her he was doing all he could to keep his distance. That if not for this blasted competition, she wouldn't have to suffer his damned company at all.

"Lemonade?"

He glanced to Caillie, who leaned across the blanket with a small glass in hand and a bright smile on her face.

"Thank you," he muttered as he took the offered refreshment.

Unfortunately, the glass was drained in two healthy gulps, which left him to awkwardly cradle an empty glass in his too-large hand.

"Have you had a chance to tell Lady Anne how well she did this morning?" Caillie asked.

Beynon narrowed his gaze at his little sister. The chit knew damned well he hadn't.

"I acknowledged her skill," he replied.

"Since neither Colin and Worthy nor the third-place archers had finished in the downhill race, I believe this puts the two of you near the top of the leaderboard."

"The games have only just begun, Caillie," the earl reasoned calmly. "And with such a wide array of events, a great deal can still happen."

"Aye, but it's still verra exciting to be in the lead. Even if it's only for a wee bit of time," the girl argued. "Wouldn't you agree, Lady Anne?"

"Ah, yes. Yes, it is exciting."

The lady's blue-green gaze flickered briefly to his before dropping it to where his hand held the empty glass. A faint furrow of consternation tugged at her elegant eyebrows.

No doubt she'd noticed his callouses and the many small scars that came from a life of physical work. His fingers involuntarily tightened around the glass and she quickly shifted her gaze to something else.

Irritation sat like a burning lump of coal in his stomach as he forced his attention elsewhere as well and noted that Colin and Ainsworth were engaged in a separate conversation. Their lowered voices and the way they leaned into each other indicated he wouldn't find a proper distraction there.

"The afternoon event should be interesting," his sister continued, clearly intent on discussing the games. "Are you looking forward to it, Beynon?"

He turned to Caillie with flash of annoyance. By her unabashed grin, he could see she was fully aware of his mood and was utterly unconcerned by it. For some reason, she'd decided to drag him into the conversation and didn't care much at all what he thought about it. Unfortunately, he'd only glanced at the schedule and couldn't recall what painful trial he'd be expected to endure next.

He mumbled a noncommittal, "Not particularly."

Caillie grinned, obviously suspecting his ignorance, as she turned to Lady Anne. "I think it'll be lovely." Then her eyes widened with a flash of excitement. "Oh, maybe it will give me a chance to practice floriography."

Lady Anne tilted her head. "Have you taken an interest in the French pastime, Miss Claybourne?"

"Aye," the girl exclaimed then slid a glance to Beynon. "Are you familiar with floriography, brother?" Caillie pressed.

Not happy at being pulled back into the conversation, he remarked, "Am I familiar with what?"

"The language of flowers," Lady Anne replied in a voice that wasn't exactly condescending but wasn't *not* condescending, either.

Still annoyed, he gave the lady beside him a dark look as he replied with intentional obtuseness. "No. I can't say I've ever heard flowers speak."

Caillie laughed and he swore he saw just a twitch of amusement at the corner of Lady Anne's mouth as she explained, "It's the practice of using the symbolism associated with certain flora to communicate a particular message."

"I read a wonderful book about it, *Le language des Fleurs*," Caillie added in a wistful tone.

"You can read French?" Beynon asked, a bit surprised.

The girl shrugged. "Passably."

"You'd love Joseph Hammer-Purgstall's *Dictionnaire du language des fleurs*. I can lend you my copy if you'd like," Lady Anne offered. "But we'll have to wait until we return to London."

"Thank you. That'd be lovely," the girl effused before turning to Beynon. "Too bad you won't have a chance to read up on it yourself before the next competition."

"I assume we're expected to do something with flowers," he noted with a distinct lack of enthusiasm.

Caillie just grinned and decided that was a good time to turn her attention back to her meal. Assuming he was finally getting a reprieve, Beynon did the same.

But as Lady Anne leaned forward to select a buttered roll from the basket set in the center of the blanket, Beynon's gaze wandered to the straight line of her spine and the gentle flare of her hips. The woman's posture and poise were flawless. No one should have so much grace and elegance white seated on the ground.

When she leaned back again to reclaim her seat at the corner of the blanket, he didn't miss the subtle stiffening in her body.

Following the direction of her gaze, he noted where the flounced hem of her skirts had shifted to nestle against his boot. For a moment, the pristine pink lay in stark contrast to the worn black leather. It was oddly entrancing.

But then the lady shifted position, tucking her skirts more securely about her legs.

Something dark and dangerous flowed through his bloodstream as he acknowledged her actions. Did she find him so distasteful she couldn't tolerate even that casual contact?

He didn't bother to hide the acrimony flowing through him when he looked up and met the lady's tempestuous gaze. Despite the strict stillness of her person, the blue-green of her eyes swirled with a quiet, mystifying light. A fervent—carefully guarded—intensity.

It was utterly unexpected and it struck him like a kick to the sternum.

In a rush, he rose to his feet, nearly upending one of the platters.

Colin and Ainsworth glanced up from their conversation and Caillie eyed his sudden movement curiously. He couldn't bring himself to risk another glance to his partner.

"If you'll excuse me."

Not bothering to wait for any reply, he turned and strode heavily through the garden to the back gate and didn't stop until he was deep beneath the cool canopy of the woods that extended westward from the house and manicured grounds.

He shouldn't care what the fine Lady Anne thought of him. He *didn't* care. At least, not beyond the fact that they were stuck together in this god-awful game for the next several days.

He'd been fully honest when he'd told Roderick he had no intention of considering a bride amongst the ladies gathered here. Not that he didn't wish to marry. The idea of having a wife and children appealed to him greatly. But he would choose a woman who'd be willing and able to work the farm right beside him. Someone who'd share in the burdens as well as the rewards of their labor. As his mother had done for his stepfather.

He sure as hell wouldn't ever consider a woman who was suited to nothing more than serving tea while perched at the edge of a settee or flitting about a ballroom dressed in silks and lace. He told himself Lady Anne's obvious aversion to the touch of her fine skirts to his worn boots meant absolutely nothing to him. But it was the cerulean fire in her eyes that made him feel like there wasn't a forest dark enough, cool enough, or deep enough to escape the unwanted heat she triggered in his blood.

Chapter Eight

F lower arranging.

That was the afternoon event.

One partner was tasked with selecting the blooms while the other was responsible for creating the most attractive arrangement. The results were to be anonymously judged by the Countess of Harte's great-aunt, Lady Chelmsworth.

So it was that Beynon found himself standing at the long gardener's table in the estate greenhouse beside the other gentlemen competitors, staring at the profusive array of choices. Flowers of every color, shape, size, and scent imaginable were on display. There were more than a few he'd never seen before and some he sure as hell couldn't identify by name.

The rules indicated you had to choose at least three different types but no more than seven.

As the other men stepped around the table, making their selections, Beynon stood in place with his arms crossed over his chest. He'd never had cause to consider what might go into making a stylish bouquet. But he couldn't remain unmoving for long. There was also a time limit placed on the event. The sooner he got the flowers to Lady Anne, the better chance she'd have of making sense of what he managed to collect.

Not that he cared about winning the event. He just didn't want it to be said he hadn't at least tried to do his part.

"Come now, brother," Roderick said with a clap on the back as he passed by. "No need to look so pained. They're just flowers."

Beynon's response was a rough grunt as he continued to glare at the explosion of blooms.

Just as he was about to start grabbing whatever was closest to him, he caught sight of something familiar. Wild honeysuckle.

Taking up a small handful, he paused as the heady scent brought on a subtle wave of nostalgia. Seeing another couple flowers he recognized, he grabbed a little of each of those, as well. In no time at all, he was suddenly the last man still making his choices. Looking at what he had in his hand, he realized they were all rather small, delicate things when he'd seen others with big blooms—roses and lilies and such. Thinking he needed something a bit bolder to balance things out, he spotted some blue hyacinths nearby. Then he took up some maidenhair ferns to add some greenery to his mix.

With a dubious look at his odd cluster, he gave a shrug.

It'd have to do.

Entering the conservatory, he was grateful there were no spectators for this event. Each partnership had been allowed their own individual table holding a large vase and a pair of shears. Lady Anne was positioned off to one side of the room. As the other couples bent over their flowers and spoke in low words, Beynon's unfortunate partner waited. Her sharp gaze landed on him the moment he stepped into the room and he felt the oddest urge to apologize.

Not bloody likely. He might have been the last to arrive but only by a few steps. There was still plenty of time for her to make her little arrangement.

As he neared, the direction of her focus fell to the posies clasped in his fist. There was an odd little twitch in her right eyebrow and a quick press of her lips before she lowered her chin.

What the hell did that mean?

With a rough sound that would have to pass as a greeting, Beynon set his selections on the table beside the vase. Unsure what else to do but noting that the other gentlemen all remained hovered over their respective tables, he took a step back and watched as Lady Anne began sorting through the flowers.

She gave no indication if she was pleased by his choices or disappointed as she chose one of the largest hyacinths and clipped a bit off the stem with the shears before setting it into the vase. She added one of the ferns next, then a bit of clover, then some honeysuckle. As she continued adding blooms, he realized the composition didn't look like any of the bouquets he'd seen around the house in the last few days.

With a scowl forming over his gaze, he glanced at the other tables and saw roses in all shades, orchids, tulips, and irises. With a harsh realization, he acknowledged most of his selections could be considered wildflowers. Or weeds.

"I'm getting a sense my choices aren't terribly fashionable," he noted.

Lady Anne paused to glanced up at him. Her eyes were soft and slightly translucent in the indirect light of the conservatory. No stormy fire today, thank God.

Rather than replying right away, she seemed to examine him for a moment. Her assessing gaze touched on the tense muscles bunched between his brows before sliding gently down the bridge of his nose to the hard line of his mouth.

His back teeth clenched and he just barely resisted the urge to shift his weight when she blinked then turned her attention back to the task in front of her.

"The various shades of purple and blue are quite lovely, I think, with the bit of yellow and white as accents."

She paused to take up a stem of dainty purple flowers he'd seen before but didn't know what they were called and tucked it carefully into a cluster of ferns. He got the sense she wasn't finished speaking, so he held his tongue. Not that he had anything in particular to say anyway.

"The ferns add a nice texture," she added.

"They grow between rocks near waterfalls back home." He wasn't exactly sure why he said that. "The clover is rather common, as well."

She nodded but didn't say anything else.

A few minutes later, a bell signaled the end of the allotted time. Lady Harte explained the judging would take place while everyone rested before dinner and the winners would be posted that evening.

As everyone began to wander from the room, Lady Anne gave him a slightly anticipatory glance. It seemed as though something were expected of him, but he hadn't the slightest idea what it was.

The lady cleared her throat. "Tomorrow is the fishing competition, the scavenger hunt, and the maze. Have you noted our scheduled times for each?"

Beynon nodded. "We're to be the first on the lake and the last through the maze."

"Which allows us all the time in between for the scavenger hunt. Should we also make a plan for rehearsing the dramatic reading we're expected to perform?"

"The what?"

Her frown was a quick dip of her brows. "Each pairing is expected to read a short dialogue from a popular play. We've been given *Faust* by Johann Wolfgang von Goethe. You should have received a copy of the reading."

He hadn't but he was familiar with the play. It was one of his mother's favorites.

"We're not expected to memorize the lines, but I suppose we should practice a bit," she added.

He couldn't help but notice the hopeful tone in her voice and an odd resistance rose inside him.

"When is the reading?"

Lady Anne blinked at his curt tone. "It's the last event. At the end of the week."

"We have time then," he answered gruffly.

It was clear his answer didn't particularly please her, but she didn't try to argue or persuade. Instead, she gave a soft little sigh and glanced to the side. It was then that he realized they were now quite alone in the conservatory. Not even a footman had remained behind.

Every muscle in his body tightened. At the same time, she brought her gaze suddenly back to meet his. Though not currently swirling with quiet intensity, there was still a surprising depth in her eyes. Like a mystical, never-ending pool.

And he found himself holding his breath. It would be frighteningly easy to drown in those eyes.

"I suppose I shall see you at dinner then, Mr. Thomas."

Not knowing what else to do, he nodded then watched as she turned and glided gracefully from the room.

He muttered a curse.

Though there had been many times since he'd first met his brothers and sister that he'd experienced a sense of being totally out of his element, especially in the months since he'd been officially introduced to London society, he'd never felt so at a loss as he did whenever Lady Anne walked away from him.

———— ⟨∞⟩ ————

THAT NIGHT, THE DRAWING room was filled with fragrant and colorful bouquets, providing an opportunity for the guests to admire and assess the creations prior to the announcement of the winners.

Though he tried not to pay undue attention to the twitters and speculation the other guests engaged in as they passed by Lady Anne's arrangement, Beynon couldn't fully ignore the occasional sly glances cast in his direction. No doubt everyone found his lack of sophistication in choosing flowers so obviously out of fashion very amusing, but he refused to feel shame for it. Such a skill had no purpose in his life.

Directing his attention away from the floral display, he crossed the room to where Roderick stood with Emma beside Lord and Lady Harte.

Beynon only had a moment to mutter good evening before a bit of a commotion drew everyone's attention toward the main doors.

Lady Harte gave a little laugh she quickly hid behind her glove as Emma murmured, "We should have known she'd made a theatrical entrance."

Beynon turned to see the Countess of Chelmsworth—an elderly Frenchwoman who preferred her hair ink black and her lips ruby red—sweep into the room wearing an emerald-green gown with a skirt displaying a veritable garden of embroidered posies. Caillie walked beside her, also dressed in a floral-themed frock of pink and green, carrying a pink silk pillow on which nestled a crown of white lilies.

Roderick gave Beynon a nudge with his elbow. "I think our little sister has a true flair for the dramatic, don't you?"

"I wonder where she gets that from," Beynon noted dryly as he gave a pointed look at his brother's waistcoat.

For the most part, Roderick's style was fashionably understated by London standards—with one significant exception. No matter what the event or time of day, he never failed to sport a waistcoat in some dramatic color. Tonight, it was a leafy green brocade.

As his brother chuckled, Lady Chelmsworth, who insisted everyone call her Angelique, paused in the center of the room.

Though quite elderly, the lady had a very commanding presence and a style all her own. Emma and Roderick had once discussed how Angelique often told tales of her life prior to her marriage to the Earl of Chelmsworth. Tales that—if all were to be believed—suggested she had lived a very colorful existence.

"'Ello, 'ello, everyone," she began in a voice that carried her accented words surprisingly well throughout the murmuring crowd. "Though it was a very difficult decision requiring consideration of a great many factors, I have chosen zee three winners."

Not particularly interested in which bouquets were deemed the best, Beynon allowed his attention to drift toward Lady Anne. He wasn't at all sure why he'd developed the annoying tendency to seek the woman out whenever his attention wasn't otherwise occupied, but he wasn't particularly inclined to resist it either.

As always, she sat with perfect posture. Her slim shoulders, partially bared by the wide neckline of her gown, were straight and proud though she held her head with a slight bow that gave a graceful arc to her neck. Her hands rested gently in her lap and her expression was one of unstudied poise as she gave her full attention to the announcement of winners.

But even from his angle and distance, he was able to detect something slightly discordant in her manner. There was nothing specific in her appearance that was incongruent. It was really just a feeling. An internal sense that her outward demeanor was just a bit forced.

He scowled. He was being ridiculous.

Then, just as he was about to look away, Lady Anne suddenly stiffened. Her eyes widened and her gaze flickered very briefly in his direction. The glance was so quick, he would never have noticed it if he hadn't been staring so intently. And though she immediately turned her attention back to Angelique, her fingers were now interwoven and clasped tightly together.

It was then that he heard the ripple of laughter chasing through the room followed by more surreptitious glances in his direction.

"What in hell?"

Beside him, Roderick to give a low chuckle. "Congratulations."

"For what?"

Roderick lifted a brow. "Weren't you listening?"

"Just tell me," Beynon growled as the looks and whispers continued. A quick peek toward Lady Anne revealed a slight blush coloring her cheeks as she spoke quietly with the ladies seated beside her.

"Angelique awarded third place to the most unusual entry in the competition."

Understanding dawned with a bit of irritation. Though he certainly wasn't happy for the pity vote, he didn't think the matter warranted the kind of attention he was currently receiving.

"She explained that although the color scheme was rather unconventional, being unconventional herself, it was one of the things she liked most about it," Roderick continued. "That and the deliciously scandalous message of the blooms."

Beynon turned a hard gaze to his brother and noted how the other man was just barely holding in laughter. "What message?"

Roderick did laugh then and clapped Beynon on the back before walking away without answering.

Beynon practically snarled in frustration. What the fuck had he done?

Chapter Nine

The sun had been above the horizon for less than an hour when Anne stepped from the house. Being so early, the garden and grounds were quiet and still and the lightly overcast sky covered everything in a muted shade of golden gray. It was pleasantly cool now, but something in the air suggested the day could get quite warm if the thin layer of clouds managed to disperse.

The boathouse was located at the end of a long path beyond the south lawn and the hill they'd raced—or tumbled—down the other day.

Fishing was not her forte, but since it seemed to be a favorite pastime amongst most gentlemen she knew, she hoped her partner might step in where she was lacking in this particular event. Five teams were scheduled for the morning and five teams in the evening, allowing everyone three hours on the lake to make their best attempt at catching the biggest fish.

As she reached the bottom of the gravel path and approached the boathouse, Anne peered ahead to see if anyone had gotten to the lakeshore ahead of her. When she didn't see any sign of movement, she wondered if she might have been a bit *too* early. But then again, being that she was a great deal less confident about this event, she intended to make the most of every minute allotted for the task.

Of course, that would only work if Mr. Thomas also managed to be on time.

She'd very carefully avoided speaking with him last evening though she could feel his black eyes staring at her intermittently throughout the hours that had followed Angelique's inciting little announcement. Though the suggestive tone of the lady's voice alone had been enough to cause a stir, she could only hope the Frenchwoman's cryptic reference to the symbols of their flower arrangement wouldn't have been understood by most people present. The practice of floriography, while popular in France for some time, was really quite new to Britain.

Since Angelique gratefully didn't go into any detail, most people could only speculate on what the "scandalous message" might be until they lost interest, which shouldn't take long. At least, that's what Anne was hoping for.

Reaching the boathouse, she continued around the building toward the lakeshore instead of going inside. If no one was there just yet, she'd look for a nice dry, grassy bank where she could sit and wait in the fresh air.

But it seemed she wasn't the first to arrive after all.

As soon as she stepped around the corner of the small building, she saw two of the Harte footmen tying a rowboat up to one of the metal rings bolted along the dock extending a short way from shore. Just as she paused, two more men came from the boathouse, carrying another rowboat between them. One man was dressed in a footman's uniform while the other was dressed as a country gentleman minus a coat.

Mr. Thomas.

Anne took a swift breath through her nose as the bones in her body suddenly went a bit wobbly. She'd never considered how much of a man's physique a simple coat could conceal or enhance, depending on the man. If she'd thought Mr. Thomas exceptionally large and burly before, she now realized she'd truly had no idea.

Beneath the thin cotton of his shirt, muscles bulged and rolled as he and the footman adjusted their hold on the boat in order to set it into the water and secure it to the dock. His sleeves were rolled up to his elbows, revealing the sun-bronzed muscles of his forearms. For some reason the way those muscles tightened and released as his large hands and deft fingers worked the rope into a proper knot made Anne's heart skip madly about.

Heat rushed through her as she realized how crudely she was ogling the man. But just as she was about to flee back around the corner of the building, Mr. Thomas straightened. Bracing his large hands on trim hips, he turned to say something to the footman beside him. He must have caught sight of Anne from the corner of his eye, because while the footman replied with a laugh, Thomas sent his heavy, dark gaze in her direction.

And then fleeing was impossible.

Breath and thought were impossible.

There was something so...raw and intense in how he looked at her. What she'd initially thought was anger, she was starting to suspect might be much more complicated than that. Or maybe it was her own reaction that was so complicated and intense. Whatever it was, it seemed to increase with each encounter, each glance, each brief conversation.

Essentially frozen in place, she watched with a little stab of disappointment as he unrolled his sleeves while he stalked purposefully to shore. After swiping up his coat from where he'd left it on the grass, he shrugged into the garment and was once again a properly clothed gentleman by the time he reached her.

"Lady Anne."

Why did his voice always sound so weighted with richness and texture? As though it were a physical thing flowing through her?

"Good morning, Mr. Thomas."

It was all they managed before the sound of voices preceded the arrival of several more guests. Then it was a few moments of activity as everyone selected their fishing poles and bait and other necessities which the footmen loaded into the boats while the gentlemen assisted their ladies onto the vessels before embarking themselves.

When Mr. Thomas held his hand out to Anne, she automatically set her fingers in his palm. Neither of them wore gloves and the sensation of his warm, roughed skin against hers sent a strange frisson through her body. The sensation was delicate but sharp and she recalled that she'd felt something similar when she'd taken his hand for the downhill race. But it was significantly more unsettling this time. She might have been able to conceal her reaction if she weren't already out of sorts from earlier. As it was, she stilled. Abruptly.

Her lips parted on a quick inhale and her attention flickered up to his face. With his head bowed as he looked down at her, his dark-set features appeared slightly menacing.

It was definitely anger that she saw in his eyes.

And for some reason, the hard edge of his glare and the firm press of his mouth just then struck her in a new way. It rather hurt, actually.

His eyes narrowed as he glanced down to where her fingers still rested against his palm before meeting her gaze again. "It's just a hand, Lady Anne. Rougher and larger than yours. But no different otherwise."

She blinked. The tone of his voice was harsh and accusing. She blinked again then widened her eyes as she realized with a pang of shock that he thought she'd been offended by his touch when the opposite couldn't be more true. Heat infused her cheeks as she glanced down. It was horribly embarrassing to think he'd believe her so shallow, but it seemed worse, however, to admit the truth.

"Of course," she murmured as she turned toward the rowboat, suddenly wishing she could just disappear.

As she stepped somewhat hastily into the unsteady vessel, it rocked a bit, forcing her to grasp tighter to his hand as she regained her balance. But as soon as she did, she released him and took her seat at the bow.

He embarked with much more assurance and masculine grace. Within another moment, the footman released the rope and gave a little shove to clear them from the dock. Two of the other teams were already gliding gently away from shore and the third was soon to follow when Mr. Thomas grasped the oars and set to rowing.

While the other gentlemen rowers maintained a steady but gentle pace, the sheer power of her partner's movements quickly eliminated the disadvantage of being one of the last to push off as he angled them toward the shady side of the lake.

Anne kept her focus on staying balanced and centered on the narrow wooden bench seat as they glided swiftly over the water. Since her partner appeared intent upon his task, she didn't bother with small talk even though she heard the murmur of conversation and periodic laughter drifting from the other rowboats.

After another few minutes, she was able to find some pleasure in watching the softly rising sun slowly disperse the layer of fog that drifted across the lake's surface. Gentle rays of light began to sparkle on the water as the greenery along shore came to life. In any other circumstance, it might have been a very romantic scene. For that reason specifically, Anne forced herself not to send even a casual glance in Mr. Thomas's direction in case he somehow misconstrued her enjoyment.

As they reached a small bay lined with large deciduous trees that created dappled patterns in the water, Mr. Thomas ceased rowing and dropped a small anchor.

Still without speaking, he secured the oars then began to ready their tackle. His movements were efficient and well practiced as he set up the long bamboo fishing poles.

Being that he was so occupied with his task, she allowed herself a moment to observe him. Avidly.

With his feet braced widely in the bottom of the rowboat, he didn't even seem to notice the occasional rocking as he leaned forward for this or twisted around for that. With surprising deftness, his large hands secured the line and set the bait to the hooks.

He was very comfortable here. In this element. Outdoors, beneath the sky, with the quiet of nature surrounding him. No doubt, he'd have been even more comfortable if she weren't there.

He glanced up and extended one of the poles toward her.

The dark force of his sudden attention unbalanced her far more than the gentle sway of the rowboat. Being alone with him like this—even though they were in full sight of the other competitors and anyone who came down to the lakeshore—felt disturbingly intimate. Until his features pulled into a grim and almost hostile expression.

"Your pole, Lady Anne," he muttered.

Moving carefully so as not to upset the boat, she shifted her weight and leaned forward to claim the fishing pole as she murmured a quick thank you. Then she watched as he turned toward one side, propped his own pole between his spread knees, and tossed the bait into the water.

She suddenly wished she could paint him exactly like that. The way the earthy tones of his buckskin breeches and chocolate-brown coat contrasted with the lush greenery on shore and the dark blue and gold of the lake. Even in his relaxed posture, with his shoulders lowered and his elbows resting on his solid thighs, he possessed such a commanding presence that was somehow not at all incongruent to the natural serenity of the setting. Perhaps she'd even allow her watercolors to blur a bit of the background so the eye was inescapably drawn to the strong lines of his form, the confidence in his casual manner, and the focus in his gaze—which was once again turned on her.

As soon as her eyes met his, he frowned and looked away.

She'd been caught staring yet again. It would seem this morning was going to be highlighted by her frequent moments of embarrassment.

Anne clenched her teeth. The two of them were going to be spending nearly the entire day together. If she didn't set aside her internal disquiet and find a way to engage in simple conversation with the man, it was going to prove unendurable. Surely, she could manage a bit of innocuous small talk.

"Is fishing one of your preferred hobbies, Mr. Thomas?"

He glanced aside at her for a brief moment before replying. "I don't have time for hobbies."

Anne forced herself to ignore his gruff tone as she continued pleasantly. "Yet you appear rather proficient at the task."

He shrugged his great shoulders. "It's not particularly difficult to bait a hook."

All right, then. Apparently, the man didn't appreciate compliments, no matter how subtle. Conversation was overrated, anyway. Concealing her sigh, she turned her attention back to the task at hand. Eying her pole dubiously, she tipped it forward and allowed the baited hook to drop into the water as she'd seen him do. Now, she supposed all there was to do was wait, though she hadn't the slightest idea what to do if she actually got the attention of a fish.

"Have you fished before?" he asked.

"What?" Looking up with a blink, she realized he was watching her with a somewhat skeptical expression. Her lack of experience was no doubt quite obvious. "Only once," she replied, "when I was very small. Whenever my father spent time in the country, he'd visit the trout stream on our estate. One time, I was curious enough to ask if I could go as well." She watched the ripples from their gently rocking boat fade out across the lake's surface. "The footman who accompanied me didn't know much more about fishing than I did."

There was a brief silence. "Your father didn't take you himself?"

She gave a soft laugh. "Definitely not. Lord Humphries is not a man to suffer the company of children. Young or grown," she muttered, then chastised herself for the display of self-indulgent bitterness. To offset her resentful tone, she offered a smile as she said, "But if fishing is not particularly difficult—as you said—I'm certain I'll manage." Suddenly realizing she was in the midst of a perfect opportunity to explore a possible new interest, she boldly risked adding, "Though if you feel a desire to offer a few tips along the way, I'd be obliged."

His answer was a short grunt as he turned his attention back to his own pole.

She frowned. It had been worth a try, but she probably should have known better than to ask such a *trying* favor of her grouchy partner.

Silence reigned once again, but only for a few minutes before he spoke with no preamble whatsoever, asking, "What did the flowers mean?"

"What?" she said again, a bit sharper this time.

Without looking at her, he clarified—though truly no clarification was needed. She knew exactly what he was asking even if she'd hoped to God he wouldn't.

"Our *scandalous* bouquet," he prompted while staring intently at the spot where his line disappeared into the water.

"Right. Nothing significant, really." She tried for a lightly dismissive tone, hoping to convince him the matter was inconsequential.

He did look at her then, one heavy black brow raised in disbelief as he narrowed his gaze. "You're not a good liar, Lady Anne."

She glanced down as she tried to keep the rising blush at bay. "Truly. I know there was no intention behind your selections. It was an unfortunate coincidence that Angelique is familiar with the symbolism; otherwise, I doubt anyone else would have noticed a thing about it."

There was a long pause before he muttered, "But you knew the meaning they supposedly conveyed the moment I brought them to you."

Anne wasn't sure why her breath caught as it did or why her belly tightened as he stared at her, but for a second, she honestly couldn't figure out how to reply.

"As I said," she finally managed, "I knew it wasn't intentional, so I didn't think much on it."

Another pause, then he looked back to where his line disappeared into the water.

"You're not going to tell me, are you?" he noted in a disgruntled baritone.

She almost smiled at his annoyance but replied simply, "No, I'm not."

Thankfully, he let the matter drop, and soon after, he hauled in their first catch of the morning.

Chapter Ten

Beynon ruffed the towel over his head as he stepped from the bathing tub. A quick glance at the clock told him he had only fifteen minutes before he was due to meet Lady Anne in the breakfast room, where they were to acquire the list of items for the scavenger hunt.

He chose casual clothing once again, assuming they'd be expected to trek about the house and grounds. As he stood in front of the mirror to tie his cravat, he gave his reflection a quick frown. His hair was in need of a trim, and though he'd shaved that morning, there was already a dark shadow along his jaw. He didn't have time now, but he'd have to shave again before dinner. Even if he did have time, the idea of shaving three times in a single day was more than he'd entertain when he sometimes went a number of days between shaving back home.

Lady Anne and the rest of the fine houseguests would just have to accept his less-than-pristine state. At least he no longer smelled of fish and lake water.

Though she had essentially no prior experience, Lady Anne had surprised him by doing a fair share during the three hours they were on the water. Since the contest required that they turn in only their largest catch of the day, anything too small was released. She'd handed him the net when needed and had held his pole while he traded out a larger catch for the one on their stringer.

She'd even managed to hook two herself, insisting rather stubbornly that he instruct her on how to hold the fish and remove the hook. Her first attempt had been laughable. Beynon had been forced to bite his lip to hold back his chuckle when the fish flopped from her hands and she gave a shriek. But she'd eventually managed the task with his assistance then insisted he show her how to reset new bait. The release of her second catch went significantly smoother and she'd leaned confidently over the side of the boat to release the fish back into the lake with a smile of accomplishment brightening her face.

Beynon had quickly averted his gaze, ignoring the odd tugging sensation in his chest as intently as he'd denied his earlier amusement.

At the end of their allotted time, they'd ended up with a pretty good entry for the competition.

Now, as he stepped into the morning room with only a minute to spare, he expected to find Lady Anne already waiting. The room was empty; however, a basket holding a collection of scrolls, assumedly containing the list of items to be found, had been placed on the small table near the leader board and event schedule. Beynon took one of the scrolls then signed them in with the time indicating the start of their hunt. They would have to return to document their end time, as well. The couple who found the most items in the shortest time would win the event.

He considered waiting for Lady Anne before signing them in, but he trusted she'd be down shortly. Deciding to await her in the hall, he turned to leave but came up short at the sight of Lady Mayhew entering the room. Alone.

"Mr. Thomas. What a pleasure to find you here."

Beynon nearly groaned his frustration at being cornered by the woman once again. But this wasn't like the other day when she'd come upon him away from the house, sheltered along a tall wall.

Anyone could walk into the breakfast room at any moment. Lady Anne was likely making her way there already. There was no reason to think Lady Mayhew would attempt anything scandalous—aside from the rather greedy look in her eyes.

Beynon had never been one to make the same mistake twice. With only a split second of deliberation, he decided his best course of action was to simply leave. Quickly and efficiently.

Saying nothing in response to her greeting, he took long strides toward the door. But he'd greatly underestimated her brazen resolve.

The freedom of the hall was in sight as he arced around her position, hoping his utter lack of acknowledgement might clue her in to the fact that he wasn't interested even if his blunt words the other day had not. But at the last moment, the lady side-stepped in front of him. He barely had a chance to grasp hold of her arms to keep from knocking her over as he plowed forward, completely unprepared for such a maneuver. As their bodies made brief and unavoidable contact, a quiet hum of satisfaction slipped from the lady's throat, triggering a flash of temper in his blood.

Though he managed to shove her away—making sure to use only as much force as was absolutely necessary—the lady insisted on leaning toward him, giving every bit of her weight into his hold. He couldn't reasonably release her or she'd tumble right back into his arms.

He did not appreciate being manipulated in such a way. He abhorred it, in fact.

Anger and frustration billowed inside him like heat from a furnace. He held his body fiercely rigid, doing his best not to touch her any more than was required to keep her upright. Glaring down at her, he struggled to find words harsh enough to convince her to leave him the hell alone without blatantly cursing her as he was tempted to do.

"Good morning, Lady Mayhew. Hello, Mr. Thomas."

Lady Anne's gentle voice lifted Beynon's gaze to where his partner stood in the doorway. Though there was a calmly pleasant smile on her face, he noted a flicker of fire in her blue-green eyes. There was also something...new in her demeanor. It was a subtle sort of irritation. Or perhaps it could be better described as disdainful antipathy.

Despite the ridiculous and humiliating situation he found himself in at that moment, he couldn't help but feel a reluctant twinge of gratitude for her sudden appearance as Lady Mayhew stumbled back a step and quickly righted herself. The look she gave Beynon before she turned to greet the other lady suggested she remained undaunted.

"Lady Anne," the woman replied with a wide smile. "I'm afraid Mr. Thomas and I had a little collision. Nothing to worry about, however," she added with a laugh and a wave of her hand. "The gentleman gallantly saved me from a disastrous fall."

Without replying to the transparent explanation, Lady Anne continued forward, shifting her attention to Beynon. With a gentle tilt of her head, she asked, "Do you have the list of items we're to hunt down, Mr. Thomas?"

Still fuming over the other woman's attempt at seduction, he simply lifted the scroll rather than reply.

"Excellent." She paused then quite deliberately turned to give her back to the other woman in the room—inciting a gasp of shocked affront—as she lifted her hand. "Shall we begin the hunt?"

Following her lead by completely ignoring Lady Mayhew, he stepped forward and Lady Anne slipped her hand into the curve of his elbow. They strode from the room in tense and awkward silence. The embarrassment of being caught by her in yet another compromising position with Lady Mayhew only heaped on top of the anger which had yet to dissipate.

In his distraction, it took a moment for Beynon to realize the lady at his side was subtly guiding him across the hall toward the front door. Once outside, they continued around the house to the west where a cobblestone courtyard separated the large manor house from the estate's stables. Only then did she slow their steps and finally release his arm.

Turning to face him, she seemed quite determined not to meet his gaze as she looked pointedly at the scroll in his hand instead. "Is that the list?"

Her curt tone was very different from the soft, melodic way she typically spoke, and for some reason, it triggered in him a fierce and sudden urge to defend himself.

"I did nothing wrong." The words tumbled roughly from his mouth before he could stop them.

She stiffened but didn't look up from the scroll she'd unrolled. After a brief pause, she said, "There's no need to explain."

"I wasn't explaining," he growled, realizing his anger was still coloring his responses. "I'm just saying it wasn't me."

Slowly, she lowered the scroll and lifted her chin so she could meet his gaze. She took another long breath then replied, "And I'm saying there's no need." Her voice was low but firm and the blue of her eyes seemed darker than usual. "I know you're aware that I heard you over the wall that day. You tried to dissuade her then. I also had a clear view of her little performance just now. I *know* you did nothing wrong, Mr. Thomas."

For a second, he got the oddest sense the woman was angry on his behalf. But then she glanced back down at the scroll and gently arched one fine eyebrow. "Now that we've wasted more time on the issue than it deserves, can we begin?"

Beynon glowered at the crown of her bowed head. She declared the matter finished, so that was it? What if he had more to say?

"I don't think so," he replied in a rough growl. When she looked up at him with a glint of confusion and subtle wariness in her eyes, he continued, "Perhaps we haven't spent enough time on the matter. Perhaps I'd like to know why some people feel as though they're entitled to treat others as objects for their personal amusement."

She blinked in that way she had, where her lashes gave a quick flutter and her eyes widened at the same time.

"I..." she began, but then didn't seem capable of going on.

He was aware his current display of wrath might be seen as out of proportion to the incident, but he didn't care. He was just so damn tired of it all. London society had already decided he was barely better than a brute, so why should he bother trying to prove otherwise?

He narrowed his gaze and lowered his voice. "I know what people say about me. The idiotic moniker they've given me." *Welsh Devil.* His mum would expire if she ever learned of that. His stomach turned. "And Lady Mayhew isn't the first to seek me out in such a fashion. In the last months, I've received countless similar demands from others of her kind."

"Her kind?" Lady Anne asked quietly.

"Selfish. Rich. Unable to imagine anything they want shouldn't be laid at their feet. I know exactly what they want from me and I assure you it's not a round of pleasant conversation or a turn about the ballroom. Women like her see me less as a man than as a beast," he added gruffly. "Something unpredictable and frightening to chase away their boredom, even if only for a few hours."

The lady bravely met his gaze though he suspected he looked every bit the uncivilized devil they believed him to be. There was a quiet intensity to her steady stare. Then she pressed her lips together before speaking in an even tone that barely rose above a whisper. "You're saying they want..." She paused and a tiny scowl formed between her brows. "They want to use you as a diversion...as a plaything."

Her simple acknowledgement burned a path through his core. Anger threatened to rise again in its wake, but he held it at bay. Barely. Lady Anne thought she understood. She'd barely brushed the surface.

"Some of them want to use me," he agreed, his voice heavy. But then he lowered his tone even more. "Others want to be used *by* me."

In her obvious innocence, she couldn't possibly grasp the full meaning of his words. But the shock in her eyes and the blush that colored her cheeks suggested she wasn't totally oblivious either.

"I'm sorry," she murmured softly and he could see she meant it.

Unfortunately, her compassion only angered him further. With a growl of frustration, he closed his eyes and heaved a breath meant to disperse the pressure in his chest. He opened his eyes again to pin Lady Anne with a dark stare.

"I don't want your pity," he snarled. She parted her lips as if to refute his comment, but he spoke first. "I want to be left alone."

There was a quick flutter of dark lashes over her swirling gaze as she blinked then looked down to focus her attention on the scroll still held in her hands. Her modest breasts lifted and pressed against her bodice before she gave a series of short and shallow nods.

"Of course. I understand," she replied.

But he wasn't sure she did. And suddenly, he felt like a raging arse. She'd done nothing to deserve his harsh words even if they weren't directed at her specifically. He knew he should apologize, but his temper was still too high and words of contrition never came easily to him.

As he stared down at her bent head, noting how the light breeze stirred the faint wisps of hair that curved against her temple and along her nape, he felt a sudden rise of urgency in his blood. It took all of his will to resist the compulsion to brush the backs of his fingers up the side of her throat to see if her skin felt as soft as it looked.

"Shall we take a look at the list?" she asked in an obvious attempt at redirecting their focus to the far less volatile topic of the scavenger hunt.

He cleared his throat, but his voice was still unnaturally rough as he replied, "What's the first item?"

"We're looking for something that possesses an edge sharp enough to score glass while giving its wearer divine ability."

Beynon scowled. "Are all the clues phrased in riddles?"

"At least they haven't been forced into awkward rhymes," she replied. Then her chin came up and triumph lit her features. "Ice skates. The blades score the ice and allow a person to walk on water, albeit frozen water," she added with a lift of one shoulder.

"I saw a large collection of them in the boathouse," he noted.

Her eyes sparkled as she met his gaze and her smile, though subtle, forced the breath from his lungs as if he'd been punched in the stomach. His temper was gone in a second to be replaced by something decidedly more dangerous.

"Well done, Mr. Thomas. Let's go."

Chapter Eleven

They managed to collect all twenty items within their allotted time, though they did have to return to the house more than once to register what they'd collected to that point before heading out again. After seeing other couples going about with large baskets or sacks—one couple even passed by with a wheelbarrow—Anne initially worried their lack of foresight in arranging something similar might cost them the win. But by the time they'd finished, she was simply grateful to be done.

The boots she'd worn were terribly new and hadn't been properly worn in yet, which caused several areas of friction that had quickly become painful blisters. She'd managed to bite her tongue and keep a steady pace while they'd completed the scavenger hunt, but when she retired to her room before the midday meal, she breathed a deep sigh once as she removed the stiff leather shoes.

Though the lighter slippers she changed into didn't cause nearly as much pain, they still rubbed against a few of the raw spots. If she'd had time, she'd have soaked her feet and properly wrapped them to avoid further discomfort. But lunch was only to be served for a short while longer, and after skipping breakfast, she was starving.

Caring for the small wounds would have to wait until later.

Unfortunately, after lunch, she ran into Angelique, who insisted on engaging Anne in a lengthy discussion on the varying qualities of wool obtained from the different breeds of sheep. Though Anne had no experience with the topic, Angelique apparently had a wealth of knowledge and continued the conversation far longer than Anne would have believed possible.

Having known the dowager countess since her debut season considering the elderly lady had served as Lily's chaperone, Anne was quite familiar with Angelique's eccentricities, which included occasions when the lady seemed a bit disconnected from reality. The elderly woman's flights of fancy were quite harmless, so it was best to humor the kind and brazen old woman. Something Anne was always happy to do since such conversations tended to be far more interesting than most.

But the delay left her no extra time before she was due to meet up with Mr. Thomas to attempt the earl's extensive hedge maze before nightfall.

With a sigh, she stepped outside and made her way toward the spot where Mr. Thomas had said he'd be waiting. Though time was getting a bit short, she could not bring herself to hurry when every step caused a sting of discomfort. When she neared the designated location and saw no sign of Mr. Thomas, she wondered if perhaps she'd misunderstood where they were to meet. Or perhaps it was later than she'd thought and the man had gone on ahead?

Worried about being the cause of any delay, she continued a bit farther down the path toward the maze. After a minute, she heard the soft bark of a dog and the low sound of male laughter. Turning toward the sound, she spotted Mr. Thomas some distance away. He was crouched beside a black and white collie that was intent on licking the man's face. The young Miss Claybourne stood nearby and a footman trailed not far behind her.

Once again, Anne found herself simply watching the man.

Why she should find him so fascinating while doing such common things was far beyond her comprehension. But there it was. Mr. Thomas *was* fascinating.

There was an earthy grace to his form as he crouched there in the middle of the path. His knee rested in the dirt, and though he ruffed the dog's fur in vigorous strokes, he was focused quite intently on his sister, who was speaking with animated gestures.

Anne was shocked to note he wasn't sporting his usual heavy-browed scowl. There was actually a subtle gentleness in his rugged features as he listened to Miss Claybourne. And was that a smile curving the typically harsh line of his lips?

She had to believe so when the low roll of his laughter soon followed. The sound was rich and easy, like warmed honey.

In the next moment, Mr. Thomas straightened just as Miss Claybourne glanced up and saw Anne standing in the middle of the path. The friendly girl gave a bright smile and waved.

Mr. Thomas glanced her way, as well, and even from a distance, Anne could see his expression change from relaxed and open to dark and forbidding.

The smile of greeting she'd given Miss Claybourne fell away and her insides twisted as the lovely girl and her dog continued toward the house and Mr. Thomas strode along the path to where Anne waited.

A prickle of irritation distracted her from the acute injury to her pride, which was quickly becoming toughened and scarred from numerous prior slights dealt by this man. She was well accustomed to being overlooked and disregarded, but what on earth had she ever done to deserve his contempt?

Nothing at all. That's what.

Honestly, after the enjoyable morning and the almost companionable few hours they'd spent on the scavenger hunt once he'd let out a bit of steam over that encounter with Lady Mayhew, she'd thought they'd turned a corner in their partnership.

Apparently not.

Not waiting for a pleasant greeting that would likely not be forthcoming, she gave a tense, "Shall we?" then turned to head toward the maze. Unfortunately, she forgot about her blisters and her first step dissolved into a graceless hobble.

"What's the matter?" he asked gruffly, still a few steps behind her.

Anne waved her hand and straightened her spine. "Nothing. We should hurry." Gritting her teeth against the pain, she marched rather stiffly along the path.

A pair of footmen greeted them at the maze entrance. Throughout the day, as they'd traipsed all across the estate, she'd noted varying groups of spectators milling about near the maze as other couples made their attempts at getting to the exit in the quickest time.

She was actually grateful they were going last and no one still lingered. No doubt, most of the other guests had retired to their rooms to rest and prepare for dinner. Anne would be doing the same if given the opportunity. In fact, the idea of a hot bath and soothing salve for her feet might be the perfect motivation for getting through this current trial swiftly.

As the two of them stepped into the maze, she glanced to her partner. "What sort of strategy would you like to employ?"

He arched a thick eyebrow. "Strategy? Isn't the point to get through it as quick as we can?"

"Of course. But this maze is known for being a rather complex labyrinth." She glanced down both possible paths in front of them. One went straight forward and showed several intersections, the other continued to the left before taking a turn to the right. "The most reliable method would be to keep our right hand on the wall at all times. It should inevitably lead us to the exit, but it will take time to traverse every turn of the wall." She frowned. "Since winning is dependent on having the fastest time, no doubt others chose to simply rush through, relying solely on luck."

"Sounds good," he noted as he strode forward.

"But we could just as easily end up utterly lost," Anne argued while following after him, extending her fingers to brush along the hedges to her right. "And once we lose sight of the entrance, we won't be able to use the wall strategy since we could end up following an internal structure that is disconnected from the wall containing the exit."

He wasn't listening to her at all as he took a fork to the left in a decidedly frustrating choice that totally negated her right-hand strategy.

Exasperation made her voice sharp. "Mr. Thomas, we should approach this with a bit more careful consideration."

He replied without even bothering to look back at her. "You just said following the wall takes time and I've no desire to remain trapped with you in this maze any longer than necessary."

Anne suspected his comment wasn't intended to be a personal insult toward her company, but she couldn't help but take it as exactly that. If this was going to be his attitude during this task, she was fully in agreement on getting through it was quickly as possible. Since he clearly had no intention of taking her advice, she didn't even bother bringing up other strategies. But she did manage to bend a branch to mark their passage as he made another impulsive turn.

She narrowed her gaze in a fierce and fiery glare at the man's broad back. He might wish to charge through the labyrinth with no forethought, but that didn't mean she had to.

"BLOODY HELL."

Beynon didn't intend to mutter the curse out loud. He'd managed to keep nearly a dozen previous curses firmly behind his teeth, but the hour they'd spent encountering endless dead ends and false avenues had steadily worn at his self-control and he no longer had the proper means of tempering his frustration.

"Mr. Thomas."

He could feel the annoyance in his partner's tone. It struck his senses like a fine whip. In truth, he was rather surprised the woman hadn't spoken up more than she had as he'd led them deeper and deeper into what he was beginning to suspect was an impossible maze. He expected a litany of complaints to start up any moment. So far, after her initial protests, she only piped up when they'd reach a divergence in the path to voice a suggestion on which way they should go. Sometimes he agreed with her recommendation. Sometimes he didn't.

When he didn't, he almost always heard a quiet huffing sigh. But the lady refrained from arguing further. He'd been grateful for her silence at first, but now he was doubting his direction and silently wished he'd put more faith in Lady Anne's strategies.

"Mr. Thomas."

Her tone had gotten sharper and—if he wasn't mistaken—farther away.

He immediately stopped to look over his shoulder. She'd taken a seat on one of the many petite stone benches set throughout the maze. Her fine features were strained and her skin slightly flushed. Though the pink in her cheeks could have been from the rather punishing pace he'd set for them, he suspected there was a healthy tinge of frustration coloring her stiff-backed attitude.

With a heavy sigh and a quick glance at the sky above, which was starting to turn from blue to a soft violet-gray, he strode to his partner's side.

"I need just a moment before we continue on," she explained.

"A moment," he conceded gruffly as he crossed his arms over his chest. "I reckon we have barely another half-hour before it'll be dark."

"I'm aware." Her tone was decidedly curt.

The lady was peeved.

He was about to say something about taking the competition too seriously when he noticed her wince. It was so slight and swift and subtle he almost missed it. He paused and narrowed his gaze.

There it was again—a brief tensing around her mouth as she adjusted her feet beneath her skirts.

Dammit.

He should pretend he didn't see it. That would be the gentlemanly thing, right? For her to be so intent on hiding whatever discomfort she was experiencing meant she didn't want him to know of it. He should respect that.

He was just about to glance away when she lowered her chin and rolled her lips in between her teeth as she closed her eyes.

Dammit.

"What is it?" he asked. He acknowledged the gruffness of his tone and so wasn't very surprised when the lady looked up at him with a firmly blank expression.

"What is what, Mr. Thomas?"

"You're in pain, Lady Anne. What is the problem?"

"There's no problem," she replied stiffly.

Hadn't he already told her once she was a terrible liar?

"Then let's get going."

He turned to walk away but then glanced quickly back to watch her.

She rose very slowly—very tentatively—to her feet. Her face was a mask of stoic resignation. It looked as if she'd forge ahead despite whatever was distressing her until she took her first step. Her whole body flinched and she bit hard to her bottom lip.

"Sit down," he barked.

He thought she might protest, but she lowered herself back to the bench with a choked sigh. "I just need another minute or two," she insisted from between clenched teeth.

"Sure you do." He lowered himself to one knee in front of her. "Give me your feet."

She gasped in indignant surprise. "I will not."

He looked up at her, his expression dark and commanding. His tone allowing no room for dissent. "Your feet, Lady Anne."

Pride flared in the depths of her fierce glare, but she braced her palms on the bench and lifted her feet into his waiting hands.

The shoes she wore were of soft satin with a sturdy leather sole. He detected nothing that might cause the kind of discomfort she displayed. But when he shifted his hold and his fingers brushed over her heels, she sucked in a swift breath.

"Lift your skirts."

Her voice was more strained than resistant when she replied, "I don't think—"

"I assure you, I've no devilish intentions. Now, do as I say or we'll be stuck in this maze for the rest of the damned night."

Her eyes were wide in shock at his use of the curse, but she recovered quickly enough. "Fine. But it's nothing. Just a couple blisters from all the walking earlier. I'll be perfectly all right once I have a chance to tend them."

As she spoke, she tugged at her skirts, sliding them up her slim thighs a few scant inches. Just enough to clear the hem from her feet and ankles.

The severity of the issue was made immediately apparent by the dark reddish-brown stains soaking the heels of both slippers. The obstinate woman was bleeding and had been for some time.

Beynon muttered a harsh curse as he loosened the fastening of one shoe before gently starting to ease it from her foot.

"What are you doing?" she asked sharply, trying to tug free of his grasp.

But he'd anticipated the reaction and had a firm grip around her ankle. Her features were set to a mulish expression but there was undeniable panic in her eyes.

"These shoes are causing more damage. They're coming off."

"But—"

He stopped her with his fiercest glower. The one he used when his youngest and most bullheaded little sister thought she could override his dictates.

The lady's protests died. With her spine still straight and her eyes flashing, she turned her head to stare at some point in the near distance.

After removing the first shoe, he did the same for the other. The lady's thin stockings had done nothing to protect her injuries from the constant friction caused by their endless trek through the maze. And he'd set such a harsh pace. Yet she'd never asked him slow or rest until now.

Stubborn, prideful woman.

Chapter Twelve

"Why in hell didn't you say something?" he demanded angrily.

There was a pause. Then, "Say what exactly?"

Her voice was tense and curt. Beynon glanced up and was surprised to see a flash of temper lighting her fairy-colored eyes.

"Really, Mr. Thomas, was there anything I could have said over the last hour that might have convinced you to take a moment of heed? Anything that might have overridden your fixed insistence on doing exactly what you wished? You made it sharply clear from the start of this wretched task that you were of no mind to consider anything I said."

Beynon glowered at her accusations. They weren't entirely untrue. But he wasn't accustomed to having his arguably obstinate behavior being catalogued so bluntly. "If you'd said you were in pain—"

"You'd have what?" she interrupted with eyebrows arched in disbelief. "Grumbled about how pampered English ladies cannot endure a simple walk?"

Dammit. She wasn't exactly wrong there, either. "So, you decided your pride was worth more than your blood?" he asked harshly.

Her eyes flashed. "Sometimes, pride is all a woman has."

The tone of her voice and the set of her chin suddenly reminded him of his mother, a woman whose warmth and grace were upheld by a will of steel.

They stared at each other for a fierce moment. Then the lady took a steadying breath. When she spoke again, her voice was calm and almost annoyingly reasonable. "I understand if you don't particularly like me, Mr. Thomas. It's fine. We don't have to be friends. It's certainly not a requirement for a proper partnership." She paused and the corner of her mouth tugged ruefully upward before she added, "But I don't think it could hurt much to cultivate a bit more cooperation."

Though Beynon felt slightly shamed by her effective little lecture, he wasn't about to admit it. Instead, he kept his expression harshly unmoved while her direct and hopeful gaze roamed tentatively over his features. But as the moment of silence lengthened, the confidence and fire in her manner slowly ebbed away. The space between her brows furrowed and a heavy sigh lifted her shoulders.

Beynon almost said something then, but his jaw remained fiercely clenched as he finally glanced away.

Realizing he still held her feet in his hands, he gently lowered them to the ground. But when he leaned forward to brace his hand on the bench in preparation to rise, her swift inhale brought his attention back to her face.

Her lashes fluttered as though she wished to lower her gaze but fought against it and he was instantly captured by the curious sparks of light shining from the depths of azure and green. He couldn't look away. Couldn't rise. Couldn't even force a distance between them that had suddenly become very necessary.

And when her attention fell to his mouth and her lips parted on a sharp inhale, something pulled tight deep inside him.

Goddammit. He was going to kiss her.

It was a fact.

Even as he acknowledged it was a horrible idea, he lifted a hand to the side of her throat. As his fingertips pressed into the little hollow at the base of her skull and his thumb brushed the edge of her jaw, he leaned toward her.

He had a swift impression of the shock in her eyes before her lashes swept over them and he pressed his mouth to hers.

Her lips were softer, sweeter than he'd imagined—not that he'd imagined the feel of them at all until a moment ago. But as he brushed his mouth across hers, he felt as though he'd been waiting for this kiss a very long time and he wondered why on earth he'd been denying himself such a pleasure.

As her initial surprise fled and the arch of her neck relaxed in his hand, he flicked his tongue against the gentle parting of her lips. Her gasp sent a shiver down his spine and tied his belly into a tight knot. But when she reached forward to curve her hand over the surface of his thigh and her tongue slid from between her teeth to glide gently along his, a shot of pure lust angled to his groin. It was so sharp and intense and immediate that he tensed as a groan filled his chest.

Unfortunately, she felt his shock and a small sound got trapped in her throat. Her fingers tightened on his thigh then released him as she gently pulled back.

Fuck. He'd ruined it. If he'd been able to rein in his reaction, he might still be kissing her, exploring her sweetness. Instead, he watched as her eyes opened and her swift, panicked breath bathed his lips.

"Why did you do that?" she asked, her voice slightly shaky.

He didn't answer. He couldn't. He didn't know why.

Or maybe he knew exactly why but couldn't form it into proper words just then.

So instead, he rose abruptly to his feet. After swiping up her shoes in one hand, he leaned forward and swept her up into his arms as well.

"No. Wait! What are you doing?"

"You can't walk on bleeding feet," he grumbled thickly, still fighting through his fierce and unexpected desire.

"I can. I'll be fine," she protested even as her elegant hands gripped at his coat in an attempt to find purchase in his arms.

"We don't have the time to argue this, Lady Anne," he noted. "As it is, it'll be fully dark by the time we find our way out of here."

"We'll find our way more quickly if you listen to me," she muttered.

"Fine," he conceded gruffly. The more intently they focused on the maze, the less likely he was to think on what had just occurred or the lovely weight and warmth of her body in his arms. "But I thought you said we couldn't use your strategy once we left the entrance."

"If you'd bothered to listen to me earlier, you'd know there's more than one strategy." Her expression managed to be smug and contrite at the same time.

Desire lit inside him once again. He forced himself to ignore it as he lifted a brow in question.

"I bent a branch anytime we entered a new passage. Two branches for any dead ends or if we found ourselves looped back to the initial mark. As long as we treat any double marks as an impassable wall, we'll eventually find the right path to the exit."

He wanted to be irritated and insulted by her lack of faith in him, but he couldn't help but admire her obstinate cleverness.

"All right, then. Which way, Lady Anne?"

"We should start by heading back the way we came since we've passed this way twice already. But you really don't need to carry me, Mr. Thomas. I imagine I'm quite a burden."

He gave a short grunt as he started in the direction she indicated. "Less burden than a full-grown sheep."

"Excuse me?" Her tone was only slightly indignant. "Did you just compare me to livestock?"

The flare of amusement was unexpected and he almost didn't manage to tamp it down. "Might have."

Silence followed for several more steps and he started to suspect he'd truly insulted the lady.

"Do you carry sheep often, then?"

He managed to shrug despite having her in his arms. She really wasn't very heavy at all. Her unusual height coincided with a slight figure. "On occasion."

"Why?"

The single word sounded genuinely curious.

"To bring them into the barn for clipping or to move them from one pasture to another."

He didn't have to look into her face to feel her wide-eyed surprise. "You move them all by hand?"

"Of course not." His slid a glance to her then and gave her an intentionally dark gaze. "Just the stubborn ones."

Something unexpectedly defiant flared in her eyes a moment before she gave a little harrumph and looked away.

It took more effort than it should have to resist the urge to chuckle.

WITH MR. THOMAS FINALLY following her directions, it only took another ten minutes to find their way free of the maze. Anne didn't know if she should be grateful or regretful they made it out so quickly. The sensation of being carried against the solid breadth of the man's chest was a singular experience. One she had no idea how to properly process through her senses as each one kept getting overwhelmed by turns.

Mr. Thomas was simply too much for her to take in all at once. The heat of his body and iron strength of his arms around her back and beneath her knees. The scent of him—dark, mysterious, and wonderfully rugged. The way his growly voice seeped through her flesh and blood to the depth of her bones. His profile, so harsh and unwavering against the dark rows of hedges they swept past. The taste of his kiss on her tongue.

She'd been so shocked in that moment when he'd leaned toward her, his large hand warm and strong around her nape, she'd barely had a moment to think on what was happening. She'd resorted to instinct as her eyes had closed and she'd held herself still and receptive, part of her afraid to do anything at all in case it might interrupt his intention.

The first lovely pressure of his mouth had been a revelation.

Anne had never been kissed before, but in all of her private imagining of what it might feel like, she'd fallen far short of reality. For a man with so gruff a manner, Mr. Thomas's lips had been shockingly soft. The sensation had been not unlike the feeling of the finest silk rubbing across her lips.

But then his tongue—that sudden flick of fire between her lips.

It had been shockingly unexpected and such a different sensation...so decadent and wicked.

She'd wanted more. She'd wanted to feel the warm, wet texture of his tongue with her own and hadn't hesitated to seek him out. But now—as she thought back to that moment—she realized that was what had stopped the kiss. She'd heard the rough sound he'd tried to contain. She'd felt the muscle of his thigh harden beneath her hand before she'd even realized she'd grasped hold of him.

Her boldness had shocked him. Proper, demure Lady Anne Humphries had actually *shocked* the Welsh Devil.

If she didn't regret how it had ended their kiss long before she was ready, she might have laughed at the idea.

As they stepped from the maze, one of the awaiting footmen offered to fetch a wagon, but Thomas grunted a refusal. "I've gotten her this far, I'm sure I can get her safely back to the house."

Anne tucked her chin to hide the blush heating her cheeks.

Once they entered the hall, she made one more attempt to get him to set her down.

"While I appreciate your gallantry, Mr. Thomas, I feel as though I should make my way alone from here."

He didn't even bother to pause his long strides as he continued to the main stairway, though he did look down at her with a hard stare that made her belly feel oddly effervescent.

"Allow me this, Lady Anne."

His words were spoken quietly, almost intimately. And she felt as though there might be a hint of apology there in the depth of the baritone.

Was he sorry for not listening to her advice regarding the maze? Or for kissing her?

Gratefully, they only encountered a few servants along the way as she directed her escort to the guest room she'd been given. With the hour so late, the other guests were no doubt readying for dinner, something she'd need to do quickly if she hoped to finally tend her feet and avoid being rudely late.

Her maid was waiting when Mr. Thomas open the door to her room without even shifting her weight. The servant turned with wide eyes at the sight of Anne in the gentleman's very capable arms.

"Oh, my lady! I was so very worried. I was just about to send someone to look for you. Have you been injured?"

"Nothing to fret over," Anne quickly assured.

Striding past the anxious maid, Mr. Thomas lowered Anne into a comfortable armchair near the fire. There was a moment while he leaned over her—his arms still around her body, his shoulders blocking out the rest of the room—that his dark gaze found hers.

Her body ignited with a million sparks.

Because the weighty intensity in his eyes was exactly as it had been in the maze—right before he'd kissed her. The harsh resistance. The silent foreboding. The *confusion*.

A part of her wanted to be insulted by the bewilderment in his eyes, but she understood it. The man barely tolerated her. The kiss had clearly been an impulsive mistake.

But she couldn't help but wonder...if her maid hadn't been waiting for her, if they were alone right now, would he kiss her again?

Even as she had the thought, he released her and stepped back to hand the ruined slippers to the servant. "Her feet will need tending."

"Yes, sir. Of course."

He was halfway across the room before Anne managed to call after him. "Mr. Thomas, we really must arrange some time to rehearse our reading."

He didn't even look back as he grumbled a reply. "Later." And then he was gone.

Chapter Thirteen

As usual, Anne was awake early the next morning. After breakfast, she made her way to the specified site of their next task—portrait painting. Each competing pair had been assigned a location by random draw, which put Anne and Mr. Thomas in a far corner of the garden. Since today's event was expected to take a significant amount of time, it was the only one scheduled for the day. Something Anne was quite grateful for. The last couple days had been rather trying. Physically...and in other ways.

At least today's event was something that gave her a great deal of pleasure and wasn't terribly taxing. Best of all, she was finally going to be able to paint Mr. Thomas, which gave her a rather intense little thrill.

The garden was quiet in the soft morning sunlight as Anne strolled slowly along the path toward the southwest corner of the garden. From prior explorations, she knew that spot to be well shaded beneath a spreading oak, with a row of tall hedges to one side and riotous flower beds showcasing a range of colors to the other. At this time of day, the lighting would be gentle and indirect, and though they were each to have their turns as artist and model, she hoped Mr. Thomas wouldn't be opposed to allowing her to take up the paintbrush first.

When she reached the little spot of grass, she saw that two easels had been set up along with a tall stool beside a table containing a variety of brushes, an array of watercolor pigment blocks in every shade, and various other items needed for the task ahead, including smocks to protect their clothing.

Anne would have preferred her own paints, but as she examined those provided, she acknowledged they would be more than adequate. Lily certainly didn't do anything by half measure.

Taking up the smaller of the smocks, she slipped her arms through the narrow shoulder straps then wrapped the long apron strings around her waist and tied them securely in front. She'd intentionally chosen a gown that had short sleeves and was devoid of any flounces that might get in her way.

She'd just started to arrange the paints and brushes to her liking when she heard a footfall behind her.

Delicate thrills passed along her nerves, igniting thoughts she'd very forcefully kept dormant all morning. One breath of awareness and her efforts were blown away.

How on earth was she to spend the next few hours staring at the man when all she could think about was how he'd kissed her? It had taken hours of analysis in the dark of her bedroom last night to convince herself the kiss had been nothing more than an odd impulse triggered by the frustration and proximity of having been stuck in the maze.

No doubt Mr. Thomas regretted the act and had likely vowed to himself that it would never be repeated. In which case, Anne had determined it would be best to act as though it had never happened.

She only just managed to remind herself of that decision when he stepped up beside her and her heart gave a violent little lurch. Forcing an appearance of calm she absolutely didn't feel, Anne tipped her head to look up at him. And forgot anything she might have said.

His nearly black eyes met hers and her knees weakened. The strength and breadth of him felt overly large beneath the oak's wide-reaching branches, yet she wanted to step into him and feel that strength surrounding her.

How could a man feel so dangerous and so safe at the same time? Foolish.

She looked back to the paints and managed to mutter a sufficient, "Good morning."

Rather than return the common greeting, he reached past her to pick up one of the paintbrushes in his calloused fingers.

His tone was contemptuous as he grumbled, "I can't believe someone thought this would be a good idea."

Already on edge, Anne took his comment personally. Simply because watercolors were often seen as a quaint little hobby for young ladies didn't mean it wasn't a true art form. "Painting is as worthy a pastime as fishing or hunting, Mr. Thomas," she replied curtly.

He leaned across her again to replace the brush and his words stirred the hair at her temple when he replied, "Not when I do it."

She blinked and lifted her gaze to find him staring rather closely—and way too intently—at her face. Trying her best not to show how deeply his nearness—and his emanating warmth and his heavy focus and his earthy scent—affected her, Anne asked, "Have you some experience with it then?"

The corners of his mouth actually lifted in a self-deprecating smile than made her bones melt.

"None at all."

First her bones and now her brain. Good lord, don't let her heart be next.

She turned to face the easel more squarely, putting her back to the man who was clearly intent on destroying her equilibrium and her sanity. Though she thought she heard him give a gentle huff of breath, she ignored it and a moment later he moved away from her to stroll toward the oak tree.

"How would you like me?"

His question was rough and impatient, proving a return of the man's typical manner. Anne was relieved. She had no idea what to do with the velvety tones he'd used a moment ago.

She looked up to see him standing with his arms crossed and his chin lowered as though he expected to face some long-awaited adversary.

She'd love to paint him that way. All fierce and defiant and magnificent.

But not today.

Today, she wanted something different. Something quieter. Calmer.

"Why don't you have a seat and lean back against the tree."

With a heavy expression that did nothing to conceal his obvious discomfort, he lowered himself to the grass and did as she suggested.

Anne shook her head. "No need to be so stiff and proper, Mr. Thomas. Try to imagine you've been walking through the country and decided to take a short rest."

He heaved a sigh as he shifted his weight, allowing more of a natural curve to his spine. Then he bent one knee to plant his foot in the grass and tossed her a look of exasperation.

It was better. If he'd just relax a bit more...

"Tell me something about your home, Mr. Thomas," she suggested conversationally as she picked up a small graphite pencil and began to sketch her idea.

Portraits were not usually her chosen subject when she painted, but there was something about Mr. Thomas that inspired her in ways she'd never previously experienced. She wanted to capture him as a man who was comfortable being an element of nature. A man of the earth and grass and trees. A man of fresh morning air and wide-open spaces. She could almost envision a pasture of rolling hills behind him with wildflowers and sheep in the distance.

Focusing on her sketch, it took her a moment to realize he hadn't replied to her comment. She paused and glanced to her subject to find him staring at her in that way he had.

Broody, silent, anticipatory.

"Why would I do that?"

She blinked. Must he always be so determined to be difficult?

"Well, it might be a nice way to fill the time. And I suppose I was hoping the conversation would help you to relax a bit," she added with a hint of challenge in her tone.

His weighty scowl deepened but he shifted his weight into a slightly more natural position. "What do you want to know?"

She hid her smile as she returned her attention to her sketch. "You mentioned sheep yesterday. Do you raise them?"

There was a pause following her question, during which Anne recalled how often the gossips had used the rumor of him being a farmer as a tool to degrade him. Worried that she might have insulted him with the topic she'd chosen, she tried to come up with a less potentially touchy subject.

But then he replied, and although his words were a bit short, there was an interesting warmth in his tone. "We raise, breed, and shear them to sell the wool."

Relieved that he was willing to talk about something she was genuinely curious about, she maintained a light tone with her next question. "If you could choose to do something else, would you?"

Finishing the basic sketch of her idea, she moved on to the wash, choosing a pale golden color that would layer well beneath the richer colors she planned to add.

His answer came after another pause. "Likely not."

Anne looked at him then. "You enjoy your work."

His answer was a gruff sound and a subtle nod acknowledging the truth of her statement.

She returned to her paints, not expecting him to say more.

But he did.

"I was ten when my mam married my stepfather and we moved to the farm. I learned quickly that my days would be filled with hard work. But it was still far better than the life we'd had before."

His voice grew heavy with the last words, and though Anne was tempted to glance up at him, she didn't want to risk disrupting his unexpected willingness to share.

"I didn't want to like the man who'd courted my mam for years before finally convincing her to marry him," he added with a hint of reflection in his tone. "But Cedric Thomas's patience was endless. Even when it came to a lad with more anger than sense. I learned everything from him. Not just about farming but what it was to be a man who protected and provided for his family. I suppose it's only natural I came to value the things he did." He took a slow breath. "The only thing he loved more than the farm was us."

Feeling the weight and depth in the last comment, Anne did glance up then to see him staring intently at a blade of grass pinched between his large fingers. There was a distinct air of sadness about him.

"Has he passed?"

He nodded. "Three years ago. I'm not his blood son, so he didn't have to pass the farm to me, but the children he and my mam share are younger." He dropped the blade of grass then brushed it from where it had landed on his thigh. "I reckon he passed it on to me because I was the only one capable of managing things."

"Or perhaps because he knew you'd love it as he had," Anne suggested softly.

His dark gaze met hers. By the heaviness and depth of his eyes, she could see he still mourned the man who'd raised him. And she suspected he worked hard every day to make him proud.

With a gentle clearing of her throat, she resumed her painting. "Tell me about your siblings. Do you have brothers or sisters?"

"Three brothers. Wretched scamps, every one of them," he grumbled, but again, the warmth in his tone was undeniable. "And two sisters. One nearly grown and the youngest just four and a great trial to my patience."

Anne smiled at the pride in his voice. "I imagine Miss Claybourne gets along with all of them quite famously."

"Miss Claybourne has never met them," he replied, a subtle hardness entering his tone. But then he added, "Though I reckon you'd be right."

She knew it was absolutely none of her business, but something inside her urged her to ask anyway. "Why have they never met?"

His sigh was heavy and ragged. "I only just found out about my sire's other bastard children a couple years ago."

She'd wondered if that had been the case. "Was it very difficult to discover the existence of half siblings you'd previously known nothing about?"

"At first," he replied gruffly. "But they're a persistent bunch."

Anne smiled. "I used to wonder what it'd be like to grow up with brothers and sisters."

"Loud. With not a moment of peace to be found."

She laughed then mused, "Still, it would've been nice to have someone."

His expression seemed to darken at her words and she quickly glanced away. She'd never admitted as much to anyone before and it left her feeling ungrateful considering all he'd endured. She had no reason to complain—as her father had often expressed.

Forcing her attention back to her painting, she quickly became engrossed in the details of her task as she mixed the exact shade of green she wanted or carefully recreated the way light angled through the wide branches of the tree. She had no idea how much time passed while she layered pigments on the paper, ensuring just the right saturation of color with each stroke and twist of her brush.

But when she finally came to the main subject of the painting, her hand stilled.

She studied her original sketch still faintly visible beneath the transparent color she'd already applied, then lifted her gaze to the man reclining against the tree.

Something wasn't quite right.

His pose was perfect. The angle of his head as he watched her at the easel, the way one of his forearms was propped atop his bent knee and the other hand rested on his outstretched thigh, the subtle physical mastery evident in his relaxed form... All perfect.

But something was still off.

He lowered his chin to send her a questioning look. "You appear disturbed, Lady Anne."

"I am," she replied then bit her lip when his brows shot up. "I'm sorry," she continued quickly, heat rising in her cheeks. "It's just...I wonder...would you mind removing your coat, please?"

There was a moment of hesitation, and for a second, she thought he might refuse. But then he leaned forward and shrugged the garment from his shoulders before slipping his arms free. He folded the coat and laid it on the grass beside him before reclaiming his previous position.

"And roll up your sleeves a bit, please."

The look he gave her was skeptical, but he did as she asked. When he was finished, he met her studied gaze once again. "Better?"

Anne nodded. There was a flutter in her belly and a tightness in her chest that prevented her from answering. It was more than better. Who knew a man's bare forearms could be so...alluring?

Forcing her gaze back to the easel, she reminded herself she wasn't here to ogle the man's physique. Narrowing her gaze, she dipped and twirled her brush in the pigment and started to add shape and depth to his figure.

After a moment, she paused again to eye the painting with a critical frown before lifting her attention back to the man beneath the tree.

She blinked when she saw what appeared to be a curve of amusement softening the firm line of his mouth. Surely, that wasn't a smile.

"What now?" he grumbled.

She wasn't quite sure.

Anne glanced back to the painting. Then to the man. Then back to her rendition.

"Ah, that's it," she exclaimed quietly.

Setting her brush down, she started toward him. Though he noticeably stiffened, she didn't shift her gaze from the offending issue. Lowering to her knees between his legs, she reached for his neckcloth. It might have been tied in a casual style, but it just didn't belong and had to go.

She didn't even realize she'd just started to untie the thing until she happened to flick her gaze upward and caught sight of his intense expression. It wasn't dark, exactly, or angry, or even shocked. There might have been a glint of amusement in his eyes, but it was surely overshadowed by the depth and heaviness there as he stared at her face, mere inches from his.

Her belly erupted with flutters and her hands stilled in the snowy white folds of his cravat as fire raced through her. Fire and a tingling shiver that touched every nerve in her body.

She tried to chase it away, and when that didn't work, she simply chose to ignore it.

With a subtle clearing of her throat, she lowered her focus back to the neckcloth and continued to unravel it.

Though her actions might have indicated a lack of concern for their sudden proximity, her body refused to allow her any reprieve.

Every inch of her hummed as her insides slowly melted and her core
twisted and turned through a silent internal storm.

Best to get the task done quickly so she could return to a safe
distance.

Grasping one end of the long bit of soft cotton, she slid it free
from around his neck and set it aside atop his coat. Luckily, the man
remained still and unmoving. Unnaturally still almost, if not for the
occasional tensing of his jaw. But when she lifted her hands to the
collar of his shirt to release the fastenings there, he made a short
sound in his throat that brought her attention back to his face.

Any amusement that might have been present earlier was fully
gone now as she met a gaze so dark and deep it appeared infinite. She
felt as though that stare of his held answers to age-long mysteries she
was desperate to explore.

His voice was rough and barely above a whispered murmur as he
spoke. "Isn't this getting rather scandalous?"

Yes! Yes, it was.

She lifted her chin as defiance tugged her mouth into a subtle
smile. "It's art."

His chuckle was warm and low. An intimate sound, mostly
contained.

Anne lowered her attention as she gently spread the points of
his collar, revealing the strong column of his throat. She inexplicably
found herself entranced by the shadow created beneath the hard
edge of his jawline. That hollow was suddenly the most intriguing
thing she'd ever seen. She wanted to smooth her fingers along his
skin there. No doubt it'd be warm and slightly textured by the faint
stubble she could just barely see. Would she feel the thrum of his
pulse? Would the muscle running from that hollow down to his
shoulder feel as strong beneath her palm as it looked?

She leaned forward, lifting her hand.

Good lord. She was losing her mind.

Realizing the inappropriateness of her thoughts and intentions, she would have drawn back immediately, but something stopped her. A firm tug at her waist.

She looked down in surprise to see his large hand wrapped in the strings of her painting smock. Staring wide-eyed at his hand, she watched with a growing, tingling awareness as he tightened his fist and slowly pulled her closer. She didn't look up until she felt his warm breath drift across her lips.

The black heat in his heavy-lidded eyes stopped her heart.

"For the art," he muttered thickly, before giving a final tug that caused her to fall against his chest as his mouth dropped to hers.

Chapter Fourteen

This was not the same breathless kiss from the maze, where his lips had so softly grazed hers. This was heavy and hot and full of intention.

His mouth was hard against hers while his large, strong body created an unyielding support for her swiftly melting spine. One arm wrapped around her back, holding her secure while the tingling flames she'd tried to ignore burst into an overwhelming inferno.

With a soft grunt, he tightened his arm around her, lifting and shifting her until her hip settled on the grass in the space between his legs. She was twisted awkwardly against him, but she didn't care. The position allowed her to feel the hard length of his thigh against her hip as her belly pressed to his groin and her breasts flattened against the wide surface of his chest. With the band of his arm around her back, she felt surrounded by him. Captured and claimed.

The sensation thrilled her.

Easing the pressure of his mouth just a bit, he shifted his hold again to bring a hand to the side of her throat—as he'd done in the maze. This time, his thumb pressed against the corner of her mouth—gently but with firm pressure—until her lips parted.

A low sound of triumph rolled through him as his tongue entered her mouth in a velvet thrust. Hot, wet, demanding.

Anne gasped and his tongue retreated. But she was ready when he thrust forward again to flick her tongue against his. Tasting him, learning the luscious feel of him. Soon they were engaged in a devilish dance, stroking and twisting and teasing. Already desperate for his taste, when he retreated once again, she readily followed to explore the warmth of his mouth.

My goodness! The taste of him. The heat. The rough, subtle encouragement as he urged her to go deeper. Taste more. Take more.

Her head spun and her body seemed weighted with some deep hunger she couldn't begin to comprehend. But maybe he did. Because the kiss continued to deepen. The strokes of his tongue became more demanding. He wanted something from her, and whatever it was, she wanted it too.

She lifted her hand to curl it around the strong column of his neck. Her fingers threaded into the wavy locks at his nape and she reveled in the feel of his pulse against her palm. His skin was so warm. His body so virile and strong. She wanted to melt right into him.

As she shifted her weight, struggling to get closer, she felt an impossibly hard thickness against her low belly. Following her instinct, she pressed against it.

His answering groan was low and deep and seemed to roll through the achy hollowness inside her. She understood now what that hardness was, and instead of being shocked or frightened by the undeniable evidence of his lustful state, she felt empowered by it.

Sliding her tongue over the fullness of his lower lip, she twisted against him, trying to get even closer.

His large hand fell to her hip and he squeezed. Hard enough that she felt the pressure of each fingertip bruising the softness of her buttocks as his thumb pressed into her belly. Then he began to knead her flesh, molding her with an urgency that increased her own as he boldly rocked her hip against his hardened groin. The amazing intensity of his firm caress and the blatant evidence of his arousal triggered something inside her and a soft moan of surrender slid from her lips.

She didn't know if it was the sound that stopped him or something else, but with a ragged groan, he eased his mouth from hers.

Anne's breath was tight and her body heavy when she opened her eyes to see him staring at her with eyes of endless black.

They remained like that a moment. Still wrapped in each other but no longer kissing. Just staring and breathing heavily as everything inside her resorted and settled into new shapes and forms.

Then he gave her hip a short, possessive squeeze that ignited the most delicious sensations in her low belly before he smoothed his hand in a weighted caress up along her side until the heel of his hand rested firmly against the outer curve of her breast.

Understanding the unspoken cue, Anne flattened her palm over the bulging muscle of his chest to leverage herself to a more stable position as she eased herself back to her knees. With her chin lowered and her gaze unfocused, she lifted her hands to her hair, self-consciously trying to ascertain just how mussed she might look.

She should say something. But what exactly could one say after having their entire world flipped upside down?

He cleared his throat and she stilled her nervous ministrations, dropping her hands to her lap.

"You should finish your painting."

His voice—gravelly and intimate—tingled over every inch of her skin.

But he was right. The realization of how easily someone could have come upon them caused a flush to heat her cheeks. Though her belly still trembled, she rose carefully to stand. The heaviness in her limbs which had felt so languid and wonderful while held secure in his arms now made her feel clumsy and awkward as she made her way back to the easel.

She supposed they would now simply pretend the kiss never happened. Just as they had in the maze.

But she didn't want to pretend it didn't happen. It had been too...wonderful. Too enlightening. Too powerfully perfect to sweep it away into some dark corner, leaving her to wonder if it would ever happen again.

Inexplicable tears pricked her eyes as she lowered herself to the stool, picked up a paintbrush, and tried to refocus on the watercolor. She hated crying. It never changed anything. And besides...no matter how beautifully stunning the kiss had been, it certainly didn't warrant such a reaction.

Breathing deep and slow, she forced herself to glance back toward the tree. He'd returned to his prior pose with an ease that shouldn't have surprised her. The open collar had been loosened even further by her grasping fingers. He looked unapologetically masculine—strong, at ease in his body, his expression both forbidding and challenging at once—and so very sensual.

Their gazes met for just a moment but for Anne it was as if he were still touching her. Her nerves ignited. Her breath shortened. And her low belly fluttered with delicious longing.

But she couldn't tell what he was thinking—only what he made her feel.

His thoughts remained as darkly shadowed as always.

She finished the painting in silence. Each breath she drew into her lungs brought a return of her usual, practiced steadiness until a focused calm replaced the wild storm of confusion and desire inside her. Instead of looking at the man, she forced herself to see only the lines and curves and shapes and colors. Her brushstrokes gradually became more confident and concise, moving over the paper with a fluid instinct as she recreated the image before her into the greater composition she envisioned.

Finally, she stepped back and she gave the watercolor a critical look. Then with a sigh of releasing tension, she put down her brush.

Apparently realizing she was done, Mr. Thomas rose to his feet in a swift, solid motion and started toward her. "My turn."

Flustered at his sudden approach and the way it started things swirling again in her core, Anne quickly started loosening the ties of her smock.

"Where would you like me to pose?" she asked as she set the smock aside and started to rise from the stool.

"Right there. Don't move."

She blinked and looked at him where he stood behind the other easel. He'd already turned it to face him and was starting to swirl his brush in some pigment.

"Do you know what you're doing?" she asked dubiously.

"I watched you," he replied.

His shoulders were tense and his brows were drawn dangerously low over his gaze while his jawline was as hard as she'd ever seen it. Altogether, he appeared a bit hostile. And frighteningly handsome.

She didn't understand it, but the more menacing and forbidding he looked, the more intensely her body reacted.

He looked up at her then and time stood still.

Utterly self-conscious, she realized her lips were parted as her breath passed quickly between them and her eyes were probably overflowing with the wanting that gripped her.

Her lashes fluttered, but a short, harsh sound from him prevented her from closing her eyes or turning away as she wanted to. Instead, she watched as his focus shifted from her face to the painting while he moved his brush in bold brushing sweeps.

She almost smiled at his rushed and haphazard technique, but the experience was too fascinating to manage it. She could only stare. Breathless and curious. And oddly...stimulated.

In barely any time at all, it seemed, he was finished.

He simply paused, gave another back-and-forth glance, then nodded and set his brush down. Still without a word, he turned away and strode to where he'd left his coat and cravat.

Unable to resist her curiosity, Anne rose from the stool and stepped around to view his painting.

And her breath caught sharply in her throat.

He clearly had no training. His brushstrokes were unlike any she'd ever seen before in a watercolor. He didn't bother with any blending at all and seemed to have simply thrown color on the page with no thought to composition.

Yet somehow it worked.

He'd painted her as she'd sat on the stool, her body partly turned away as she looked over her shoulder at him. In minimal sweeps of his brush, he'd managed to capture the hint of sunlight on her hair, the faint pink coloring her cheeks, and the strange blue-green of her eyes. It was undeniably her, even as it felt nothing like her.

It was too bold. Her gaze was too direct and confident. Her lips too sensual and her manner far too regal.

"Incredible." She hadn't meant to utter the word aloud and peeked quickly in his direction, hoping he might not have heard her.

But he gave her a sideways glance as he shrugged into his coat. "I'm no painter," he grumbled.

"It's beautiful," she muttered quickly, not wanting him to think she was criticizing in any way.

"I just tried to recreate what I see."

"*This* is how you see me?"

His black eyes met hers. For a long, breathless moment, Anne felt seen in a way she'd never experienced before. And then he looked away. "I can't stay," he muttered gruffly. "Excuse me."

Anne could only stare in stunned confusion as the man abruptly walked away.

BEYNON BLINDLY TURNED the corner around a tall garden hedge and nearly plowed right through a man coming from the other direction. As they both righted themselves, he forced himself to hold back a snarl of annoyance.

Running into his oldest brother at any time contained potential for a certain degree of discomfort. But to encounter him now, as his entire being seethed with frustrations barely kept in check, could only result in unintentional disaster.

"Beynon." After nearly two years, the ever-proper Earl of Wright had only just started calling him by his given name.

Of course, Beynon had not exactly given the man much cause to assume the familiarity sooner. His first trip to London had lasted barely a couple weeks. This visit was certainly longer and he might have grown accustomed to the idea of having three half brothers and a young half sister since first learning of it, but there was still a small part of him that resented their father's heir and only legitimate child.

It was an irrational resentment and Colin had proven himself many times over. But Beynon had a horrible tendency to hold a grudge and his oldest brother had unfortunately taken on some of Beynon's residual resentment toward their father.

Still reeling from his experience with Lady Anne, Beynon didn't manage to return the greeting before Colin's attention shifted to something behind him.

By the subtle twitch of his brother's brow, Beynon suspected Colin had spotted Lady Anne making her way back to the house.

"Is everything all right?" the earl asked, his tone even.

"Wonderful."

The faintest frown touched Colin's features before he smoothed it away. "How are you getting on with Lady Anne?"

Beynon clenched his teeth. Was he really going to have this conversation? Now? "Fine."

Holding his gaze, Colin continued, "I don't know the lady well, but she seems a gentle sort—rather shy and reserved. I hope you keep that in mind in your interactions with her."

Beynon narrowed his eyes as irrational fury started to replace the desire he'd finally contained. "Are you afraid I'll break her?"

"Not at all," the earl replied, clearly taken aback by the vehemence in Beynon's tone. "I just understand how it might be difficult for someone like her and someone like you to find common ground."

"Someone like me?" Frustration curled Beynon's hands into tight fists. "The Welsh Devil, you mean?"

Colin's expression flashed with something akin to anger before he had the emotion swiftly concealed. Then he sighed. "No, Beynon. I mean someone with feelings and thoughts that run so strong and deep." He lifted one eyebrow in a sardonic expression that was a near replica of one his wife often displayed. "You do realize you come off as rather antagonistic at times."

Beynon couldn't exactly argue that. He was well aware he wasn't always able to keep his more vehement emotions from showing in his manner and countenance. But although Colin might be right about him, he suspected the man was quite off when it came to Lady Anne. Gentle? Perhaps. Reserved? Maybe most of the time.

But definitely not *all* the time.

And he doubted the woman had an ounce of shyness in her. More likely, she simply preferred her own company over the forced socializing in which everyone else engaged.

"You underestimate her," he muttered.

Colin tilted his head thoughtfully. "Do I? You may be right."

"Either way, you've nothing to worry about. The lady and I are getting along just fine."

Colin didn't believe him. But he didn't really care. He just wanted out of the blasted conversation so he could go walk off the tension riding through him, especially now that he'd recalled just how *unreserved* the lady in question had been only minutes ago.

"If you say so," the earl replied evenly. "Just be careful."

Beynon gave a curt nod before stepping past his brother. "Excuse me."

"I'll see you at dinner," the earl called after him.

He didn't bother to reply.

Chapter Fifteen

Considering the frightful mood he was in, Beynon did his best not to glower through the evening meal that night, but he suspected by the many apprehensive glances he received he was failing rather spectacularly.

He did, however, manage to avoid looking overly long at Lady Anne. Unfortunately, by preventing his gaze from lingering on the one person he wanted to observe, he basically ensured his thoughts remained locked on her.

If he closed his eyes for even a second, he could clearly see the way she'd looked after he'd finished kissing her beneath the oak.

When her thick lashes had lifted to reveal the bright green and azure swirling in her unfocussed gaze and her breath had slid shallowly from her lips—glistening, pink, and plump from his kiss—he'd been shaken right down to his core. He'd never seen anything so damned beautiful as Lady Anne ensnared in a web of blissful desire.

Too beautiful.

Colin may have been a bit off in his perception of the lady's vulnerability, but he'd been right about one thing. She was no match for Beynon. Not socially. Not physically. And sure as hell not romantically.

By the ton's standards, she was so high above him, he couldn't even see her exulted perch. He was raw and unrefined while she was the epitome of gentle grace. Anyone who looked at them for a second could see they didn't belong in each other's worlds. They didn't even exist in the same universe.

So why in hell could he so clearly envision her naked in his bed? *Bloody hell.*

"Hello, brother," Roderick greeted as he stepped up beside him. His usual annoying grin was firmly in place.

Beynon had hoped that by taking up a position in the corner of the large drawing room, he'd make it clear to others he was not in the mood to socialize. His brother clearly didn't get the message.

"Move along, Roderick," he warned. "I'm wretched company this evening."

Roderick eyed him closely. "That's exactly why I came to talk to you. So no one else would have to."

"I should just leave."

"Stay right there."

Beynon eyed his brother curiously. He'd never heard that sharp tone before.

Seeing his expression, Roderick added, "I've something to say to you and you're going to stand there and listen."

Beynon gave him a glare. "Why do I get the feeling I'm about to receive a lecture?"

"Because it would seem you're due for one. Colin says you and Lady Anne are having something of a quarrel."

Beynon glanced to where Colin stood with Lady Wright talking to Mr. and Mrs. Turner, who'd just arrived at the country estate early that day. Mrs. Turner being the youngest sister of Roderick's wife and their hostess.

He turned his accusing glare back to Roderick. "The two of you talk about me when I'm not there?"

Roderick shrugged. "Colin and I talk about you. You and I talk about Colin. No doubt you and Colin occasionally talk about me.

And all three of us talk about Owen. The only exception is Cailleach who we all know prefers to express herself more directly."

Beynon scowled at that. The man was right. But it didn't make the issue any more palatable.

"What happened?" Roderick pressed.

Beynon could already feel his temper rising as he suspected where his brother's obvious concern was directed. "Nothing."

"I can tell when you're lying, you know."

This brother's intuition was frustratingly astute but that didn't mean Beynon had to bow to his curiosity. He ignored Roderick to sweep a glance over the room. Unfortunately, his attention fell almost immediately upon Lady Anne where she stood talking with several other ladies.

After spending the last hours very purposefully avoiding even the barest peek at the woman, he now couldn't seem to drag his gaze away.

Tonight, she'd dressed in rose-colored silk. Not a pale pastel, but a deep, vivid shade of pink that was not unlike the color of her lips after he'd so thoroughly kissed her.

With a harsh tightening in his stomach, he forced his gaze away, only to have it slam disconcertingly into his brother's scrutinizing stare.

Fuck.

"You know," Roderick began, "Lady Anne has been a close friend of my sister-in-law since her debut. Though I sure as hell don't make it a habit to concern myself with such things, I believe it prudent to offer you a bit of warning."

Irritation flared even more brightly. First Colin. Now Roderick.

And the worst part of it all was he couldn't even argue their concern was misplaced. Imagine if they knew he's already kissed the woman. Twice.

Either unaware or unconcerned with Beynon's internal struggle, Roderick returned his glare with a hard look of his own. "I've heard you say a thousand times that you've no intention of marrying a lady of London high society"—he lowered his brows forbiddingly and dropped his voice—"to which Lady Anne decidedly belongs. Whatever is occurring between the two of you needs to stop or you'll find yourself with a bride after all."

That was it. Beynon had enough.

Neither of his brothers could possibly say anything to him he hadn't already been saying to himself, and far more harshly. He didn't need their warnings or their advice or their noble insistence on protecting the meek and fair Lady Anne from his dastardly intentions. Even if it came from a desire to protect Lady Anne, his older brother had a way of putting Beynon's back against the wall like no one else. And when he felt cornered, he had a tendency to lash out.

Squaring off to face his brother more directly, he decided to be as clear as possible.

"Have you any idea how ridiculous you sound? The thought of something even remotely worthy of concern occurring between myself and Lady Anne is absurd. I assure you, I've absolutely no intentions toward the woman. Dishonorable or otherwise. The type of woman I take to wife will need to be far hardier of character than the delicate Lady Anne. If not for this infernal competition, I'd do everything in my power to stay as far from her as possible. I'd sure as hell never consider bringing such an unsuitable woman to Wales as my bride."

With his blood running so hot and his words filled with self-condemnation, it took Beynon longer than it should have to acknowledge the look of alarm that crossed Roderick's face midway through his tirade.

But he did note the subtle shifting of air behind him followed by the distinct tones of Lady Anne's voice as she spoke.

"I apologize for interrupting. Clearly, I should've waited for you to finish your conversation before approaching."

Beynon turned to face as her with his stomach tied in a painful knot. There was no way she hadn't heard everything he'd just said. Though his vehemence had been self-directed, no doubt it could easily have been mistaken as vitriol against the woman herself. The blush on her unnaturally pale skin and the flatness of her gaze made it very clear his thoughtless, angry words had injured her.

And all Beynon could do was stare at her, his hands still curled in fists, his teeth clenched so hard his jaw ached.

Her gorgeous, magical eyes swirled like the sky in a summer storm.

"To ease your mind, Mr. Thomas, I've absolutely no desire to go to Wales," the lady stated with an odd note hovering in her voice. "In any capacity." She turned to Roderick and gave a short nod. "If you'll excuse me." Without giving Beynon another glance, she turned and strode from the room. Her manner, her movements, her unreadable expression, a perfect study in grace and dignity.

Beynon watched her leave. The fire inside him spinning dangerously out of control. And at the center, a point of regret so sharp and fine it seared through his core.

"Fuck," he muttered under his breath.

"Indeed," Roderick agreed, his tone equally regretful.

Chapter Sixteen

Anne made it halfway down the dim and quiet hallway that ran behind the main staircase before the tears welled in her eyes. Unable to go any farther, she pressed her back to the wall and lifted her hands to cover her face, pressing her fingertips against her closed eyelids in an attempt to stem the flow.

He wasn't worth the tears. He was a solemn, brooding, judgmental arse who didn't deserve an ounce of the emotion welling up inside her. He was rude and rough and dismissive and arrogant and it was clear now he'd hated her from the start.

Despite the way he'd kissed her just that morning and the tenderness and care he'd shown her in the maze or the fact that she'd started to believe there was something more to the man than what everyone believed.

She'd obviously been fooling herself.

"I didn't mean it."

The rich, weighty sound of his distinctive baritone interrupted the silence of the narrow hallway. Anne gave a start as her heart fluttered and her body was flooded with tingling awareness and urgent panic.

Without glancing his way, she pushed off from the wall and continued walking. She had no idea where the hallway led and didn't care as long as it took her away from him. Away from the humiliation and pain his words had caused. Words that really shouldn't have surprised her, though they did. He'd never suggested he had any tender thoughts toward her.

"Lady Anne," he called after her, his voice gruff.

She ignored him and quickened her pace. When he responded with a low growl, a raw shiver of fearful exhilaration ran through her but she didn't slow or turn around. Whatever it was that made her feel the way she did in reaction to the man was futile and foolish. She might have given in to the rush of feelings once, but she wouldn't make that mistake again.

But it seemed Mr. Thomas had no intention of letting her escape him. And as she felt his large hand encircle her wrist, stopping any further escape, a strange wildness rose up inside her. It was fierce and reckless and perhaps just a bit terrifying.

Rather than resist his far superior strength, she spun to face him without any forethought or particular intention. But as soon as she looked up into his dark features, made even darker by the deep shadows of the unused hallway, she lost a large portion of the fight inside her. All of a sudden, she just felt small and sad and tired.

She gave a testing tug of her wrist still caught in his grip but he didn't loosen his hold. If anything, his fingers tightened as he took a deliberate step closer. His body was so large it took up the full width of the narrow passage and his voice, though nothing more than a low murmur, seemed to fill all available space between them.

"Go on," he urged thickly. "I know you've a sharp tongue when you choose to wield it. Cut me down for my cruelty."

Anne took a deep breath. She wanted to. She really did. But no words came. She wished he'd just stayed in the drawing room. She didn't want him to see how deeply his words had wounded. She didn't want him to have the satisfaction of knowing he had the power to hurt her at all.

"I've nothing to say to you," she replied.

"Yes, you do," he growled as he stepped into her, turning her until her back came up against the wall once again. Only this time, he held her there by the sheer force of his proximity. "Call me a fucking bastard if you must. A savage brute. The Welsh Devil. I don't care."

With each word that fell roughly from his lips, he slowly closed the distance between them until he was pressed against her from knee to chest. His head was lowered toward hers—close enough for a wavy lock of his hair to brush her temple.

"We both know I deserve it," he muttered. The harsh, unforgiving lines of his firm lips hovered just above hers. His eyes sparked black fire in the darkness.

Overcome by sensations too wild and hot to manage and emotions that stabbed too deep, Anne closed her eyes, forcing an inconsequential barrier between them when all she wanted was to sink into him. Sink into the hard heat of him, the potent savagery of his anger, the raw sensuality.

But she knew now she couldn't trust him. Not with the tenderness growing inside her or the confusion and the longing that had become ever present in the most private corner of her soul.

"Why are you doing this?" she asked on a breathless whisper.

With her eyes still tightly closed, she was able to feel his response. The tightening of his fingers around her wrist pinned to the wall behind her. The swift intake of breath that expanded his chest and flattened her breasts. And then the ragged exhale that bathed the side of her throat.

"I don't know," he confessed and the tortured defeat in his voice lashed at her pride.

She opened her eyes as the muscles bracketing her spine tensed to steel. Lifting her free hand, she pushed against his shoulder, having every intention of stepping away. But with her wrist still firmly in his hand, when she shifted her weight away from the wall, it only brought her body more fully in contact with his. And when he set his large hand to the inner curve of her waist, the warmth and weight of his hold on her there felt like an act of possession, a claiming.

A sound of gentle frustration and willful surrender escaped from her lips.

She didn't want to walk away. She wanted to be here with him. In the darkness and the quiet. But not in anger or guilt or injured pride.

She wanted to feel cared for—like she mattered—as she had when he'd tended to her in the maze. She wanted to feel what she'd felt when he'd kissed her in the garden—the wildness and the hunger. She didn't want to feel despair as they stood so close. She wanted desire.

Without pausing to consider the decision, she lifted her hand to the hard curve of his shoulder and rose to her toes as she tipped her head back.

The pressure and warmth of his mouth immediately covered hers, as if he'd been waiting for exactly this. She whimpered softly and parted her lips to flick her tongue against the edge of his teeth. Desperately seeking the taste of him.

His groan was heavy and raw. He answered her demand with a velvety glide of his tongue and the harsh bite of his teeth on her lower lip.

He might not like her, but in this...she suspected he needed her as badly as she needed him.

She arched against him and grasped his coat in a tight fist as she tried to fit herself more completely to his powerful form. Desperation pressed outward from every corner of her being. Making her strain in his hold and gasp into his mouth.

After only a moment, he growled and wrapped one arm tight around her waist, lifting her from her feet. He thrust his tongue into her mouth and she whimpered again at the lush invasion.

In the back of her mind, she acknowledged the sound of a door opening. He executed a quick turn and she caught just the bare impression of some sort of storage closet before the door closed again, leaving them in pitch-blackness. With his arm still locked around her waist and his mouth ravishing hers, he pressed her back against the closed door.

They were alone. Shut off from the rest of the party—the rest of the world—in a private darkness all their own.

A thrill unlike anything she'd ever felt before rushed through her body, making her fingers and toes tingle and her blood pulse wildly through her veins. Desperation spread like an inferno, as though suddenly freed from some invisible confinement.

Anger and hurt were still present somewhere inside her—quietly seething. But the need rolling through her blood, sparking in her soul, was far too powerful to ignore. She willfully allowed herself to be consumed by it. She didn't *want* to feel pain and rejection. She wanted—*craved*—this heat and hunger. As long as she focused on the undeniable passion, everything else became irrelevant.

Somehow, he managed to shed his coat and tossed it aside without breaking from the kiss. Her hands roamed frantically over the toned heat of his chest and shoulders, loving the strength and power so evident in his form, while he urgently explored her mouth with plunging strokes and fiery licks. But that wasn't all he explored.

He'd lowered one large palm to grip firmly at the curve of her rear while he wrapped his other hand high around her rib cage. When he shifted his hold to boldly brush his thumb over the swell of her breast, she turned her head to drag in a ragged, panting breath. The second brush of his thumb found the aching point of her nipple and he paused there, circling the sensitive peak through the thin material of her evening gown. The caress sent shockwaves through her system, triggering a deep swirling low in her belly.

She dropped her head back and deepened the curve of her spine, a weak attempt at pressing herself more fully into his hand. She wanted him to cover her completely. Claim her. Mold her flesh with the warmth of his palm and the strength of his fingers.

Every time she didn't think she could feel any wilder, any more unbridled, he urged her to a new level of desperation. With an almost savage growl, he lowered his mouth to the side of her throat, sucking her sensitive flesh against the edge of his teeth as he grasped a handful of her skirts and lifted them to her waist. His movements were impatient and coarse as he delved beneath the gathered material to grip her rear in both hands. Before she could even think to protest, her feet were off the ground and her legs were wrapped around his narrow waist.

And then, as he pressed her more firmly to the door at her back, protesting was the last thing on her mind.

Shock and the maddest passion claimed her when the hard, hot length of his erection lodged in that hollow between her thighs. Molten desire pooled there. She rolled her hips, hoping to ease the sweet aching, and for a bare moment, she almost found the perfect ease to her torment as a delicate part of her rubbed against his hardness. She moaned from the pure pleasure of it. But it was far too fleeting and frustration followed swiftly in its wake.

With his mouth roaming over the top curve of one heaving breast, he muttered something roughly in Welsh. She couldn't understand the words, but they felt undeniably erotic sliding over her skin.

And then he rocked against her.

It was a strong, subtle movement that caused the thick ridge of his erection to grind with aching perfection against her heated, swollen core.

She gasped and met his next rolling thrust with a purposeful tilt of her pelvis.

Yes. This was what she needed. This bold pressure. This wonderful friction.

The guttural sound he made while he dipped his tongue into the shallow crevice between her breasts shattered whatever tenuous vessel contained the last bit of reticence she'd been holding on to.

She wanted all of him in that moment. Every inch, every gravelly moan, every harsh grip of his hands. She wanted nothing between them. She wanted to take him into herself and claim him as he claimed her with every pull of his mouth and short, heavenly thrust between her legs.

He lifted his head and his lips found hers. He delved his tongue past her teeth and claimed her breath with every harsh inhale. As she lost herself in the kiss, she vaguely felt him shift his hold before he reached between them.

The first touch of his fingertips—long and broad and slightly rough, sliding along her sex—stole her breath. Her drawers had been soaked by her body's reaction and clung to her like a second skin, allowing her to feel every nudge of his thumb against her swollen bud. The erotic caress was heavenly wicked and she never wanted it to stop. But then he found the open seam, and a second later, his finger slid more intimately along her opening.

The exhilaration she experienced in allowing him such liberty with her person—in craving his touch so acutely—was utterly unexpected.

And when his finger pressed past her entrance to slowly claim space inside her, she lost her breath to the sensation. Every thought, every second, every thud of her heart was intently focused on the experience. Somehow, his touch managed to be unrelenting but gentle at the same time as he filled her, softening her inner flesh and bringing more sensations to life. The pleasure he awakened with every deliberate, demanding stroke of first one finger then two started to tumble over itself as it expanded through her body—reaching to her fingers and toes, snaking up her spine, tingling across her scalp.

Anne moaned and arched against the door. Her thighs squeezed tightly around his hips. She felt reckless and out of control. She loved it.

Thrusting his fingers in and out of her body in a rhythm she began to crave like her next breath, he spread open-mouthed kisses along her throat and the curve of her shoulder. All the while, murmuring rich, gravelly words she couldn't understand.

When he brought his mouth back to hers, she grasped his head in her hands and dove into the heat of his mouth with an urgency she couldn't quite explain.

He answered her with deep strokes of his tongue and harsh scrapes of his teeth. There was nothing gentle about the kiss. Nothing calm or sweet or tentative. It was primitive and savage and it consumed her.

So much that she nearly cried out when his fingers left her.

The knuckles of his hand bumped and rubbed against that tightening bud at the apex of her sex as he seemed to fumble with something between them. She gasped at the sensitivity and intensity of the brief contact and twisted her tongue more wildly with his.

And then it wasn't his knuckles nudging against her, but something smoother, hotter, and far broader than his fingers. She knew what it was—of course she knew—and oddly, the realization brought a deep sigh of contentment followed quickly by a sharp inhale as he slowly pushed into her body.

He bowed his head beside hers, resting his forehead to the door. His heavy, panting breaths spread hot air against her neck and his hands gripped hard to her buttocks as he held her in place to accept the pressure of his body claiming space inside hers.

With her heart in her throat, she clung to him. Her legs locked around his hips and her arms tight around his neck. Tucking her face into that hollow beneath his jaw, she breathed deeply through her nose as he filled her.

She expected a bit of pain or discomfort, but all she felt was a delicious stretching and the wonderful hard heat of him. Once fully sheathed, he immediately began to withdraw. A slow, lovely glide, then another slow, claiming thrust. But as he continued, each pump of his hips became more urgent, more forceful, and more spine-tingling than the one before.

Something began to build strength inside her. Something stronger and more demanding than desperation. Fiercer than hunger. It was a heaviness...and a pleasure that went deeper than what she'd experienced so far. It made her teeth clench and her heart pound so furiously her chest ached. She couldn't speak—could barely breathe beyond a quick, shallow panting—and though she wanted to beg him to ease the unbelievable torment clawing through her, she wanted him to never stop the lush, deep thrusts that were slowly driving her mad. Surely, she wouldn't survive much more.

When he released a heavy groan that reverberated through her body, she wondered if he could possibly be feeling the same. *Goodness, she hoped so!* And then he tightened his grip on her hips and tilted her pelvis. The sudden, subtle shift caused a breath-stealing new sensation as his thrusts reached something inside that made her inner muscles clench around him.

When the ultimate pleasure came, it burst so quickly and so forcefully she cried out. He swiftly covered her mouth with his, muffling the sound. He consumed her gasping moans as the climax rippled through her body, spreading shaking pleasure to every corner of her existence.

Swept up in the maelstrom of sensation and surrender, she forced herself to acknowledge the stunning beauty of that moment. His taste on her tongue, the imprint of his hands marking her softness, the sound of his ragged breath, and the throbbing hard heat of him filling the aching emptiness inside her.

Chapter Seventeen

A surge of animalistic possessiveness roared through Beynon as her deep, fluttering spasms caressed his cock. The pleasure was too intense, the demand for release too strong. His throat closed on a growl and his legs trembled. Then he tensed from head to toe as his orgasm exploded with a depth and power that stunned him.

By the time her soft, gasping sighs died and his shaking limbs regained a bit of strength, the shocking reality of what had just occurred hit him like a cannon ball to the gut.

He sucked in a hard breath and flexed his hands against the soft flesh of her arse.

Fuck.

The muscles of his thighs bunched as he realized almost all his weight was shoved against her. His belly pressed firm to hers. He could feel every rise and fall of her breasts as she struggled to slow her breath and the thundering pace of her heart resonated through his chest.

When he shifted his pelvis and withdrew from her gently pulsing sheath, she murmured softly but said nothing. A moment later, she slowly, shakily lowered her feet to the floor.

A great and terrible clenching moved through his body. Not quite regret or denial but something similar. He'd never experienced such a consuming passion, such a raw need to claim. And the pleasure! The intensity of his climax hummed through him still.

But now...

With a pain he'd never experienced before, he acknowledged that an experience like the one he'd just had came with a set of severe consequences.

As her arms slid away from around his neck, he didn't need to be able to see through the darkness still surrounding them to know there was a flush of exertion on her pale cheeks and her lips were plump and glistening. Her gown was likely beyond ruined—crumpled and twisted between their heated bodies.

After unwinding his neckcloth from his throat, he used the soft cotton to wipe away the wetness seeping from her body, then cleaned himself as well. Despite having just shared the most intense form of physical intimacy, neither of them spoke while he tended to the aftermath of their reckless passion.

He couldn't stop himself from gently smoothing his hand up her inner thigh before stepping back to allow her skirts to fall over her legs. Her breath stuttered a bit at the caress, but still...she said nothing.

Beynon refastened his breeches then bent to pick up his coat. After sliding the garment back on, he tucked the damp neckcloth into a pocket. Then he shoved his hands back through his hair as he finally directed his focus to the woman standing against the door as though she'd crumple without its support.

His sight had adjusted enough to see that she watched him intently. Her focus was quiet yet fierce but the slight part of her lips nearly tempted him to claim another taste of her.

"Are you all right?" His voice was hoarse, making the words sound gruffer than he intended. Her subtle flinch twisted at his insides. He'd never felt more like the vile man who'd sired him than he did in that moment.

She nodded then licked her lips. "I'm fine."

Her reply was tremulous and another stab of self-disgust angled through him.

He should say something assuring. Something to ease the shroud of uneasiness that had dropped around them the moment the pleasure had receded. But what assurance could a man give to a woman who was no doubt already cursing him for being every bit the devilish brute people claimed he was?

In truth, he knew exactly what he needed to say. He just couldn't get the bloody words past his clenched teeth.

He took a step back and bumped into something set on the floor. Looking down, he noted the thing he'd nudged with his foot was a wash bucket.

Fucking hell. A servant's closet. He'd taken her in a bloody servant's closet.

"We can't stay here," he muttered.

"Probably not," she replied, her tone utterly unreadable.

Beynon's shoulders burned with tension. "Shall I escort you to your room?"

There was a pause and her lashes fluttered as though she were struggling to meet his gaze. But the moment of vulnerability was gone in another instant as she looked up at him with steadfast focus.

She gave a gentle shake of her head. "No. I believe I'd prefer to go alone."

Though she seemed properly composed, Beynon sensed her tension. It thrummed in the air between them, as though hovering on the verge of full panic.

His stomach clenched, halting his breath.

This was all wrong.

She didn't deserve this. *Him.* Her innocence and her future destroyed in one reckless moment. She'd hate him. And rightfully so.

He lowered his gaze, no longer capable of meeting her stare with so much regret snaking through him.

"I'll guard the way to ensure no one intercepts you."

Without replying, she slowly stepped to the side so he could open the door. The hallway was as silent and dim as it had been. His hand tightly gripping the doorknob, he turned to her before leaving.

Her gaze was deep and tumultuous, her cheeks were flushed, and her hands visibly trembled as she clasped them together. But there was an undeniable poise in her manner. She was far more self-possessed than he could ever hope to be. Even now, as he looked at her, all he wanted to do was sweep her up in his arms and carry her to the nearest bed so he could peel away her clothing and make love to her properly.

He couldn't, of course. *He shouldn't.* But neither could he just walk away.

Stepping toward her, he looped an arm around her narrow waist and hauled her up against him. Her gasp of surprise turned to a soft whimper that angled sharply through his chest when he covered her mouth with his. She curled her fingers into the material of his coat, clinging to him as he thrust his tongue past her teeth then sucked harshly on her lush lower lip. He released her as abruptly as he'd claimed her—before he could lose himself again. Then he left her, denying the urge to look back in fear he'd decide to stay in that damned closet with her the rest of the night.

The faint sounds of the other guests still gathered in the drawing room met him as he stepped into the entry hall. He hovered there, lurking near the entrance to the hallway, but no one even left the drawing room let alone crossed toward him. And after some time, he assumed Lady Anne must have found another way upstairs that did not require passing through the main hall and he ascended the grand staircase to his own bedroom.

He should have insisted on escorting her.

But he knew now as he'd known then that if he'd gotten her upstairs to the quiet halls of the guest rooms, he'd have been just as likely to bring her to his bedroom as her own. And he wouldn't have let her go until morning.

Finally alone in his room, he fisted his hands as his mind filled with the image of her soft blonde hair slightly loosened from its pins to brush her cheeks, her expression so intently watchful despite the faint haze of sexual release still present in her gaze. Beautiful. Soft. Sensual in a way that shocked him to his toes just by thinking of it.

Dammit.

How could he have so completely and disastrously lost his head?

There was a strong reason he'd never intended on courting any of the fine ladies of London. His life in Wales was a distant cry from the elegance and sophistication of high society. Any wife of his would have far more pressing matters of concern than the latest style or ballroom dance.

Lady Anne, perhaps even more than most of the ladies he'd met since entering London society, was made for the gentle living she'd been born into. He couldn't imagine for a second she'd find any joy or peace as a common farmer's wife.

And yet he'd doomed her to exactly that.

His fisted hand ached with the urge to punch something.

Because even now, as he castigated himself for his lack of control and foresight, he couldn't help but feel another surge of desire for the woman. Those stolen moments when she'd held him secure with her legs around his hips and her arms around his neck had felt more deeply satisfying than anything he'd known before.

Her quiet gasps and sighs and moans had flowed through his blood like molten honey—rich and sweet and so fucking erotic.

He was a selfish beast of a man to want her again so fiercely after having been buried deep within her barely an hour ago. Would she be sore? Her body tender where he'd touched her? Had she been frightened by the strength of his hunger?

His desire was replaced by a fresh wave of guilt and regret.

But he'd laid his course. The way forward was clear. His stomach clenched. He had no choice.

And neither did she.

Chapter Eighteen

A nne woke with a disturbing sense of foreboding. It was the same feeling she'd had when she'd eventually fallen asleep the night before. Except worse.

Because despite the very passionate kiss Beynon had given her before he'd left her, the expression clouding his darkly handsome features had been...stricken.

Her heart seized painfully at the memory.

Though she couldn't possibly doubt his passion for her in the moment, it had been shockingly clear afterward that he'd regretted the experience. A truth made all the more wrenching by the fact that she'd never felt anything so heart-achingly beautiful as what she'd discovered in his arms. He'd triggered something inside her with his deep kisses and strong hands. Something wild and willful and a bit dangerous.

She'd finally been released from whatever invisible bonds she'd so ignorantly accepted all her life. But her liberation was covered by a dark shadow. Because he hadn't felt the same.

In fact, she'd never seen a man look more like a bear caught in a trap than he had last night.

Of course, she understood most ladies would anticipate a formal proposal after engaging in such scandalous activities with a gentleman. But Anne knew better than to expect such an offer. The man's words to his brother still rang clearly in her head.

No, Beynon Thomas had no desire to take her as his wife. What happened between them had been about physical lust—an eruption of passion and sensual need. She was not so naïve she couldn't understand that.

And why would she want to marry the man anyway? They were entirely incompatible. He was stubborn and rude and never listened to her. And it's not as though she had to worry about a lack of innocence keeping her from marrying anyone else. She'd already resigned herself to spinsterhood.

As soon as she had an opportunity, she'd make it clear to Mr. Thomas that she had no expectations and would certainly not demand any sort of declaration from him. Not now or ever.

Unfortunately, setting the man's mind at ease proved to be difficult when he was nowhere to be found. Not that she was actively searching—quite the opposite, actually, since she did her best to keep busy with various tasks throughout the day so as *not* to seek the man out. No matter how strongly she felt compelled to do so.

Tonight was the last event of the competition—the dramatic readings. She and her partner were to perform a short dialogue from Johann Wolfgang von Goethe's *Faust*. Anne was familiar with the play and the rather emotional scene they'd been assigned. She certainly would have liked to go through it few times with Mr. Thomas before reading it in front of others, but the practice wasn't entirely necessary.

Still, as the hours passed without even a distant glimpse of Mr. Thomas's tall, broad form, Anne began to worry. She didn't think he would be so cowardly as to actually try to avoid her, which meant something must be keeping him occupied. She only hoped it wasn't something unfortunate.

An explanation finally came from Miss Claybourne.

Anne was strolling along the path beyond the garden when she encountered the girl returning from a walk with her collie.

After a pleasant greeting, Anne decided to simply ask the girl if she happened to know where Mr. Thomas might be found. To her surprise, Miss Claybourne's expression turned downright mutinous.

"As a matter of fact," the young lady replied, "I do. No thanks to my overprotective brothers, who still dinnae see fit to give me fair knowledge and equal say in Max's affairs even though they ken bluidy well how I feel about being left out."

Taken aback by the vehement response, Anne replied cautiously, "I'm afraid I don't understand."

Miss Claybourne gave a quick shake of her head. "I'm sorry, Lady Anne. I reckon Beynon didnae tell you of our brother Max Owen."

"He did not."

"It's ridiculous, really, to think such a thing can remain a secret."

Worried their conversation might be betraying a confidence, Anne suggested, "If it's a secret, perhaps you shouldn't say any more, Miss Claybourne."

The girl's chin came up sharply. "It's my secret, too. I can share with whomever I wish." Clever hazel eyes narrowed. "The truth is, Beynon left late last night, along with Colin."

Anne's heart gave a strange stutter. "He left?"

Left the estate? Without even a word to her?

Not that he owed Anne a detailed report of his activities, but surely...she was due some consideration. A moment of thought. They were partners, after all, if nothing else.

"Aye, in the middle of the night while I was asleep and couldnae insist on going along."

"But why? Where did they go?"

"All Worthy would tell me this morning was that they had to go to London on an urgent matter. She said I had no need to ken anything more than that. But I'm not a bairn. Something so urgent it couldnae even wait till morn must be related to Max, which means it's also related to me."

The girl was getting fired up again, swinging her hands about in dramatic gestures as she spoke. "He'd better not've been taken by the magistrate again," she muttered under her breath.

"The magistrate?" Anne asked, eyes wide and blinking. The girl's explanation was getting more confusing by the minute.

"Aye." Miss Claybourne tilted her head. "Beynon really told you nothing about him?" When Anne shook her head, the girl heaved a great sigh. "You're aware that Beynon, Roderick, Colin, and I are all half siblings? Colin being our sire's only legitimate offspring, of course," she added with a dismissive wave of her hand. At Anne's nod, she continued, "Well, there's another brother born between Beynon and me. Max Owen. We only just managed to track him down a couple months ago and it turns out..." Dramatic pause. "He's the feared leader of a criminal gang based in St. Giles, London."

Anne gasped as the girl obviously intended judging by the theatrical drop in her tone as she confessed the last.

"Although Owen was thrilled at the idea of being yet another of the Earl of Wright's bastards, he has no intention of leaving his gang. If Beynon and Colin had to run off to London in the middle of the night, I've no doubt it has something to do with Max, which means I should've been informed of it," Miss Claybourne finished with a huff of exasperation.

Anne was shocked, and although she did her best not to show it, the girl gave her a knowing little smile. "It's all right, Lady Anne. It is a wild tale, but true nonetheless. I just hope Max hasnae gotten into serious trouble. Again."

"I'm certain Lord Wright and Mr. Thomas will be able to handle anything that might have occurred."

"They'll try, I ken. But it still upsets me when they leave me out of such things. And now that I think on it, it's a wee bit odd Roderick didnae go along as well."

There was a pause as the girl seemed to be thinking through something, but then her expression shifted into one of bright excitement.

"Are you looking forward to the ball tomorrow evening, Lady Anne?"

Anne blinked at the change in subject. She'd totally forgotten there was to be a ball in celebration of the end of the competition. "Yes, I suppose so," she answered.

"Worthy and Colin are allowing me to come down and *observe* for a little while."

Though the girl rolled her eyes dramatically at the word *observe*, it was clear she was excited by the opportunity not typically afforded a child her age.

"I do hope Beynon makes it back for your reading tonight," she added thoughtfully. "It would be a shame if you had to forfeit the event. Depending on how everyone votes on the paintings, the two of you have an excellent chance of winning the games."

"Really?" Anne was honestly surprised. She hadn't been following the results after the first couple days and hadn't realized they'd done so well. She'd have thought their disaster in the maze would have ruined their chances. And she'd totally forgotten all the paintings had been displayed in their respective pairs in the portrait gallery for the guests to vote upon by silent ballot throughout the day.

"Personally, I think your depiction of Beynon was unbelievably romantic," Miss Claybourne continued wistfully. "And Beynon's painting was verra...surprising," she concluded with a grin.

Anne smiled. "I appreciate the vote of confidence, Miss Claybourne."

"Oh, I've invested more than that," the girl replied with a wink. "Angelique and I have a wager. But I suppose I should be getting Bramble back to the house." She gave a sharp whistle, which brought her collie swiftly back to her side with a flopping tongue and fiercely wagging tail.

After parting from Miss Claybourne, Anne did her best not to worry about Beynon.

A part of her wished he'd have thought to inform her of his abrupt departure, but she disabused herself of that notion quickly. She had no claim to his personal time especially when it came to a private matter regarding his family. Though she hoped he might be back for the last game event that evening, she was more concerned with the possibility that something serious might have occurred with his younger brother. If all Miss Claybourne had said was true, the young man lived a dangerous life.

Considering the possibility that Beynon could be caught up in something perilous even now, an acute sort of fear snaked through her blood. She quickly forced it away, telling herself he was more than capable of handling himself. Besides, Lord Wright was with him. Surely, the levelheaded lord would ensure Beynon didn't go charging into anything truly dangerous.

Chapter Nineteen

Beynon and Colin made it back to Earl and Countess of Harte's estate just after dusk had fallen. Tired yet relieved that their journey had been successful, Beynon was anxious to change into clothing that didn't stink of his horse.

When he'd realized last night that he'd need to marry Lady Anne and quickly before any whisper of her downfall at his hands became known, he'd gone in search of his eldest brother. Though he'd considered going to Roderick first and the thought of asking Colin for help grated on his pride, he knew the Earl of Wright would have far more influence in his quest to obtain a special license. And he'd been right. With the special license in hand, all he needed now was the signature of Lady Anne's father. And the agreement of the lady herself.

Although Beynon had considered speaking with Anne before leaving for London, he feared being denied by the archbishop. In which case, advising the lady of his intentions beforehand would serve no good purpose. Not when she'd likely have significant cause to protest the union. He hoped the special license might help to convince her that—like it or not—marriage was the only option.

And now that he was back, he was anxious to see the matter resolved, which meant he didn't bother hiding his annoyance when the butler intercepted him before he could rush upstairs to change.

"Excuse me, sir, but this letter arrived for you this morning," the staid servant noted as he handed Beynon a crumpled missive. "And a Lord Humphries also arrived more than an hour ago and has been awaiting your return in the lord's private study."

Assuming Beynon would follow, the butler turned and began leading the way.

Beynon stuffed the letter into his pocket for later. Though he would have liked to clean up first, the matter of Lord Humphries was far more pressing. He glanced up to where Colin had paused on his way up the stairs. Having heard the butler's announcement, his brother lifted a brow in question, and after only a moment of hesitation, Beynon gave a nod. Colin immediately turned around and came back down the stairs to join Beynon as they were shown to the study.

Beynon wasn't entirely pleased to have his brother present for the meeting with Lady Anne's father, but he also acknowledged the fact that Colin had a way of soothing ruffled feathers when Beynon was mostly skilled at ruffling them further. And if he wanted this conversation to go his way, he'd best accept all the help he could get.

Lord Humphries stood in front of the fireplace with his feet braced wide and his hands clasped behind his back. Tall, lanky, and in possession of a hawkish face and sharp eyes, the aging lord had no trouble pinning Beynon with a stare of hard condescension and an almost fierce impatience.

"Lord Humphries," Beynon began as he approached the lord, "thank you for responding so quickly to my request for an audience."

Humphries blatantly ignored Beynon's offered hand as he narrowed his beady gaze. "Mr. Thomas, I presume."

Taking a deep breath to dispel a natural inclination to give in to the rise of temper at the other man's rudeness, Beynon reminded himself what was at stake. "That is correct. And this is Lord Wright," he added, indicating Colin, who stood back a bit, just inside the closed door.

Without even bothering to glance toward Colin, Humphries passed a scornful glare over Beynon. "You're the man who has compromised my daughter and now thinks to claim her hand and her dowry." Before Beynon could reply, he continued in a scathing tone, "I suppose I shouldn't be surprised the twit would lower herself in such a way. Though after so many years of humiliating failure, I'd hoped she'd take herself off to the country rather than go to such lengths for a husband." His expression turned to one of disgust. "I've always known she had nothing of value to offer a gentleman, but I wish she hadn't decided to whore herself to a blasted pig farmer."

The spittle from his vitriolic declaration barely left his lips before Beynon's temper got the best of him. In two strides he had the lord pinned to the wall with his forearm pressed firmly beneath the old man's loose jowls. Colin was instantly behind him, a solid hand on Beynon's shoulder. "Let him go. This serves no purpose," the earl urged firmly.

But the shock and flicker of fear in the lord's tiny dark eyes wasn't nearly satisfaction enough for what the wretch had just said about his own daughter. A fist to the nose might be a start. That or a knee to the gut.

"Brother," Colin warned.

Recalling that he still needed the lord's signature, he slowly eased up the pressure of his arm across Humphries's throat. The older man immediately began to sputter and shake in his rage.

But Beynon held fast to his cravat. "You're a disgusting excuse for a father," he muttered thickly, his temper just barely in check.

"At least now the useless chit will have the husband she deserves," Humphries retorted. "A pig farmer and a bastard. Good riddance to the girl. She's been nothing but a burden since her damnable birth."

Beynon's hand tightened in the man's neckcloth. How had Anne managed to endure such a hateful sire?

"Then you won't object to signing the special license," Colin noted calmly from behind Beynon.

"I can't wait to get the bloody chit off my hands."

Releasing him before he changed his mind, Beynon stepped back and withdrew the license from his coat pocket. Stalking to the desk, he slammed the license down before swiping up a quill. His movements stiff and jerky with the fury still rolling through him.

Lord Humphries took a long minute to smooth out his coat and fluff his cravat before he strode forward and took the quill to sign his name in a hasty flourish. Then he flashed a disturbing grin. "Good luck with your useless new bride, bastard. She comes to you with nothing but the clothes on her back since you won't be seeing a damned penny of her dowry. Whether she goes through with this marriage or not, from this day forward she shall not receive a single thing from me. She is disowned. Now and forever."

Beynon replied in barely suppressed fury, "Fuck off."

Humphries laughed—a grating, ugly sound—then strode from the room.

ANNE WAITED UNTIL THE last possible moment to seek out Lily and advise her that she and Mr. Thomas would have to withdraw from the evening's event. Though she was deeply regretful for having to disappoint her friend, with the dramatic readings due to start in less than an hour and still no word of Beynon's return, she saw no other choice.

She was crossing the main entry hall in search of someone who might know where Lily was to be found when the door to the lord's study opened rather forcefully and a shockingly familiar figure stepped out. Locked in place, Anne could only stare wide-eyed and blinking.

Lord Humphries's stride was sharp and swift and his slightly stooped shoulders were stiff with tension as he strode toward the front door. On his long, weathered face was an expression she'd often seen in her youth—when he'd still taken something of an interest in her.

It was the look of disgust teetering on the verge of full rage.

She hadn't seen her father in nearly two years and hadn't witnessed one of his tempers in longer, but it still affected her just as it always had. Her entire body flinched then froze. Her chest tightened so swiftly it caused her to choke on a gasp when she realized she needed to keep breathing.

The sound had her father turning just his head to pin her with a hard glare. He didn't even slow his steps and his voice was as cold and unfeeling as ever.

"I never expected much from you, girl. But I sure as hell expected better than this. I wash my hands of you."

And with those cruel and cryptic words, he continued through the front door and was gone.

Shock and a peculiarly nostalgic sort of pain held Anne in an unrelenting grip. She remained where she was—poised mid-step in the middle of the hall. Her blood was chilled while her cheeks burned with embarrassment and an anger buried too far below the surface to be released.

It wasn't until after her father's footsteps had faded to silence that confusion finally overcame her shock.

What on earth had he been doing here?

Her gaze flew back toward the study, realizing he likely hadn't been alone in the room.

Beynon stood in the doorway—his thick-muscled arms crossed over his chest, his forbidding features drawn into such a ferocious glare it caused a frisson of alarm to slide across her nape, and his black stare focused intently on the door through which her father had just left. A few steps behind him, just visible over his broad shoulder, stood Lord Wright. His attention was fixed on her, a subtle yet undeniable expression of compassion shadowing his handsome face.

Another wave of embarrassment washed through her. Running hotter and deeper than the last. She ignored it. Turning toward the study, she didn't hesitate when Beynon's fierce gaze landed on her with the force of a cannonball. She kept her head high and her gait unhurried. Holding his gaze, she approached both gentlemen.

Then she paused and glanced to the earl before returning her focus to Beynon.

She might have overcome the rush of humiliation her father so easily triggered in her, but there remained a heavy dread—an acute fear—encroaching upon her like a black cloud swallowing the moon.

Staring into Beynon's menacing gaze, she forced a steady calm to her voice. "Why was my father here?"

Beynon's scowl grew ever darker—heavier—as he stared at her. The muscles of his jaw were so hard beneath the shadow of beard growth they looked turned to stone and the line of his mouth was so firmly drawn she wondered if she'd ever detect softness there again.

When it appeared he wasn't going to answer, Anne glanced past him to Lord Wright.

"My lord?"

"Please, Lady Anne, join us for a moment and all will be explained."

What on earth was going on?

She glanced to Beynon once again but encountered only a forbidding wall of intensity and fury. Then he took one step back and turned to the side so she could enter the room. She could see nothing of the man who'd kissed her so passionately just last night. But as she stepped past him, she still felt the magnetic pull of his body. The solid heat of him, the lure of his strength and hardness. Especially in this moment, when she felt so small and alone.

But she'd been alone all her life.

Whatever was happening now, she could weather it. She'd surely faced worse.

The earl gestured for her to take a seat in the chair set before Lord Harte's large desk.

She gave a small shake of her head and continued to the center of the room, where she turned to face them while tight bands of foreboding wrapped around her lungs, cinching tighter with every breath.

"Leave us."

The harsh words were spoken by Beynon to his brother. The earl frowned and looked to Anne. "I don't think that's prudent."

Anne's voice was firm as she was quick to interject, "It's all right."

Concern tugged at the earl's mouth, but he nodded. "I'll be just outside."

Once the door closed behind him, leaving Anne and Beynon alone, she forced herself to meet his gaze without faltering. "Why was he here?"

"I requested his presence."

Anger was starting to overthrow the trepidation inside her. "Why?" she asked sharply. "I thought you'd gone to London. My father spends his summers in Surrey."

He cleared his throat and finally lowered his arms to his sides as he took a few steps into the room. But not toward her. He stalked first toward the desk before hesitating and stopping behind the chair Lord Wright had intended for her to sit in. He braced his large hands on the curved back as his dark gaze found hers.

"I did go to London but not before sending a note to Lord Humphries, asking him to meet with us here."

Her eyes narrowed and her belly gave a hard lurch as a terrible suspicion gripped her. "Why would you do such a thing?" And what had he said in the note to bring her father from his summer estate so quickly? He was not a man to follow the whims of others.

"I required his permission."

"For what?" The words flew from her lips in a near shout as panic caught her in its grip.

He glanced to the desk. The surface was extremely neat and tidy, which made the paper lying in the center stand out in stark clarity.

A strange numbness began to spread up from her toes.

"What is that?" she prompted.

"A special license. Obtained from the archbishop this morning."

The hollowness of his voice echoed in her head as she stared at the document. Even from where she stood, she could clearly make out her father's sprawling signature.

A special license.

Emotions too intense to name swirled inside her as she boldly met Beynon's dark glare. "You can't be serious."

There was a swift tic at the corner of his jaw, but he held her gaze. And said nothing.

Of all the things rolling through her in that moment, she was grateful for the fury that came to the fore.

"You decided this last night. Without speaking to me about it. Without *asking me.* You flew off to London and sent for *my father,* all without even pausing to consider what I might have to say about it."

Her words got steadily louder and more shrill. Yet still he said nothing.

Anger propelled her forward. Two swift steps before she stopped herself.

"How dare you?" she muttered from clenched teeth. "How dare you make such a decision for me?"

"We made the decision together," he answered gruffly. "Last night in the closet. Remember?"

Anne gasped. For some reason, his stark reference to those stolen moments caught her off guard. The anger in his voice hurt.

"What did you expect me to do?" His question was a near growl.

A leaded feeling turned her stomach. "I didn't expect *this*," she whispered. Then she straightened her spine and strengthened her voice. "What we did...what happened between us last night did not give you the right to make a decision that would affect the rest of *my* life without consulting me. Did you consider the possibility that I might not *want* to marry you?"

His answer was a low growl as his hands curled over the back of the chair as if he wanted to tear the thing in half. "Of course I considered it," he shouted before giving a rough shake of his head. "But it doesn't matter."

"Yes, it does!" she shouted back. She'd never in her life imagined her first marriage prospect would come in the form of an angry man making the offer out of some misplaced sense of duty.

She cast a glare toward the offending paper. "You can toss that thing into the fire, Mr. Thomas. I do not agree to it."

With that, she strode swiftly to the door.

"You've no choice," he said in a voice barely above a murmur.

His words make her want to scream, but she held it in, along with the fury and shame and despair rolling through her like a wildfire. Lord Wright was standing just outside as he'd promised but she walked past him without a glance.

Chapter Twenty

Beynon wanted to throw something. Tossing the chair through the nearest window might be properly satisfying to his current mood. But the relief would be temporary.

Lady Anne's reaction to their situation was essentially what he'd expected. He knew damned well she wouldn't want to marry him. He had to admit to himself it was partly the reason he'd gone to get the special license without telling her. He'd spent every minute since leaving her last night preparing himself for her righteous anger and dismay.

No. It wasn't her reaction that had gotten him to such a high temper.

It was that bloody bastard who called himself her father. The man was more of a monster than Beynon's own sire. Considering the prior Earl of Wright had fathered a handful of illegitimate children out of spite and vengeance, that wasn't an easy feat to manage.

Beynon still regretted not breaking the lord's prominent nose.

"I'm sorry, Beynon." Colin's level voice interrupted another rise of temper.

"It doesn't matter," Beynon grumbled, releasing his white-knuckle grip on the chair. "She knows what must be done. She'll see it through."

She had no choice.

He hated that the phrase kept repeating in his head. But it was the god-awful truth.

"You don't have to look upon this situation as a death knell," the earl noted calmly. "Many marriages begun under such circumstances have managed to thrive. And there is something undeniable between you and Lady Anne. If you focus on that—"

"Enough, Colin," Beynon interrupted. "It is what it is."

He left the room in angry strides. People were starting to gather downstairs in preparation for the evening's event. He stalked past all of them, noting Anne was nowhere in sight.

He calmed his almost panicked need to find her with the acknowledgement that he'd see her shortly at the evening event. An event he sure as hell couldn't attend in his current state.

After a quick bath, a shave, and a fresh set of clothes, Beynon felt only marginally calmer. The fury he still felt had been pushed as far down as he could manage as he told himself that the only good thing that might come of this debacle was that Lady Anne would never again have to suffer her father's cruelty.

In his hurry to get to her side, he cut through the Earl of Harte's portrait gallery on his way back downstairs. He'd forgotten that all of the competitors' paintings would be on display, and despite his rush, he found himself slowing.

He was suddenly desperately curious to view her painting of him.

He hadn't even glanced at it that day in the garden. He'd been far too intensely focused on the lady herself. After their heated kiss, it had taken all of his willpower to stop himself from touching her—kissing her—the way he really wanted to. To distract himself, he'd trained his focus on watching her as she'd finished his portrait.

It had been fascinating—and not entirely effective in cooling his ardor. Her expression had been so quietly intent. Her eyes vivid and captivating. Her movements so confident and graceful. When it had finally been his turn at the easel, he'd been determined to capture the vibrance and tenacity she usually kept so carefully subdued.

As he stopped now in front of the portrait she'd done of him, an edgy dread rushed through him. Twisting his stomach into a knot.

The painting was lovely. The talent and skill undeniable.

From the vivid greens and golds of the background and the accents of color in the flowers creeping into view around the edge to the use of light and how faithfully she rendered his likeness. It was a beautiful scene.

But what cut through him so sharply was the realization that this was how she saw him.

Rustic. Unrefined. Not a country gentleman of leisure but a field laborer at rest. He could even see a flock of sheep dotting the hills in the background.

And she was right. About all of it. The unpolished boots, the open collar and rolled sleeves. The careless locks of his too-long hair. And most true of all—the bold, ungentlemanly stare. Nothing else in the world could have shown him his true place so well as Lady Anne's painting.

He suddenly wanted to smash it to pieces.

"I'd intended to give you a stern talking to for your disloyalty, but I'm rethinking that plan since you're looking verra murderous at the moment."

Beynon tensed as the first sound of his impertinent sister's voice. But he didn't shift his gaze from Lady Anne's painting. "What do you want, Caillie?"

Despite the forbidding tone of his voice, the brave girl stepped closer until she stood beside him. "I wanted to yell at you for going to London without me."

Confused, Beynon slid a quick sideways glance to the girl to find her staring rather intently at his portrait, her head tipped slightly to one side. "It was an urgent matter. And a personal one. There was no reason for you to come along."

Her frown was fierce and full of accusation. "How could you say that? You ken how I feel about being left out when it comes to Max."

Now he understood. "My trip to London had nothing to do with our brother."

Caillie's eyes narrowed as she turned to face him more fully, as though she intended to peer into his mind and extract the truth by sheer will.

"Do you really think Roderick would've stayed behind if there was some new development pertaining to the lad?" he asked.

Her brows furrowed. "I suppose not."

"When we said we'd keep you properly informed, we meant it. At least, I did."

And it was true. His first encounter with this sister two years ago had occurred because she'd traveled across London by herself to speak with him when Colin and Ainsworth had erroneously thought it best to keep certain details from her knowledge. Beynon knew better than to take such a risk.

After another moment, his sister sighed and gave a little nod. "I believe you. So, why did you run off to London so suddenly?"

Beynon hoped his scowl would deter her curiosity. "As I said—a personal matter."

Unfortunately, it seemed to do the opposite. Hazel eyed widened then narrowed dramatically as she crossed her arms over her chest. "Does it perchance have something to do with the fair Lady Anne?"

Bloody hell. The girl was proving herself to be as annoyingly astute as Roderick. Beynon really didn't like being so easily read, which was why his reply came out far harsher than he intended. "Of course not."

Caillie actually smiled. "That's a bold-faced lie, Beynon Thomas." Then she squinted at him in harsh suspicion. "What did you do?"

"I'm not discussing this with you."

Beynon took a step back, intending to walk away, but the stubborn girl stepped to swiftly block his path. "Good idea. Let's not discuss it. You can just listen."

"I'd rather—" he managed to grumble before she interrupted him.

"I dinnae give a damn what you'd rather."

The profanity stopped him short. He dipped his chin with a forbidding scowl. "What would Ainsworth think of such language?"

"Worthy knows a well-placed curse is sometimes entirely necessary."

Probably true. The Scotswoman wasn't one to hold back when a situation warranted blunt speech.

He folded his arms in a pose matching hers. "Out with it, then."

There was a pause as she stared at him, utterly unintimidated. Then she sighed. "I ken that you and I havenae had a lot of opportunities to spend time together. But from our first meeting, I've felt a kinship with you. I understand you, Beynon. And because of that I feel I can say with full confidence that you're at risk of mucking things up in a verra bad way with Lady Anne."

Her statement was far too insightful. "I'm not going to muck anything up. I'm bloody trying to fix it."

She gave him a look of disbelief as she planted her hands on her hips in a perfect imitation of Ainsworth's forbidding stance. "Then why are you up here when Lady Anne and everyone else are gathering downstairs for tonight's event? Why aren't you at her side? Why aren't you rehearsing your reading? If you've any hope of winning, you have to do well in tonight's event."

Bloody hell, the child was talking about the games.

Of course. He didn't know why he'd thought she was referencing the wretched issue of his sudden proposal. She couldn't possibly know about that.

"I've put my money on you and Lady Anne and I won't have you ruining it when you're so close to winning."

He gave her a hard look. "You bet on the outcome of the games?"

"I've made it verra clear I've been rooting for you and Lady Anne from the start," she evaded none too subtly. "Now, I ken you havenae been a verra enthusiastic participant, but you cannae be thinking of backing out now."

Beynon shook his head and shoved a hand back through his hair. All too often, his conversations with his sister tended to leave him feeling a bit wrung out to dry. "Don't worry, I'll be heading downstairs in a bit. I won't muck things up."

"Good." Caillie gave a sharp nod. "See that you dinnae. Lady Anne deserves better than that."

A bolt of unease shot through him as he glanced back to the lady's painting.

His sister was right. The lady sure as hell didn't deserve a man such as he. For a partner or otherwise.

Chapter Twenty-one

Anne was still seething even after her vigorous walk about the gardens when she finally reentered the house to speak to Lily about withdrawing from the final event. She couldn't possibly perform the reading in the state she was currently in. No doubt her friend would see instantly that something was wrong, but Anne had no intention of explaining the source of her upset. She just couldn't bring herself to state out loud that she had finally received an offer of marriage, but it had come from a man with absolutely no real wish to wed her. A man who held no honest admiration or tender feelings for her. And that he hadn't even asked her for her hand but had gone about arranging the thing behind her back. He'd decided what must be done and engaged her father in the matter before even bothering to consider her own thoughts.

As her father had made so abjectly clear throughout her life—she was nothing more than an obligation to be managed. A responsibility preferably ignored except for when her existence became an unavoidable nuisance.

And now, Mr. Thomas had apparently decided that, because of last night, she'd become *his* unfortunate burden.

All the insecurities of her childhood pressed up from the darkness she'd worked so hard to bury them in. She'd already spent far too much of her life believing herself unworthy of time and consideration and *love*. She'd vowed never to resign herself to the same in her marriage.

Barely containing the pain and resentment roiling about inside her, Anne entered the conservatory, where the party guests were gathering for the dramatic readings. She scanned the room for Lily. Most of the chairs had already been claimed, but several people still lingered on their feet along the edge of the room. Lily and her husband amongst them. Anne had hoped she'd be able to simply duck in and duck out again, but it appeared she'd have to skirt the rows of chairs to reach her friend at the front of the room.

Steeling herself against the desire to flee, she made her way forward. She was still several paces from where Lily stood when she felt an ominous presence come up behind her. Close. Then the warm, firm touch of a large hand grasping her elbow.

She stopped immediately, her entire body freezing in place even as unwanted warmth suffused her insides.

He dared to approach her here in front of everyone? No doubt, he knew she wouldn't wish to cause a dramatic scene. Tense and heated with anger, she slowly turned her head to glance up at him.

He stood near enough to stir the fall of her skirts. And his head was lowered intimately toward hers. She could see his pulse beating at the side of his throat.

How could she still so strongly wish to press her fingers there? Her lips?

Her head spun and her knees felt suddenly weak.

"Shall we take a seat?" He spoke in a low murmur but the rich baritone flowed heavily through her.

She tensed her jaw. "I'm not staying."

He didn't reply, but his eyes turned dangerously dark as he held her subtle, silent glare.

"Welcome, everyone," Lily called out from the front of the room where she stood between two chairs positioned to face the audience. "I'd like to get started, if we may."

Lady Anne was stuck. It was too late to cry off now, especially since her partner was present and apparently still intended to go through with the reading.

Once again, the power to make her own choice was taken from her.

As subtly as she could, she pulled her arm from Beynon's grasp and started toward the nearest empty seat. Unfortunately, it was next to another unoccupied chair, which her partner promptly claimed.

Keeping her gaze forward, she only half listened to Lily explaining that the order of the readings had been chosen at random before she announced the partnership who was to go first.

Anne could endure this. Ten short scenes, including their own. Perhaps after she and Beynon gave their performance, she'd be able to slip from the room unnoticed.

As the first couple started their reading, the man beside her shifted in his chair. The new position pressed the length of his thigh against hers. An unwanted thrill chased along her skin at the contact as heat rushed through her.

Was she so weakened by her desire for him that such a simple touch could reduce her to trembling?

Just as subtly, she reestablished the breath of space between them.

From the corner of her vision, she saw his large hands, previously resting atop his thighs, curl slowly into fists. For a second, she thought he might reach out...touch her. Then she almost laughed at her foolishness.

He didn't want her.

Even as she acknowledged the painful truth, her memory was seized by a visceral recollection of being held in his arms, her body wrapped around his, while his heavy breath warmed her throat and his hardness throbbed inside her.

He'd wanted her then.

But passion and sexual hunger—even as intense as what they'd surrendered to last night—did not equate to true feeling. And no matter what society's expectations happened to be, she did not believe it justified a hasty marriage. She'd rather spend her days a spinster than commit herself to a life as another man's unwanted obligation.

Mr. Thomas could glower all he wanted. She wasn't going to marry him.

She remained stoic and resolved through the next few readings, but when it was finally their turn to step in front of the room, she felt an odd trembling deep inside.

Beynon stood first and held his hand to her.

She set her fingers in his without thought—a reflexive response to the common gesture. But when his warm hand curled around hers, her belly twisted and her gaze lifted to catch his for a split second before he directed his gaze forward.

What she saw in his eyes in that moment worried her. It wasn't his usual broody stare. No flash of temper or burning ire gleamed from the depths. Instead, she saw a hard, unmovable resolve.

It frightened her in a way nothing else could have.

By the time they took their seats facing the other guests, a silent wariness had claimed her.

Lily smiled encouragingly as she handed each of them copies of the abbreviated scene they were to read before turning to her guests.

"Lady Anne will be reading the part of Margaret and Mr. Thomas will read the part of Faust in the dungeon scene of Johann Wolfgang von Goethe's *Faust*, Part One." With a glance back to Anne and Beynon, she whispered, "You may begin whenever you're ready."

As Lily took her seat beside her husband in the front row, Anne glanced down at the lines. Taking a deep breath, she tried to focus on the words rather than the man beside her.

An uncomfortable hush settled in the room around them as everyone waited for the scene to begin. The first lines were Beynon's and Anne finally lifted her gaze to see him staring intently at her, his gaze dark and his expression severe.

But then he glanced down at his scene and read. The heaviness of his voice brought a stark, painful gravity to Faust's impassioned words as he sees his former love in the dungeon cell. Anne's response as Margaret was a pained appeal filled with confusion as the imprisoned woman fails to recognize the man she'd once loved.

As the scene continued through the emotional turmoil of a woman lost to grief and guilt and a man desperate to redeem himself by freeing her from the tragic fate that awaited her, Anne surrendered to the emotion of the scene. She surrendered to the pain in Margaret's pleas for mercy as the woman remembered all she'd lost. And she surrendered to the rough, almost angry insistence of the man who'd led to her ruin but was now fighting to save her.

Beynon's reading of Faust's passionate demands as he urged her to leave with him, to flee the dungeon before it was too late, forced Anne to fight past the emotion clogging her throat to respond as Margaret struggled against the weight of her own shame and despair.

By the time they reached the end of the scene, Anne felt weak and raw.

Because she'd *felt* Beynon's reading as if he'd been Faust himself. Desperate and fighting to fully understand the woman he wished to save and the strength of the darkness that gripped her.

With her heart racing, she met Beynon's heavy stare. His dark eyes were weighted with silent passion and, again, that unforgiving resolve.

As desperate as she was to reject his proposal, he was just as fiercely determined not be swayed from his intention.

And she suddenly wasn't so sure she was strong enough to resist him.

Rising abruptly to her feet, she tried to maintain some veneer of decorum as she walked up to Lily, who had risen to her feet with an odd sheen of tears in her eyes. After muttering a quick word about not feeling well, Anne continued quickly past the seated guests to the open doors behind them. Passing Lord and Lady Mayhew, she was struck by the odd look of fury in the lady's eyes, but she didn't slow her steps.

Once free of the room, she continued to the stairway that led to the guest wing and the solitude of her bedroom. Even as her eyes began to blur and her heartbeat thundered in her ears, she prayed her maid would not be waiting for her.

Blessedly, her bedroom was empty. But as she sighed in relief and turned to close her door, she couldn't.

Beynon's large form filled the threshold. She hadn't even heard him behind her.

Her stomach plummeted and her heart bounced to her throat.

"We need to talk." Even now, his dark tone resonated with something deep inside her.

She shook her head, taking a step back. "I've nothing more to say."

His glowering countenance was menacing in the dim candlelight. "Then you can listen." With fierce purpose, he stepped across the threshold and closed the door behind him. Turning the key in the lock for good measure.

Though she was now locked in her bedroom alone with a very intense, very strong man, Anne wasn't the slightest bit frightened. She was far too emotionally battered and deeply incensed to feel something so tame as fear.

Staring boldly back at him, she closed her thoughts behind an unreadable mask. He could never know how hurt she was by his betrayal—his utter disregard for her basic right to make her own decisions.

He said he wanted her to listen? Fine. He could say whatever he wanted, then he could leave.

Chapter Twenty-two

This was a mistake. A huge error in judgement.

He never should have followed her. Everyone downstairs had witnessed it. Her hasty departure with him following swiftly on her heels. Not that the impropriety would matter much after their engagement was announced.

No, the risk Beynon perceived as he stared at Lady Anne's stoic expression and fiercely proud stance had nothing to do with society's perception and everything to do with the lady's.

He took a step forward and her chin lifted. Her gaze became uncharacteristically steely as she waited silently for him to speak.

What could he say? She was clearly furious—and rightfully so. But it couldn't change anything. What had been done could not be reversed.

Resisting the urge to look anywhere but at the woman in front of him, he cleared his throat. "I understand your anger." A quick arch of her brows suggested her skepticism. He scowled. She wasn't going to make this easy for him. "I should've spoken with you before sending for Lord Humphries. At the time, I thought it best to move forward as quickly as possible."

When she said nothing in reply, he turned to stalk toward the low burning fire. Needing something to do, he crouched before the hearth and set about rousing the flames back to life. Having his back to her made it easier to continue.

"I wanted time to overcome any objections your father might express."

There was a pregnant pause following the statement. Then Anne asked in a voice that was tense and quiet, "And did he? Object?"

Beynon's stomach knotted sharply as he used an iron poker to stir the coals.

Lord Humphries's response to Beynon's confession of having compromised his daughter still shocked and infuriated him. He'd fully expected the man to be furious that someone so socially inferior would be taking his daughter as bride. He'd braced himself for a father's righteous outrage that his daughter had been dishonored in such a way. But he never would have anticipated the man's utter disrespect of his own child.

The silence following her question lengthened until she finally spoke in a voice leveled and flat. "What did he say?"

Beynon rose and turned.

She was still standing where he'd left her—tall and proud and unflinching. She deserved so much better.

Beynon had no intention of repeating anything the despicable man had said. Clearing his throat, he replied simply, "He offered no objections to our marriage."

She didn't seem surprised by her father's acquiescence. "I imagine he was quite relieved to be rid of me," she observed with calm resignation.

That she would take her father's lack of protection and concern for her well-being so readily infuriated him all over again. What had she endured from the man to expect so little from him?

"It doesn't matter," she noted. "I object. And my agreement should be the only one that matters."

She was right. But it was far too late. As frustration mixed with the guilt and regret inside him, he slowly approached her. No more prevaricating. No more apologies or skirting of the truth.

Her nostrils flared and her lashes fluttered subtly before she steeled herself once again and tipped her head back to stare up at him as he came to a stop in front of her. Vulnerability and stubborn pride were still obvious in her posture, but there was a glitter of temper in her eyes, buried deep and tightly reined, but present none the less. The sight of it stirred him. So gently refined yet so fierce.

Fierce and passionate.

He recalled the way she'd melted in his arms even as she'd clasped him to her. How she'd wrapped her long legs and elegant arms around his body as she accepted him into hers.

In an unwitting attempt at halting the rise of temperature in his blood, he lowered his gaze from the fire in her eyes. But the graceful arch of her neck was no less enticing. The steady, frantic thrum of her pulse visible beneath her soft skin. He wanted to claim that pulse with his mouth, lave it with his tongue, and scrape it with the edge of his teeth until her head fell back in surrender and her body arched into his.

His body hardened with shocking swiftness and intensity. Every inch of him was suddenly desperate to feel her against him. To feel her surrounding him with heat and sighs and lovely grasping hunger. A frantic fuck against the door hadn't been nearly enough to assuage the yearning inside him. The desire to do better by her—to take his time—to lay claim to her pleasure over and over.

Despite how dreadfully unmatched they were and how unsuited she was to life as a farmer's wife, he still wanted her. His body strained for hers. His insides clenched with need.

And her bed was only steps away.

His forced his gaze to meet hers again, even though he knew it was a risk. There was no way she wouldn't see the heat and lust in his eyes, in the furious tension claiming his body, the hard clench of his jaw.

But her expression told him a great deal as well. Her eyes widened and her lips parted on a sharp, deep inhale as her arms fell heavily to her sides. If she recognized his sudden desire for what it was, she was not unaffected by it. One purposeful step forward and he could take her in his arms.

But that's what had gotten them into this in the first place. And once again, he'd prove himself the brute everyone believed him to be. He had to fight it. Deny it. Refuse to surrender to the need clawing through him even now.

His voice was rough as he spoke. "You cannot convince me you didn't understand the ramifications of what we did last night."

Her lashes flickered, but she held his stare to say with a hint of challenge, "I'm afraid such things were rather far from my mind at the time."

Though her words inspired another jolt of lust through his system, he forcefully ignored it. "I took advantage—"

"Don't you dare," she warned in a heavy whisper.

Beynon scowled. "I had no right—"

"Don't make me a victim," she demanded with quiet ferocity. "I was there, Beynon. You took nothing I didn't willingly give."

Again, the details of her passion rushed through him like tingling flames, making his belly clench and he curled his hands into tight fists. His throat was raw as he muttered in reply, "Then you cannot deny what must happen now. Restitution must be made."

"No, it needn't," she argued, her voice rising in subtle panic. "As long as no one knows—"

"*I know*," he growled. "And so does Wright and your father."

The choked sound that caught in her throat tightened his own breath. She shook her head as a new sadness entered her gaze.

"It didn't have to go this far."

The despair in her voice cut deep, the edge of the blade ragged and sharp. He gathered himself against the rawness growing inside him. She was right. This whole thing should have —*could have*—been handled so much better. He thought he'd done the right thing by calling for her father, but it was the worst thing he could have done. His decision had backed her into a corner.

"Neither of us wanted this," he said bluntly, "but it no longer matters. We will be married, Lady Anne."

Her eyes glittered with emotion as she met his gaze. "And if I refuse?"

His stomach dropped, but he answered with dark conviction. "You won't."

Her eyes widened and she blinked hard in affront. "You think me so biddable? So lacking in my own judgement I'd just submit to your dictates?" Her voice was sharp with anger. Then her eyes widened. "Or do you simply believe me to be that desperate?"

He forced himself to meet her angry, distrustful gaze. He'd have to tell her the rest. It was the only way she'd accept that there was simply no choice in the matter.

"You *can't* refuse."

She stiffened and her eyes widened. Something in his tone must have gotten through the haze of her wrath.

In a low whisper, she asked, "What do you mean, I can't?"

Fuck. He really didn't want to have to say this out loud, but he couldn't be a coward about this. She had to know.

And as badly as he wanted to spare her the pain of her father's betrayal, it was likely the only thing that would convince her to go through with marrying him. His jaw aching from grinding his back teeth, he held her gaze as he replied, "Whether you marry me or not, your father..." Beynon curled his hands into fists. The words felt like lead bricks in his mouth. "He disowned you."

To his shock, she remained utterly still as he forced the last words. The only evidence of any emotional response being her slightly quickened breath and the undeniable turbulence in her gaze.

Then she turned and walked across the room to the window. Her steps were slow, as though she had to concentrate to put each foot before the other. For a length of silence, she stood there—her spine straight and her shoulders unbowed as she stared out into the night.

Beynon had to physically force himself not to go to her. She wouldn't welcome him.

He was suddenly struck by the awareness that although this woman's fortitude was a quiet thing, it was no less powerful for that fact. And he once again wondered how he had ever mistaken her for being meek or dull. She was a force unto herself and the subtlety of her inner strength was woven through her voice when she finally replied.

"Then it would seem you were quite right, Mr. Thomas. I have no choice at all."

Then she turned, and without even a glance in his direction, she walked to the door. Opening it wide, she stepped aside and only then looked back at him. Her expression was stoic. Her eyes dark and quiet. "You'd best leave."

His body tensed sharply in rejection. He wanted to refuse. Every urging inside him clamored to stay and offer...

What? Comfort? Or sympathy? When what he really wanted to do was send a fist into Lord Humphries's prominent nose?

If only Colin hadn't stopped him. At least the pain of bloodied knuckles might offer Beynon some satisfaction in this godforsaken moment.

Lady Anne's blue-green gaze stared hard into his soul. He'd never seen her so...unfeeling. The violet hue of her gown and the pale halo of her hair gave her an ethereal appearance in the dim lighting. Ethereal and intrinsically unyielding, once again bringing to mind those fearsome fairy queens from the stories of his childhood.

"I'd like you to leave, Mr. Thomas," she noted firmly when he still hadn't moved. "Now."

He strode from the room in silence. What more could he possibly say? He was the bastard who'd gotten her into this situation—in more ways than one. *He* was the man who deserved a few fists to the face.

A good brawl might do the trick to make him feel as bad on the outside as he did inside. Unfortunately, his chances of finding a proper opponent were slim to none.

Chapter Twenty-three

The ballroom was beautifully decorated in swaths of snowy-white tulle and ivy garland. The parquet floor had been polished to a reflective gleam and the two chandeliers overhead cast the space in a golden glow. With the night so warm, the balcony doors lining one whole wall had been thrown open to the fresh air, allowing a cooling breeze to drift about the room. In addition to the Hartes' houseguests, invitations had been extended to surrounding neighbors and already the large room was becoming quite crowded.

Anne was very careful to conceal the anxiety riding high within her as she began to stroll the perimeter of the ballroom. Her previous years in society had taught her how to make her way through crowds without appearing lost or out of place, no matter how intensely she might feel exactly that.

She expected there to be some curiosity about her swift departure after completing the reading last night. And she couldn't imagine anyone missed the fact that Mr. Thomas had followed so quickly after her.

In all truth, she couldn't bring herself to care what people thought of the incident. But she really didn't want to have to endure any curious gossipmongers hoping to question her about it under the guise of concern.

She made it about a quarter of the way around the room when she spotted Miss Claybourne standing in a small alcove off the corner of the dance floor. Lady Wright was at her side and it appeared the two were engaged in a mild argument. When Miss Claybourne caught Anne's eye, she quickly gestured for her to come over.

Lady Wright looked up as Anne approached and released a visible sigh. "Ah, Lady Anne, you're looking verra lovely this evening."

Anne smiled. "Thank you, my lady. As are you."

It was true. Lady Wright's deep emerald gown was stunning against her auburn hair. Anne could only wish she had the courage to wear such a bold color.

The Scotswoman gave her a slightly pleading look. "I wonder if you'd do me the favor of staying with Caillie while I step away for a moment. I cannae leave her alone or the crafty lass might sneak off to sample the ratafia," she added beneath her breath.

"What's that, Worthy?" the girl asked, all innocence.

"Nothing, lassie."

"Of course," Anne replied readily. "I'd be happy to remain with Miss Claybourne until your return."

"Thank you, Lady Anne. You're an angel."

As Lady Wright disappeared amongst the guests, Anne turned to the girl. "Is it everything you imagined?" she asked with a smile.

"Verra much so," Miss Claybourne breathed. "I cannae wait until I'm old enough to dance at my first ball."

Anne suppressed a jaded sigh. "I'm sure your debut will be everything you hope it to be."

But instead of agreeing, the girl gave a shrug. "I ken there'll be some who'll reject me out of hand for my illegitimacy."

Remorse swept through Anne. She couldn't believe she'd forgotten that. Her comment was terribly insensitive.

But before she could utter an apology for her thoughtlessness, Miss Claybourne flashed a grin. "Of course, there's always Roderick's club. I've heard he hosts some of the best parties in town. If I cannae dance with the ton, I'll simply secure one of his invitations."

As Anne struggled to form a proper reply to the brazen suggestion, the girl lifted a gloved hand to her mouth to smother her laughter.

"Oh, Lady Anne, if you could see your own face just now." She reached forward to pat Anne's arm in a reassuring gesture. "I ken how scandalous such a thing would be."

Anne breathed a sigh of relief that was a bit premature as the girl added, "Of course, that doesnae mean I willnae do it if I have to."

Anne could only shake her head as a smile crept across her lips. "Miss Claybourne, you certainly have an adventurous spirit."

"Thank you!" the girl beamed. Then her round face lit up as she spied someone in the crowd. "Oh, there's Roderick and Beynon. I must say I have the most handsome brothers, don't you think, Lady Anne?"

As soon as the girl mentioned Beynon, Anne's body tensed as a fine shower of sparks rained across her nerves. She'd hoped to avoid seeing the man for a while at least. But now it would be odd *not* to look.

The two brothers stood almost directly across the ballroom, yet despite the distance and the constantly shifting array of guests between them, her partner stood out.

She'd thought him arresting while dressed casually in the clothes of a country gentleman, but in formal evening wear, he was something else entirely.

Ruggedly handsome and quite unapologetically unrefined.

Though he stood beside Mr. Bentley with his chin lowered as he listened to whatever the other man was saying, his dark gaze—made darker by the downward tug of his heavy brows—was angled sharply toward Anne. The potent intensity of his stare sent a shiver down her spine and a flutter through her low belly. Her body tingled and a subtle pulse ignited deep inside.

But her heart ached.

"Thank you so much, Lady Anne."

She gave a tiny start as she turned to see Lady Wright approaching with Lord Wright a step behind her. She was instantly reminded that the earl had been present during Beynon's meeting with her father. Had he also been there when her father cut her off?

The pain over her father's renouncement had dulled to a single point of pressure in her chest. She hadn't been terribly surprised to hear her father had forsaken her. Lord Humphries had made it clear long ago that her worth to him was strictly limited to her ability to make a good match—one that would be advantageous to him either financially or in regard to political standing. When she'd failed to garner even a hint of interest in her first season, he'd essentially turned his back on her then.

This situation with Beynon had simply made it official. And now she was destitute in fact rather than just figuratively. Her father had made sure she would be forced to go to Beynon with nothing—a punishment for him as well as her. For some reason, she was more aggrieved at the fact that Beynon wouldn't receive her dowry than she was for herself.

If he received some financial compensation, perhaps she wouldn't feel like such a burden.

As Lord and Lady Wright reached them, Anne forced the tragic thoughts from her mind and offered a quick smile.

"Thank you, Lady Anne," the countess said before turning to Miss Claybourne. "Here, Caillie, I brought you some punch. Once you've finished, I'll be bringing you up to your room."

"So soon?" the girl exclaimed.

"Our agreement was for fifteen minutes," Lady Wright noted firmly. "It's certainly been that."

"Lady Anne," the earl said, stepping forward. "I wonder if you'd care to join me for the next dance?"

His expression was calmly unreadable, but she thought she detected a glint of pity in his eyes. Embarrassment threatened to heat her cheeks.

"I imagine your wife is anxious to partner you, my lord."

"Dinnae worry about me," the Scotswoman noted with a husky laugh. "I'll have my turn."

As the next song started up, the earl turned to offer his arm. To refuse now would be unconscionably rude. Settling her hand on his arm, Anne allowed him to lead her to the dance floor.

"I'd like to offer an apology, my lady," he said in an earnest tone.

"It's really not necessary," she began hastily.

"Nevertheless," he insisted gently as they took their positions.

As the music started and they moved through the patterns of the country dance, Anne hoped the earl would not attempt to continue the conversation.

She was disappointed.

At the next opportunity, he continued, "I'd assumed Beynon had spoken with you before we left for London."

"Well, he hadn't," she replied, her voice curt. Then the earl's regretful expression made her feel awful. She shouldn't be taking her anger out on anyone but the man responsible. "I don't blame you, my lord," she added hastily. "It is Mr. Thomas alone who has earned my wrath."

She could see the earl wished to reply but he didn't get another chance until the song ended. As she took his arm and allowed him to lead her from the dance floor, he kept his gaze forward and his tone earnest. "Beynon can be hotheaded at times but he's a good man."

She said nothing. What *could* she say? She already believed him to be a good man—if also a difficult one. She'd suspected for some time that his harsh exterior was simply a shield against a society he had no reason to trust. Unfortunately, she was included in that society.

For a second, it looked as though the earl might say more but lost the chance as they reached the edge of the dance floor and found Mr. Bentley waiting to intercept them.

Bentley's blue eyes sparkled as he flashed Anne a charming smile. "May I claim your next dance, my lady?"

What was this?

She glanced back and forth from Lord Wright to Bentley. Were the brothers colluding to soften her attitude toward Beynon? She nearly refused out of spite, but before she could utter an excuse, Bentley tilted his head to add, "What if I promise not to mention my brother even once?"

Seeing no easy way out, she gave a short nod and transferred her hand from the earl's arm to Mr. Bentley's.

Gratefully, there was very little time to talk as the dance was already starting. The lively pace reduced conversation to very brief comments and Bentley kept his word as Beynon never once came up.

But Anne could see he was dying to say something. By the end of the dance, she decided to allow him the opportunity if only to get it out of the way so she wouldn't have to anticipate another ambush at a later time.

As he led her from the dance floor, she offered an opening. "You've sufficiently fulfilled your promise, Mr. Bentley. You may as well say what's on your mind."

He smiled at her, not at all put off by her candor. "I knew you were a clever one, Lady Anne. Which is why I wanted to be up-front with you. Though I don't know the details surrounding your sudden betrothal to my brother, I'd like to make it clear that, in marrying him, you'll be joining a large—and still growing—family. And that we'll all be there to support you in any way we can."

The words were shockingly earnest and totally unexpected.

A family. A supportive family.

She could barely comprehend the concept.

Then Mr. Bentley chuckled. "I've no doubt you're going to need it. My brother is coarse and tactless most of the time and can be downright boorish at others. And that's when he's not being insensitive and rude."

As he spoke, Anne slowed her steps to stare at the man with a deepening astonishment that shifted quickly into affront. "Mr. Bentley, you grossly misrepresent Mr. Thomas with such comments. He is...a difficult man to understand, perhaps, but your words are decidedly overharsh."

The man shrugged. "Perhaps, but no one would argue that he's not at all a proper match for a gentle lady with delicate sensibilities to protect."

Anne narrowed her gaze. "You underestimate me, Mr. Bentley, and do me a disservice in the process."

His black brows arched. "Do I?"

Seeing the tug of a smile at the corner of his mouth, Anne stiffened. Lifting her chin, she gave him a stern look. "I know what you're doing."

He grinned. "I'm not surprised."

"If you're trying to make me feel better about marrying your brother, I'm afraid your aim is quite off the mark. His rough manner or perceived social inadequacies do not bother me in the slightest."

"No..." he noted thoughtfully as he tilted his head. "But something does."

"Something that happens to be none of your concern," she said with a tempered smile as she turned to face him. "Thank you for the dance, Mr. Bentley."

"Of course," he said with a polite bow, thankfully allowing the matter to drop. "It was my pleasure."

"If you'll excuse me." With a nod, Anne walked away, then immediately wished she'd had a destination in mind as she found herself winding rather aimlessly through the crowd once again. Every covert glance cast her way and every whisper caught on the breeze made her more and more self-conscious.

After three years of being an invisible wallflower, the sudden curiosity and attention was more than she could handle. Suddenly desperate to escape the crowd, she turned toward the refreshment room and was brought to a swift halt as Lady Mayhew stepped into her path.

The other woman had a stiff smile plastered to her lips, but the look in her eyes was anything but amiable. "Lady Anne, how exquisite—and flushed—you are this evening."

Anne forced herself to respond in kind though the urge to escape had only intensified with the unexpected encounter. Her smile was tight as she replied, "You're looking fine, as well, my lady. And you're quite right, I am feeling a bit heated and was just about to seek some refreshment."

When she tried to gracefully step away, Lady Mayhew grasped her wrist in a shockingly tight grip. Anne blinked in surprise as the other woman sneered in a lowered voice, "I know your game, Lady Anne. You play all innocent and harmless until the moment you steal the man I want right out of my hands."

Anne could barely believe what the woman was saying. Lady Mayhew was utterly deluded. And Anne had lost her patience. "The man you want doesn't want you back," she stated bluntly. "He never did and never will."

The other woman actually laughed at that. "That's ridiculous. I knew the moment I saw him that he'd end up in my bed. Your sad eyes and clingy, grasping hands won't keep him from me. Mr. Thomas is mine and I *will* have him."

"Not this time."

Alarm shot through Anne at the sound of Lord Mayhew's softly spoken words. She turned to see him standing not two steps away, certainly close enough to have heard his wife's declaration. His gaze was riveted upon Lady Mayhew, a look of deep grief and resignation in his eyes.

As though Anne weren't there, Lord Mayhew continued, "I told you what would happen if I discovered you were up to your tricks again."

"But, darling," his wife pleaded in that cajoling voice she'd used in the garden that day.

Lord Mayhew interrupted her with a firm shake of his head. "Release Lady Anne this instant. We're leaving."

Surprisingly, Lady Mayhew did as he said. Her husband immediately grasped her firmly by the elbow, pulling her tight to his side. "My sincere apologies, Lady Anne."

Then he turned and forced his wife through the crowd as the lady appeared to continue pleading her case to no avail. Anne felt for Lord Mayhew—the pain his wife's betrayal had been clear in his expression—but she couldn't dredge up an ounce of sympathy for the selfish woman.

Feeling the intent curiosity the small scene had inspired around her, Anne ignored the sharp glances as she sped toward the refreshment room. Though a good number of guests were gathered around the punch bowl, Anne stepped back against the wall and did her best to be unnoticeable while she caught her breath.

Barely a moment later, Lily stepped into the room. As soon as she caught sight of Anne, she turned to approach her with a wide smile. "There you are. I was hoping I'd have a chance to talk with you before the announcement."

An awful feeling rolled through Anne. Surely, Beynon wouldn't think to announce their engagement here. Tonight. Without even speaking to her first? But then again...wouldn't he?

"What announcement?" she asked, her voice full of dread.

Lily's smile slipped as she suddenly seemed to notice Anne's tension. "I'll be announcing the winners of the games tonight. I wanted to let you know ahead of time that you and Mr. Thomas took first place. Anne? Are you all right?"

Though she was greatly relieved to know an engagement she hadn't fully come to terms with wouldn't become more fodder for the gossips tonight at least, it seemed the shock of yesterday's events had finally gotten to her. Anne wanted to assure her friend, but the words necessary to do so simply wouldn't come.

But before Lily could press further, they were joined by her sisters.

"Lady Anne, why do you look as though someone just kicked you in the stomach?" Lily's younger sister Portia asked in her typically blunt fashion, though there was genuine concern in the voice.

"I'm fine," Anne managed to reply though the words sounded a bit strangled.

Emma Bentley assessed Anne with a quiet gaze. "Are you, really?"

Anne began to nod. But she wasn't all right. She was a mess, to be honest. And the nod slowly devolved to a morose shake of her head.

"Come on, then," Lily whispered with a quick glance to her sisters. "Let's go somewhere a bit more private." Then her soft gray eyes seemed to focus in on something over Anne's shoulder. "Portia, dear, would you mind?" she asked with a subtle tip of her forehead.

Portia seemed to know exactly what Lily was referencing as she gave a smart nod. "Gladly." The younger woman stepped away and Emma took her place before Anne could see what the issue might be.

The three of them moved easily through the milling guests to a small door that led into an adjoining sitting room which was blessedly unoccupied. As Lily started to close the door behind them, a familiar voice called out, "Wait for me!"

Bethany swept into the room with a look of admonishment. "I saw you all spiriting Anne away and knew I'd be needed." Turning a concerned gaze to Anne, she noted gently, "What has that broody Mr. Thomas done to upset you now?"

"Why don't we all sit down and get more comfortable before we harangue Anne with questions," Lily suggested in a firm tone.

"Shall I call for some tea?" Emma asked, but the question was interrupted as Portia slipped swiftly into the room and closed the door firmly behind her.

"How about Scotch, instead?" Portia asked as she strode purposefully toward a small bookcase where she pulled out a few books to withdraw a bottle of whisky hidden behind them.

"You stashed a bottle of Scotch in my sitting room?" Lily asked, aghast.

The younger woman shrugged as she lounged with a brazen lack of decorum in a high-backed armchair. "In case it might come in handy," she explained. "Unfortunately, there was no room for glasses, so we'll have to do as the pirates do," she added with a saucy wink before pulling the cork with her teeth and tipping the bottle to her lips.

Shaking her head, Anne looked to each of the four women who had taken up positions around her. "I don't mean to cause such a fuss."

"Nonsense," Emma replied quickly. "It's no fuss at all."

"After all, it's not every day a woman is forced to marry someone she'd rather not," Portia noted, then added with a frown and a groan, "then again, it is, isn't it?"

Anne looked to the young woman with wide eyes. "How did you know?"

Portia gave a cagey smile as she leaned forward to pass the bottle into Anne's hands. "It's what I do. I know things."

"What's this?" Bethany asked, fiercely indignant. "You're being forced to marry?"

Anne avoided answering by taking a tentative sip of the whisky. A delightful burn rolled over her tongue and down her throat to instantly warm her belly.

"I'm sorry, Anne," Lily, seated beside her, said with genuine remorse as Anne passed the bottle to her. "I had no idea your partnership with Mr. Thomas would lead to...this."

"Please don't, Lily. The responsibility for what happened lies securely between myself and Mr. Thomas."

"I knew that man was a scoundrel, right from the start," Bethany declared.

Anne shook her head. "No. It's not like that."

"Would you like to tell us what did happen?" Emma asked.

There was just a moment of embarrassment—more because such things were not often spoken of freely than due to any true shame—before Anne gave a short sigh. "I'm afraid we quite crossed the lines of propriety."

There was a brief moment as the other women stared at her—no doubt shocked to hear the ever-proper Lady Anne might have engaged in something scandalous.

Portia recovered first. "I've never understood why a few stolen kisses must result in an engagement," the young woman noted in obvious frustration.

Anne coughed. "It went a bit beyond stolen kisses."

Lily's eyes widened. "How far beyond?"

Anne's answer was a quick blush.

Bethany gasped in delight. "Anne, you perfect hoyden!"

Lily's smile was understanding and Emma leaned forward to add pragmatically, "You're not the first, my dear, and won't be the last."

"Just to be clear," Portia interjected with an uncharacteristically sober expression, "you were an enthusiastic participant in these activities?"

Understanding the other woman's concern and appreciating it even though it required an uncomfortably honest answer, Anne quickly replied, "Yes, of course."

Portia gave a satisfied nod and settled back into the corner of her chair.

"Mr. Thomas is not what everyone says he is," Lily commented. "I've come to see him as a rather sensitive and compassionate sort. He just struggles a bit with society's expectations, I think."

"I agree," Emma stated with a nod. "He can come off a bit disgruntled at first, but he may just be one of the most loyal and constant men I know."

They weren't saying anything Anne didn't know already, but she remained firm in her response. "None of that means he'd make me a good husband."

Emma tilted her head as a furrow formed between her brows. "Are you concerned about his lack of wealth and station?"

Anne met the other woman's questioning stare. "Not at all. Such things have no bearing on my reticence."

"Then what, exactly, is the problem?" Bethany asked bluntly, confusion and compassion clear in her tone.

Glancing down at her hands linked tightly in her lap, Anne admitted the true origin of her distress. "I don't think it's too much to ask for the man I marry to actually *want* me."

As soon as the words left her lips, she realized how pitiable they sounded, and she hated it.

"Oh, Anne," Lily breathed.

"Here. Have another," Portia said, offering the bottle again.

Anne accepted it gratefully.

Chapter Twenty-four

Though he searched for more than an hour, Beynon could not catch a glimpse of Anne anywhere in or around the ballroom after briefly spotting her in the refreshment room. He'd been on his way to her when he'd been unceremoniously intercepted by Emma's brazen youngest sister, who'd thought it a good time to question him on how he was enjoying his stay in England. By the time he'd extricated himself from the conversation, Anne had slipped away unseen.

Frustrated but also slightly relieved, he'd realized quickly he had no idea what to say to her anyway. But it didn't stop him from scanning the crowd every five minutes for her return.

He just wanted to see her. To look into her eyes and confirm the haunted pain he'd seen last night was gone. He needed to ensure she was all right.

But how could she be?

He wasn't all right. And apparently, it showed.

Even his brothers were giving him a wide berth, though the nearly identical blue eyes they'd inherited from their arsehole father followed him about with careful scrutiny, as if they feared his next move. Their concern only fueled his temper, which was firmly rooted in self-disgust at the moment.

As yet another young lady cast a sharp and wary glance past his position in a corner of the ballroom, he decided he'd made enough of an impression for the evening. But as he started to wend his way toward the main exit, he finally caught sight of Anne's pale hair through the shifting crowd.

He immediately altered direction but didn't make it far before a ringing bell drew everyone's attention toward Lord and Lady Harte, who stood together on a raised dais at the far end of the room.

"Good evening, everyone," the countess said, addressing the room. "The time has come for the long-awaited final results of this year's games. Lord Harte and I would like to thank everyone who participated..."

Beynon only half listened as he peered through the crowd in hopes of getting another glimpse of Lady Anne. He finally saw her again across the room where she stood with her friends.

A frown furrowed his brow as he noticed something a bit off about her. It wasn't terribly obvious and he likely only noticed it because he'd observed her so intently in various situations over the last week, but it seemed to him that she appeared unusually...relaxed. Her spine wasn't quite so stiff as usual and her shoulders displayed a gentle curve.

Perhaps she was faring better than he'd expected. And why did that possibility only make him more anxious?

"The scores have been tallied and the winning pair of this year's games is...Lady Anne Humphries and Mr. Beynon Thomas!"

The gathered crowd erupted with applause and smiles as everyone glanced about in search of the winners.

"I'd like to ask our winners to lead us all in a waltz," Lady Harte announced.

As the people closest to him began to part and create a pathway to the dance floor, Beynon realized he had no choice but to do as the countess requested.

He reached the open dance floor first and crossed it slowly to where Lady Anne was stepping away from her friends to join him. Her approach was slow but not hesitant. And her gaze found his readily. She appeared composed and as proud and graceful as she ever was, but there was still a hint of something different in her manner. He couldn't quite place it.

His heart thudded heavily against his ribs as she came to a stop in front of him, and though he knew he was likely glowering quite fiercely, he couldn't seem to stop himself. At least Lady Anne didn't appear to be affected by his dark countenance. There was just a subtle flicker of her lashes as she slid her fingers into his outstretched palm and stepped into proper position.

Beynon had learned the waltz and other social dances only a few months earlier. The steps hadn't come naturally to him and he still felt stiff and awkward any time he tried it. But when he looked into Anne's vivid eyes and the first notes of the song drifted around them, the necessary movements came easily. Soon, other couples joined them on the dance floor and he found himself relaxing into the steps and turns as his body moved in an instinctive rhythm with the woman in his arms.

With a sharp stab of desire, he suddenly wished he could make love to her like this. All languid and soft and unhurried. Their first time together had been a rush of feelings and sensations too powerful to regulate. It had been frantic and passionate and desperate. Fire and need.

Though his body was already responding with the same deep hunger and restless desire he'd felt then, he imagined a gentler scene. A slow, deliberate exploration. A quiet, unending feast of the senses—of pleasure in all its forms.

"You need to stop."

Anne's quiet admonishment interrupted his lurid musings but barely had an effect on his physical ardor. He met her gaze with a heavy frown. "Stop what?" His voice was unnaturally rough. "The dance just started."

She glanced to the side then flicked her gaze back to his. "Not the dance. You must stop thinking whatever it is you're thinking. Surely you know how much you reveal in your expression."

Her tone didn't sound berating or offended. If anything, there was a gentle amusement running through the words. And her eyes, as she gazed up at him, sparkled with life.

He lowered his head toward hers, allowing himself to sink into her soft and verdant stare. "And what is my expression telling you now?"

Her lips parted yet her gaze sparked. "That you'd like to find the nearest closet."

His heart stuttered and his brow twitched at her unexpected boldness. His fingers tensed against the curve of her spine as he glanced about them. But no one seemed to be watching them. He didn't know what had caused this shift in her usually staid demeanor but he found himself responding in kind.

"Right now," he murmured, "I'd prefer a feather bed, covered in velvet and silk."

Her indrawn breath was quiet but still audible. The sigh that followed carried a rich undertone of...whisky?

His chin came up as he peered more intently at her. "Lady Anne, have you been indulging in spirits?"

She gave a quick little shrug. "Only a little."

So that's what she and the other ladies had been doing. It certainly explained her unusual manner. His brows drew low over his gaze. "You're foxed."

Tipping her head, she met his sudden glare with amiable defiance. "I don't think so. I'm simply feeling far less tense and angry than I was an hour ago. I quite like it," she added with a nod. Then her lashes lowered a bit over her gaze. Her next words were soft and husky. "Now, tell me more about this bed you were imagining."

Beynon nearly groaned.

"What's the matter, Mr. Thomas?" Her tone was distinctly challenging. "If we're to be married despite my wishes to the contrary, I'd at least like to have something pleasant to look forward to."

Right. Because nothing else about their union was likely to bring anything enjoyable.

"I'll do my duty as a husband," he muttered darkly.

It was clearly not what she wanted to hear. Her features immediately tightened as her chin came up and her gaze sharpened. "Your duty. How lovely. On second thought, Mr. Thomas," she said curtly as she stiffened and slowed them both to a stop, "I believe this dance *is* finished."

Then she pulled free of his arms and strode gracefully away, leaving him standing awkwardly at the edge of the dance floor.

He was tempted to follow her but he had no desire to make more of an arse of himself than he had already. So, he turned on his heel and headed in the opposite direction, his chest aching with a weight he feared he'd be carrying the rest of his life.

He should have known better than to indulge in fantasies that could never be between them. It was best to keep sight of reality.

She didn't want to marry him.

Just because they'd allowed passion to reign once did not mean it could be expected to continue into their new circumstances. Lady Anne might still feel some thread of desire for him, but it was clear she hated him for forcing her into matrimony.

Very soon, she'd become his wife and return with him to Denbighshire, where her life would never be the same again. They both had to accept that. And everything that came with it.

The next morning, he caught sight of the letter he'd stuffed into his pocket just before he'd gone to speak with Lord Humphries. In his rush to change that evening, he'd tossed it onto the valet stand and had forgotten about.

As he took a closer look at it, he realized with a clutch of trepidation that it was from his oldest sister. It had been dated almost two weeks earlier and contained news that couldn't be ignored.

His time in England had come to an end.

ANNE AWOKE THE NEXT morning with an ache in her head as well as her heart. The indulgence in spirits the night before had certainly eased her distress at the time but did nothing for her in the light of a new day.

Despite her current discomfort, she couldn't help but feel a tiny thrill as she recalled those brief moments during her waltz with Beynon when they'd managed to speak freely of their desire for each other. It had given her a lovely glimpse into what things could be like between them. Once again, she wished he'd simply talked to her that night instead of sending for her father and riding off to London. She might have been able to convince him they could continue as clandestine lovers without the weighted consequences.

Would she really have been prepared to do something so scandalous?

Closing her eyes, she imagined what it might be like to sneak off with Beynon to quiet corners and darkened rooms where they could explore the passion that flared so intensely between them. Her skin tingled as she thought about how safe she always felt in his presence. In his arms.

Yes. She could have managed an affair very well. If it was with him.

But now, instead of passionate lovers, they were to be unwilling spouses.

It was all so hopeless and unnecessary. To have tasted something so wonderous and enlightening only to have it ruined by the dictates of a hypocritical society. It had taken Anne far too long to decide to live life on her own terms only to have her autonomy swept away by notions of duty and honor and the unrealistic expectations of purity and perfection.

But what choice did she have?

None. Her father had ensured that. As had Beynon when he'd decided to take steps to repair something that hadn't been broken.

Rubbing her forehead, she rose from her bed and rang for the maid. Perhaps the servant would have some concoction that might help her aching skull and uneasy stomach.

Nearly an hour later, Anne's head felt much better.

After a quick breakfast, she decided to make use of the clear morning to do a little painting in the garden. The hobby always managed to soothe tumultuous thoughts and ease stresses she could not otherwise contain.

Without really intending to, she found herself back under the oak where she'd painted Beynon. She settled on the grass near the rosebushes that formed a border along the walkway. After positioning her small easel and arranging her paints, she took some deep breaths and forced herself not to think of her father or Beynon or Wales or anything at all.

She focused on the roses, still dewy from the night, and took a moment to admire their vivid colors and the graceful curves and curls of their lush, layered petals. Within minutes, she was fully immersed in the task of recreating the luxurious blooms and rich foliage.

But even so, she was not so lost to her painting that she didn't know instantly the moment Beynon found her.

Her body reacted with a waterfall of delicate sparks along her nerves. Her belly tightened and her heart leapt with what might have been joy or dread.

Turning her head, she saw him there.

He stood several paces away, still on the path, as though he'd come to a sudden stop when he caught sight of her. He looked as handsome and strong and devastating to her senses as he always did. But when she forced herself to look into his face, she stiffened. He was tense and worried. The scowl riding his brow was heavy and his jaw was tight. His eyes appeared darker than usual and their focus was distracted, almost harried.

"Good morning, Mr. Thomas," she said as she set her brush down atop the wooden case.

She remained seated even as he started toward her again. With each step he drew nearer, she became more convinced that something had upset him. Something that seemed to involve her.

As he reached her spot on the grass, she had to tip her head back to continue looking at him, but only for a moment as he lowered to a crouch beside her. His eyes settled on her watercolor first and she got the impression he was deliberately not looking at her as he clearly struggled to find words.

He'd sought her out for a reason. Something that clearly had him concerned.

When the silence lengthened, Anne's worry got the best of her. Lifting her hand, she set it on his bent knee, finally drawing his attention to her. She saw a wary regret in his eyes. Her throat tightened. "What is it?"

He took a deep breath. "I received a letter from my sister Eirwyn." He glanced down to a spot of grass beside her hip. His voice lowered roughly. "She says our mam fell sick and has been abed for some days."

"I'm sorry, Beynon," Anne muttered. The news was obviously worrying him. "Will she be all right?"

He gave a slow shake of his head. "Mam is not one to take to her bed. The only times she's done so in my memory were for the births of my siblings." He cleared his throat. "That Eirwyn felt it necessary to write to me at all tells me this is not a simple illness. And already the letter is weeks old." His gaze became intent as he stated the rest. "I cannot wait to hear if she's recovered or worsened. I must return to Gwaynynog as soon as possible."

Though his decision to leave England was not a surprise under the circumstances, Anne tensed with delicate distress. Even after all that had happened, she didn't want him to leave. She realized with subtle shock that she would miss him. "Of course," she replied, trying to hide her reaction. "I understand."

Holding her gaze, his scowl deepened as he replied in a roughened tone, "You'll have to come with me. As my wife."

Her eyes widened and her stomach flipped as her hand fell away from his knee. "What?"

"There is no way of knowing when I'll return to England," he explained in a rush. "It could be months. Or years."

Anne tried to find some mental purchase within the emotional riot he'd just inspired with his declaration. "I understand your desire to get home, but surely there's no reason to rush to the altar." She forced a rueful smile. "I assure you I'll still be here when you're able to return."

"But you'll be on your own," he reminded her regretfully. "Without the protection of your father or myself. And"—he paused and his eyes flickered with an odd light before he seemed to force himself to continue in a rough rumble of words—"there could be a child."

Anne's body tensed sharply in acknowledgement of his unexpected statement even as her thoughts suddenly flew wildly about. *A child.* She hadn't even once considered that. But yes, it was entirely possible.

Oh my.

And why did the thought fill her with such a rush of hope and wonder when it should be fear and uncertainty that claimed her?

She blinked hard, and although she realized by the tightening of his expression that her shock was no doubt quite evident, she couldn't seem to bring herself to speak.

His jaw clenched and released as he furrowed his brow. Then he lowered his gaze to the grass once again. After taking a deep breath, he spoke in a tone she'd never heard from him before.

"My mother was only seventeen when she had the great misfortune of encountering the prior Earl of Wright at a summer festival. In her youth and innocence, she thought him a romantic hero. A hero who coerced and manipulated her then disappeared. When she learned she was with child, her parents set her from the house. They were barely able to feed the children they had and refused to take responsibility for another mouth to feed." He cleared the roughness from his throat. "Mam moved about for a bit, doing odd jobs for food and lodging, until she came to a village where the local inn was in need of a laundress. She told everyone she was a widow, but"—his voice lowered with an anger that seemed to come from the very root of his being—"that's not what they called her behind her back."

Anne almost reached out to him again, wanted to ease the edge of pain in his voice, but he gave a hard shake of his head and she stilled.

"Though no one said anything to her face, in the privacy of their homes, they were far less circumspect. When I was very young, I believed I could protect her from the evil things the other children said to taunt me. I thought I could be her shield and sword against the cruelty of others." He shook his head. "I was an idiot. The more I fought, the worse it got. I only proved my savagery as a wretched bastard and the unfairness of it all increased my recklessness and anger. When Mam eventually remarried and we left the village for the farm, I was sullen and angry. But Cedric gave me his last name and became the father my own had refused to be. I can't imagine the man I'd have become without his guidance...but I'll never forget the way my mother was treated. Or the fact that I was a constant reminder of the betrayal she'd suffered."

He lifted his gaze to meet hers. His expression was fierce and a storm swirled in his eyes. His next words came out in a quiet growl. "I refuse to be the cause of such hardship. I'll not father a bastard."

Feeling the depth of emotion in his tone, Anne held his gaze as she drew long and steady breaths. She could see it all in him. The anger and pain of his childhood as he fought over and over to protect his mother from the consequences of his father's callous disregard. His almost furious determination to be better than his sire.

And he was. In a thousand ways and a thousand times over.

She suddenly understood so much more why he'd reacted as he had after they'd been together. It didn't excuse his decision not to consult her, but it did explain it a bit more.

And now, for whatever purpose toward whatever future, they were inexorably linked. They were to be married, whether sooner or later, and that meant they would need to learn to support each other as true partners. How could she expect it of him if she couldn't offer it herself? If they were ever to get past the circumstances that brought them to this point, they would have to start somewhere.

"How could we possibly arrange anything so quickly?"

There was an undeniable flash of relief in his gaze as he huffed out the breath he'd been holding. "We already have the special license. I intend to speak with Lord Harte and find out if there is a local officiate who'd be available to perform a hasty ceremony. I hope to leave for Denbighshire as soon as possible."

She nodded as her thoughts roamed over all of the preparations that would need to be done. Focusing on practical issues helped to keep her from delving too deeply into how she was feeling. "I see. I shall have to start packing. Under the circumstances, the ceremony should be a private affair, but I imagine you'd like your brothers and sister there. And I'd like to have my friends present."

"Of course," he replied gruffly.

Shifting to her knees, she began to pack up her art supplies. "You'll advise me of the results from your conversation with Lord Harte?"

"I will."

After closing her box and folding the small easel, she began to rise, already thinking of what instructions she'd need to pass on to her maid. When Beynon stood and offered a hand, she placed her fingers in his without hesitation. Tingling warmth instantly ignited across her skin. Her gaze lifted to his as they stood—close but not touching beyond her hand in his.

Holding her fingers firmly, he looked intently into her eyes as he muttered, "No doubt this isn't the wedding you imagined. I cannot erase my recent errors, but if I had the power to change things, I would."

Though his words had probably been intended as an apology of sorts, she couldn't help but hear his own deep regret as she was reminded that he had no true desire to wed her.

Drawing her hand from his, she replied, "As you've stated more than once, Mr. Thomas, there is no other choice." She bent and gathered her things. "Let me know what Lord Harte is able to arrange. I'll do my best to be ready."

Without waiting for him to reply, she turned and walked away. Though she kept her gaze steady on the house in front of her, she could still see the aching remorse in his eyes, and it was all she could do to hold back the sadness pressing upward in her chest.

Chapter Twenty-five

And so it was that Lady Anne Humphries was wed to Mr. Beynon Thomas in a private—though not terribly small—ceremony that took place in the Earl of Harte's personal study. Witnesses included Lord and Lady Harte, Lord and Lady Wright, Miss Cailleach Claybourne, Mr. and Mrs. Bentley with their two young sons, Mr. and Mrs. Pinkman, and Portia Turner, whose husband had to rush off to London on some urgent business. Also present was the Dowager Countess of Chelmsworth, known to all as Angelique, who had somehow discovered the wedding was going to take place—though no one admitted to telling her—and insisted on being present.

The groom wore a casual suit with a chocolate-brown coat and a pale green waistcoat and the bride wore a simple gown of sky blue with lace trim and a crown woven of pink and purple posies selected from the earl's garden by Miss Claybourne.

After the ceremony, the Earl of Wright gave a lovely but succinct toast wishing the new couple happiness and health. There was just enough time for a few felicitations, and as Lord Harte talked with the officiate, Lily drew Anne into a quick but emotional embrace, whispering heartfelt well-wishes in a tearful goodbye. Bethany and her husband were next. Then Emma Bentley, who offered a genuine assurance that all would work out just as her husband stepped up to add that, if it didn't, Anne was to remember what he said—that as a member of the family, she would forever have his support and assistance should she ever need it.

Gratitude and a strange sort of sadness welled up in Anne's heart with the acknowledgement that she'd finally acquired the kind of family she'd always hoped for only to be leaving it for something utterly unknown.

Glancing to where Beynon stood talking with the Earl of Wright, she suddenly wished they were standing side by side. That the kind words were being offered to the both of them as a new married couple rather than individually. The distance between them felt suddenly insurmountable.

As Miss Claybourne approached with Lady Wright, Anne forced a bright smile to her lips. The girl was obviously very pleased with the outcome of her brother's partnership with Anne and would've gone on about having known they were meant to be if Lady Wright hadn't stepped forward to take the girl in hand as Lord Wright joined them to offer his own goodbye, suggesting the possibility of a visit to Wales in the future.

A moment later, Beynon was there. His large, imposing form took position at her side as he muttered about needing to be on their way. Recalling why he was in such a hurry to return home, Anne nodded and slipped her hand into the bend of his arm just as Portia Turner stepped in front of them.

"Before you go," Lily's younger sister said with a wide smile that did nothing to soften the somewhat calculating look in her eyes, "I'd just like to say that I truly hope for the best in this union." The lady paused to give a pointed look at Beynon before turning to address Anne specifically. "However, if you find yourself needing to escape an unbearable situation, I've means to assist in such an endeavor."

Anne blinked in shock. Portia hadn't even tried to lower her voice, clearly having wanted Beynon to hear the thinly veiled threat, which he did with a fierce tensing of muscles and a forbidding frown.

"Thank you but such assistance won't be necessary," Anne replied quickly.

Portia just patted Anne's hand and gave a wink. "Even so." Then she walked away.

With a grumble of annoyance, Beynon offered a general goodbye to the friends and family gathered in the study before leading Anne from the room. Barely twenty minutes after the officiate intoned his first words and only eight hours after Beynon approached Anne in the garden, they were hustled into a carriage and started their journey to Beynon's home in Denbighshire, Wales.

Throughout the proceedings, Anne felt as though she were moving through a dense fog. She had a vague sense of everything that was happening, but it seemed to be filtered through a haze of disconnection. As if she were viewing it from a slight distance rather than experiencing it all firsthand.

And Beynon's fiercely solemn manner didn't help matters.

Every time she found herself looking into his dark and shadowed gaze, the breath would leave her lungs as though she were being crushed between immovable stone walls.

She wouldn't have guessed it possible, but the tension got so much worse once they were alone in the carriage. The journey was expected to take about five days and would require four nights in posting inns along the way.

Typically, Anne didn't mind lengthy travel. She enjoyed viewing changing scenery and stopping in different villages and being able to see areas of Britain that were new to her.

But the idea of spending so much time in the closely confined space with a man who hadn't bothered to utter a single word to her in the—goodness! It had to be at least a few hours already since they'd left the Hartes' estate—honestly made her feel like she might scream.

Five days of travel with this man.

This man.

Her husband.

Anne closed her eyes and dropped her head back against the cushioned rest. It just didn't seem real.

At least the carriage loaned to them by Lord Harte was as luxurious as they come. The trip should be more comfortable than most, if not actually pleasant. Perhaps if she didn't look at the man sitting so stiffly across from her, she wouldn't feel so bereft at the chasm of silence extending between them.

When she opened her eyes again, she realized she must have fallen asleep for a bit. The summer afternoon sun had faded to a hazy slant of rays through pink and lavender clouds. Blinking a few times to clear her vision and awaken her thoughts, Anne cast a quick glance toward Beynon.

He was decidedly awake and though his head was turned to the side as he stared out the window, she had no doubt he knew she was alert and looking at him. The clenching of his jaw was a clear giveaway and the slow curling of his large hands into fists on the plush-cushioned seat was another indicator. And it appeared he was annoyed.

Apparently, he'd preferred her asleep.

Poor man.

She'd intended the thought to sound scathing and sarcastic in her own mind, but she realized there was too much truth in the sentiment.

He didn't want her and now he was stuck with her until death should they part.

And she was stuck with him.

But the saddest thing about it was how easily it would be for her to feel not stuck at all.

Since he was so intent upon keeping his attention elsewhere, she allowed her focus to drift over his broad, muscled form. From the thick column of his neck and that delicious shadow beneath a jaw darkened by a day of beard growth to the hard breadth of his chest, which had pressed so firmly to her breasts when he'd had her pinned against the door. To the strong arms that bulged with muscle when strained, then his narrow hips, then his sturdy thighs and wide-spread, booted feet.

Her slow perusal brought a quickening to her breath and ignited heat beneath her skin.

Everything about him was so different from any man she'd ever known. There was an unapologetic authenticity—an innate physical confidence that confused her even as it lured her. There was something about him that was so...tangible. It made her want to grab hold of him and not let go.

She'd floated through so much of her life. Ungrounded and uncertain. Never truly feeling she had a place she belonged. And then she'd met Beynon.

From the start, his attitude had challenged her. His gruff manner had occasionally inspired a temper she'd never known she possessed. His rugged honesty had shocked her into behaving in ways she never would have believed herself capable of.

And she liked who she'd become since meeting him. It was new for her to feel like she could dissent against expected behaviors. She finally felt empowered in a way she hadn't while under her father's roof. She felt strong and confident.

Although she preferred to think such traits had always been in her—buried deep or perhaps disguised by a lifetime of trying to meet the expectations of her father and then society—she couldn't deny how easy it had been to allow those aspects of her nature to come forth when she was with him.

And of course, she couldn't ignore the more scandalous discoveries she'd made about herself.

She liked being the kind of woman who opened a man's collar before kissing him deeply beneath a tree in full view of anyone who should pass by. The kind of woman who enjoyed harsh words being growled against her throat and large, rough hands gripping firmly to her bottom. The kind of woman a man could take passionately against a door while a houseful of guests gathered only rooms away.

Desire flooded her system, swift and consuming. Anne shifted in her seat, instinctively trying to ease the deep throbbing that had begun low in her body. The movement finally drew his attention.

He looked at her first from the corner of his eye, as though he hoped to glimpse at her without her knowing. But when their gazes locked, he gave up the pretense. His head turned toward her as his chin lowered. His brows were heavy, adding shadow to his stare. Adding heat, as well.

Anne's fingertips tingled and her belly thrilled at the brooding, penetrating intensity he delivered so easily through those dark eyes. In the silence of his direct focus, her bones melted and her awareness centered on a single, intimate longing.

A need to surrender.

To him. To their future. To her intense desire for him.

She wanted to toss herself across the carriage and be crushed in his arms. She wanted to feel like she belonged there, pressed against him. Their hearts and lips aligned.

As her belly tightened with sensual yearning and her breath shortened, an ache spread out from her chest.

She looked away, directing her focus out the window.

No matter how much she might wish it, she did not possess such a reckless willingness to throw herself into inevitable rejection. Very simply, it would hurt too much. He might accept the physical connection they both seemed to crave, but what of the rest? Deep down, she knew he'd never accept her in full. She'd never be the wife he would have chosen for himself.

So, they remained silent, shrouded in an atmosphere of bitterness and regret as the sun slowly set and darkness filled the carriage.

By the time they stopped that night at a posting inn, Anne was desperate to get out of his company and release the tension and emotion she'd been holding at bay. She didn't say a word as he requested two rooms and ordered food to be brought up. She went to her room alone while he ensured their driver, the carriage, and the horses were all properly settled.

She ate her meal by the dim light of the fire burning low in the hearth, not bothering to light more than a single candle set beside the narrow bed.

She had no illusions about her wedding night.

At some point during the last few hours of travel, she'd come to the determination that he wasn't going to come to her. Not here. Not tonight. The request for two rooms confirmed it.

So, when she finished her meal and set the tray outside the door, she turned back to the room and the single trunk that had been unloaded from the carriage containing only what she'd need for the journey. She laid out a voluminous cotton nightgown and sat on the bed to unpin her hair.

As she pulled her fingers through the loosened tresses, she had to swallow down the bubble of emotion rising in her throat.

Was this what life was going be like going forward?

Dark, lonely nights. Silent, tension-filled days. Taking action out of habit rather than any true joy or personal desire? Would she eventually become just a shadow of herself?

It was a fear she'd first had as a girl, when she'd realized how little she mattered in the world her father existed in. When she'd finally accepted that the one person who was supposed to love and cherish her...didn't.

She remembered her recent vow to start living for herself alone. To discover her true self beyond the expectations of others. She'd imagined such a personal quest taking place within the somewhat liberating state of spinsterhood.

A state that was now firmly out of reach.

But she wasn't resigned. If anything, her new circumstances made her all the more determined to finally put her own desires ahead of others' expectations.

She already knew she'd never be the kind of wife Beynon wanted. So perhaps she shouldn't waste her time trying.

Perhaps...she could truly start living as she desired. Her husband was already disappointed in her; she doubted anything she could do would make it worse. And more than that, she was past caring.

She was on her way to a new home. A new beginning. She'd create her own contentment. Her own space to live and breathe.

And Beynon could do whatever he wished.

No doubt, he intended to do exactly that anyway.

THE NEXT MORNING, SHE woke feeling surprisingly well rested.

Her maid, as an employee of her father, was unable to accompany Anne to Wales. Even if it had been possible, Anne doubted a personal servant would be practical in her future life. Without her dowry, she was uttered financially dependent upon Beynon, and she certainly didn't wish to become an even greater burden than she was. Thankfully, the maid had packed her travel trunk with clothing that would not require assistance in dressing. Anne chose a comfortable traveling dress in a light sage green. It was a fresh color representing growth and new beginnings. She enjoyed her breakfast at a small corner table in the common room of the inn, where she observed fellow travelers as they went about their morning. She was nearly finished when Beynon finally appeared.

She saw him before he saw her, and for a moment, she couldn't hide the longing that gripped her as she took in the full sight of him. The careless waves of his black hair framed his rugged features, failing to soften their harsh lines. A brown woolen coat did nothing to conceal his breadth and strength and his long, muscled legs were encased in fitted fawn breeches and dusty black boots.

He was the perfect embodiment of unrefined masculinity. Grit and brawn wrapped with a quiet, raw authority. It was undeniably attractive.

And she wasn't the only one to think so, she noticed, when she could finally tear her gaze away. A middle-aged serving woman slowed her steps while carrying out a tray of food to blatantly stare at Beynon as he settled their account with the innkeeper. And a much younger woman fanned herself in the door to the kitchen, fluttering her lashes.

Anne might have found it amusing. If she were a better woman.

As it was, jealously ripped through her with unexpected force, shocking her and then saddening her.

It was then that Beynon finished his business with the innkeeper and turned to scan the room. He didn't even seem to notice the two women practically drooling for his attention as his gaze found her across the room. In an instant, his expression hardened to stone and his eyes darkened to pools of black regret.

Anne's stomach turned. But then she recalled the promise she'd made herself last night.

She'd create her own place. And if she couldn't have happiness, she'd find contentment.

Rising to her feet before he could start toward her, she met him near the front door.

There was no greeting, just a tense locking of eyes before Beynon cleared his throat. "The carriage is ready, if you'd—"

"I'm ready," she noted. "We can go."

Then she turned and strode across the gravel drive to the carriage, where their driver helped her into the well-sprung vehicle.

Beynon stepped in a moment later and their tense and silent journey continued.

Chapter Twenty-six

As they passed through the village where Beynon had lived for the first ten years of his life, he couldn't seem to stop himself from watching Anne's reactions. Covertly, of course. He couldn't disrupt the carefully orchestrated distance he'd created between them over the last several days of travel. It was the only thing helping him to maintain his sanity and it was wearing frightfully thin.

After the wretched way he'd handled the special license followed by the rushed wedding, he'd vowed to give her all the space she needed to come to terms with the new life she'd been forced into. A vow that was proving far more difficult to keep than he could have anticipated when he wanted so badly to know what she was thinking and feeling with each minute that they grew closer to his home.

Though the village often triggered a wide range of emotions inside him, the place and its inhabitants were a part of his soul. They'd shaped him from very early on. Even after he'd gained the confidence and composure to walk down the main road without glaring defensively at anyone who looked at him, the people here remained a poignant part of his personal history.

Passing through the village also meant they were less than an hour from the farm.

With his stomach knotted, he observed his bride.

She sat with perfect posture despite the long days of travel. Since she had no maid, she'd been doing her pale hair in a simple style, parted in the center then twisted and pinned to the back of her head.

She looked fresh and young and vibrant with understated elegance. Despite the occasional roughness of their accommodations—the quick meals and lumpy beds—and the constant, undeniable tension that filled the carriage throughout every day, she'd remained quietly enduring. Never once complaining or displaying discomfort.

She'd also never once asked why he insisted on getting them separate rooms each night and she'd never tried to force him into conversation during the day. She'd basically left him to brood in silence while she observed the passing scenery or napped or read from the slim novel she'd acquired at their second stop. The tense silence between them seemed perfectly to her liking.

And now, she stared attentively out the window, leaning forward on occasion to gaze at the mountains rising from the landscape. He noted how her gaze would follow the rugged rocky outcroppings with curiosity and perhaps a bit of wonder. Just outside the village, they began to pass the small farms that dotted the lower hills. Some had sheep, others had cows. The crop farms were becoming less and less common in the area, but there were a few remaining.

He watched how she seemed to soak in the sight of the stone cottages and the country laborers going about their late-afternoon tasks, finishing up their work before the sun would set on the day and they could settle in for the night, resting amongst family before starting all again at dawn.

He'd worked himself into a fine state of uncertainty by the time the carriage finally slowed to turn down the lane that would lead to his home, the farm left in his care after his stepfather's passing. The house and land where he'd finally discovered his place and his purpose.

Though he hadn't been in any hurry, he'd occasionally imagined the day he'd bring a bride home. He'd assumed it would be a local girl. A farmer's daughter. A female already well versed in what would be required of her as Beynon's life partner. He'd at least assumed there would be a sense of optimism as they started their lives together. A life he'd deeply wished to model after the example set by Cedric.

A life that would never be his.

Because he'd been unable to resist the subtle enticement of a woman possessing fairy-like grace that disguised a wealth of quiet passion within.

He missed Anne's passion.

The way her eyes would swirl when she was angry with him. Or desirous.

Lust and longing hardened his body in a rush. He clenched his teeth.

As though sensing his attention, she momentarily shifted her focus from the passing countryside to cast a quick glance in his direction.

When she saw he was looking back at her, she'd quickly look away again, after giving a subtle, delicate flinch. And just as he had from their first meeting, he saw it. He always saw it—that uncontrollable reaction as her body tensed and something flickered deep in her gaze. He'd first believed it to be a wary sort of fear. But he knew better now. The woman was not fearful of anything, let alone him. So, why did she still react in such a way? As though her body responded involuntarily.

Unfortunately, he had no answer, which only worsened his bad mood as they rounded the bend and the house came into view.

In the fading daylight, the old gray brick took on a golden hue where it nestled in a wide, curving valley between rising green mountains. The riotous beds of flowers his mam had planted out front were in full bloom to soak up the last of the sun's rays for the day. Only a corner of the barn could be seen as it peeked out from behind the house where the narrow gravel drive curved out of sight.

For a moment, the quietness of the scene startled him. His stomach turned.

Where was everyone?

But then, he heard the bark of a dog quickly followed by a child's shout. A second later, their dog, Harry, came barreling from around the house—something white flappping in his great jaws. The sheepdog had never taken to herding so had become a pet for the children. Three boys in different sizes appeared next in swift pursuit of the dog with a tiny girl child following a bit behind but doing her best to keep up. More shouts joined the first, but they were heavily laced with laughter, until a young woman came into view and gave a sharp, ear-splitting whistle that brought everyone to a tumbling halt, except for the dog, which made a sudden about-face and trotted happily to the older girl's side, where the stolen object—a stocking—was removed from his jaws.

Some of the uncertainty and worry loosened from around Beynon's chest.

The children were all right.

Suddenly very anxious to give them all giant hugs and to find out how their mother was faring, he barely waited for the vehicle to come to a complete stop before opening the door and leaping to the ground.

Though all the children had stopped and turned to stare at the fancy carriage with wide eyes, Eirwyn spotted him first and smiled widely as she darted toward him to toss herself into his arms. The others followed quickly behind and there were a few moments of several voices rising in volume and speed as they all bombarded him with questions and expressions of shock at his sudden arrival. It took him another few minutes to calm them all down enough to make out anything they said or even attempt to reply.

Then the first thing he heard happened to be, "Who's she?"

The blunt question came from young Edwyn and Beynon cringed at the realization that he'd left Anne sitting the carriage. Turning a glance over his shoulder, he saw that the driver must have helped her to the ground as she stood back a few steps watching their chaotic reunion with the faintest suggestion of a smile. Despite the pleasantness of her expression, he could see the tension in her fine jaw and noted that her fingers were tightly linked.

Far too late, he realized he should have given her some advanced notice of what to expect of his family. He'd mentioned his siblings to her briefly before, but she probably would have benefitted from having more information before being thrust amongst them.

Stepping aside, he held a hand out to her in a gesture for her to come forward. Though she stepped up beside him, she didn't put her hand in his.

Realizing he and the children had been speaking Welsh, he shifted to English. "This is my wife, Lady Anne."

Their eyes all went wide, though he couldn't be sure if it was due to him calling her his wife or the fact that she was a genuine lady, a distinction she didn't lose even though she'd married so far beneath her station. The stunned silence that followed his introduction was broken quickly enough by Daryn. The boy could always be counted on to say exactly what everyone else was thinking but not uttering out loud.

"Why'd she marry you?" the ten-year-old asked with a scrunched brow and tilted head.

Beynon gave the boy a hard stare. "It's a long story."

ANNE WAS TEMPTED TO laugh at the boy's brazen question, but the overwhelming sense of displacement held her amusement in check. As Beynon had disembarked from the carriage, she'd seen the look of concern on his face and she'd waited a moment to give him a chance to acclimate to being home.

The farm was as lovely and picturesque as the others they passed along the way. It was also decidedly much larger. The house itself was no stone and thatch cottage but was built of rough-hewn brick and stood two stories with a wide front door and riotous flowers growing all about. If not for the two large barns that could be seen beyond the house and a nearby pasture filled with sheep, it could have been mistaken for a small manor rather than a farmhouse.

When the sound of children's shouts drew her attention away from the house, she'd taken a moment to claim a few deep breaths.

Beynon had greeted his siblings with boisterous hugs as they all spoke at once. The Welsh words were unidentifiable to Anne, but the sentiment behind them was not. The children were all very excited for their brother to be home. And though his expression remained tense, Beynon clearly shared the sentiment. The obvious relief in his body and the warmth of his greetings to each of his siblings were touching and not entirely unexpected considering the warmth he'd displayed when he'd spoken of them that day beneath the oak.

After the driver helped her from the carriage, she'd waited patiently for the reunion to finish, not wanting to interrupt the happy scene. But now that she'd been noticed, she offered a smile and stepped forward to address the children directly.

"I imagine my appearance is a bit of a shock but I'm sure your brother will explain everything. Since you all know my name, I wonder if you might not mind introducing yourselves to me?"

She ignored Beynon's dark scowl as the oldest child came forward first. A girl around sixteen years, Anne would guess, with black hair in heavy waves to her shoulders and lovely dark brown eyes similar to Beynon's, though not nearly so guarded. She gave an impressive curtsey and replied, "My name is Eirwyn, my lady. Welcome to Gwaynynog."

"Thank you, Eirwyn. I look forward to seeing more of it."

"I'm Aron and this is Daryn." The boy who spoke was clearly a few years younger than his older sister but topped her height by an inch or two. The boy he dragged forward with him was another couple years younger and had been the one to so bluntly question Anne's choice in husband. If not for their age difference, the two brothers could have been twins as they shared such similar features with dark brown eyes and the same mops of unruly black curls.

"Lovely to meet you both," Anne replied before looking to the third boy, who might have been around six by her estimation.

Though she smiled in encouragement, the youngest boy wouldn't step forward and neither would the small girl beside him.

"These two are Edwyn and Carys," Eirwyn offered, setting her hands on the shoulders of her youngest siblings.

Anne stepped toward the smaller children and lowered to a crouch. Her smile was soft as she said gently, "Hello, I'm very happy to meet you."

Edwyn gave a quick nod but said nothing.

The little girl, however, eyed Anne with a sideways glance of suspicion then gave a little snort. "You're pretty but you talk funny."

Anne heard Beynon's grunt of surprise and the choked giggles from the older boys, but she ignored them.

"That's a lovely compliment, Carys. I think you're very pretty, as well." It was true. The girl's black hair fell in long ringlets down her back and her eyes were a rich green. "And you're also very clever. I do talk funny," she added bluntly, inciting a delightful giggle from the girl.

As Anne straightened again, Beynon asked, "How's Mam?"

"Oh, she's doing much better," Eirwyn said quickly. "Did you get my second letter?"

"No. I only just received the first last week. We left as soon as we could after I learned she was unwell."

"Well, she'll be happy to see you anyway," the girl replied as she sent a quick, tentative glance to Anne. "She's probably resting, but I imagine you'll want to see her right away. And introduce your...bride."

Beynon gave Anne a quick glance. "Perhaps it should wait."

His relief at hearing his mother was faring better from her illness was obvious in his expression. As was his sudden reluctance to bring Anne before her.

"Why don't you go see your mother while I settle in and freshen up a bit." She looked to Eirwyn. "Would you have a moment to show me to my room?"

"Of course, my lady."

The girl curtsied again. Anne would have to tell her that wasn't necessary, but she'd wait until they were alone. She didn't want to embarrass the young woman.

Beynon looked to his sister first, then back to Anne. Then, with a firm nod, he turned and entered the house in long strides.

"Why's he so glum?" Daryn asked as soon as his oldest brother was out of hearing. The question earned him a punch in the shoulder from Aron, who then leaned toward him to mutter something in Welsh as he slid a sly glance toward Anne.

Whatever the boy's answer, it clearly had something to do with her. And judging by Eirwyn's sudden blush and Carys's giggle, it likely wasn't complimentary.

It was on the tip of her tongue to ask when the man *wasn't* glum, but she decided against it.

"Boys," Eirwyn chirped with a clear note of authority, "help the driver unload the luggage and bring it inside while Carys and I show Lady Anne to her room."

Though her brothers gave a few grumbles, they shuffled their feet toward the back of the carriage, where the driver had already started unstrapping the trunks.

Then the girl turned to Anne and gave a quick smile. "This way, please."

Anne hoped Eirwyn's formality would soften with familiarity but the wish wasn't necessary for little Carys as the girl slipped her hand into Anne's and gave an insistent tug.

"Come on!"

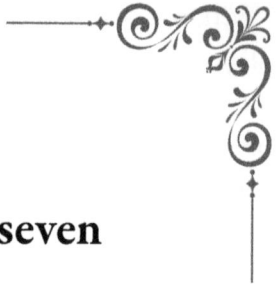

Chapter Twenty-seven

After Eirwyn left the room—tugging a reluctant Carys with her—and closed the door, Anne sat heavily on the large bed and released a deep sigh.

She was here.

At her new home.

With her new family.

A rush of inexplicable emotion closed her throat and curved her spine as she lifted both hands to cover her face. Pressing firmly to her eyes to staunch the threat of tears, she took deep, even breaths.

She could do this. She was resilient. If nothing else, the last five days in a carriage with her new husband had proven that.

Husband.

Could she even call him that?

The union hadn't been consummated. They'd never shared a room or a bed. They'd barely shared a full conversation since their wedding.

Before she could even begin to contemplate what she should do next, a sharp knock sounded on the door. Welcoming the distraction, Anne rose swiftly to her feet and crossed the room.

It was Beynon.

Just as always, the sight of him caused an immediate reaction through her body. A tingle and a spark. A tightening. A warming. Then she noticed the deep scowl on his face and the obvious tension present in his large form. Something had upset him.

An unsteady fear gripped her. "What is it?" she asked, stepping through the door into the hallway. "Is your mother all right?"

His expression remained fierce and forbidding as he looked down at her.

For a second, she had an impossible urge to comfort him—to step forward and wrap her arms around him. But she had no doubt such an act would immediately be rebuffed.

"Mam's recovering," he replied gruffly. "I suspect she'll be well enough very soon."

"That's good news," Anne replied tentatively.

Then he took a breath and his gaze slid momentarily to the side. "She wants to meet you."

"Now?" Anne took a step back. Of course his mother would want to meet her. She wasn't at all sure why the thought suddenly made her feel so uncertain and nervous.

"This way," he replied as he turned to lead her down the narrow hallway to a door at the far end.

Anne followed dutifully behind, her steps even behind his heavier footfalls on the polished wood floor. His knock on the closed door was immediately answered by a woman's call to enter. He opened the door then stepped to the side, gesturing for Anne to pass him into the room.

The first thing she noticed was that it was a lovely bedroom, full of light from the midday sun shining through two large casement windows through which the branches of a large willow could be seen against a mountainous backdrop. The floor was covered in a rug woven of various shades of blue in an intricate and lovely pattern and the bed set up in a corner opposite the windows was also covered in blue.

Beynon's mother sat propped against the pillows.

The woman was dressed in a white dressing gown and navy-blue robe and her thick black hair, threaded with silvery strands, was plaited in two braids that rested over her narrow shoulders.

She was smaller than Anne expected—quite petite actually—and despite the bit of gray in her hair, she looked very young. And when she smiled, Anne could easily see the cherubic features which had been inherited by her youngest daughter.

"Lady Anne, allow me to present my mother, Mrs. Thomas. Mam, this is my bride, Lady Anne Thomas."

"You'll call me Glynnis, of course," his mother quickly noted before giving beckoning gestures with both hands. "Come in, my lady! Come in. Please don't tarry by the door. I hadn't expected such a wonderful surprise today and I'm anxious to indulge my curiosity."

Anne approached the bedside as requested, suddenly feeling very tall and gauche.

But Beynon's mother continued to smile as she indicated a chair that had been pulled up aside the bed. "Sit, my dear. Please." Then she shifted her attention to where Beynon still stood by the door. "You may go."

"But, Mam," he began, but she stopped him with a swift wave of her hand.

"Off you go. I'll see you at dinner."

Anne glanced back as she took a seat in the empty chair and managed to catch Beynon's very put-out expression as he skulked from the room.

"Oh my, now let me look at you," his mother said.

Anne met the woman's dark brown eyes that were so similar to Beynon's. And not just because of their near black shade. She saw a similar depth and emotional intensity in this woman's gaze, though it was decidedly less angry and forbidding.

"Tell me, my dear," the older woman said in a thoughtful tone, "what on earth brought you and my son together?"

Anne stiffened at the bluntness of the question. She blinked as she tried to consider what Beynon might have said.

"I, ah...Beynon—"

Glynnis gave a swift shake of her head. "I already heard Beynon's explanation. I'd like to hear from you now, if you don't mind."

Anne realized the woman's small stature and the sweetness of her features were slightly misleading. Her new mother-in-law possessed an inherent toughness and a sharp perception she wasn't afraid to use.

Anne made a quick decision to be as forthright as possible. What point was there in beginning this new chapter of her life on a deception, even if it was by way of omission or glossing over the facts?

Clearing her throat, she met her mother-in-law's steady but not unkind stare.

"We were partnered for a series of games at my friend's house party," she noted simply. "Reluctantly partnered, I should say. Beynon wasn't very interested in participating."

Glynnis gave a subtle roll of her eyes then nodded for Anne to continue.

"Our partnership was occasionally contentious," Anne admitted, "but I'd like to think we got to know each other through the competition." She paused, hoping that might be enough of an explanation, but the older woman simply arched her brows and waited for her to continue.

At this point, Anne had to lower her gaze to the detailing embroidered on the counterpane.

"Eventually...one evening...we found ourselves..." How exactly did one admit to such a thing to their mother-in-law? She really wished she knew what Beynon had said to her.

"Overcome?" the woman offered.

Anne's eyes flew back up to meet her mother-in-law's pointed stare. All she could manage was a brief nod.

There was a moment of silence, then Glynnis said, "Well, that explains the rushed wedding, I suppose."

There wasn't exactly censure in the older woman's tone, but there wasn't delight, either.

Determined not to start her new life upon a foundation that even hinted of deception, Anne decided to take a page from the young Miss Claybourne's book by being painfully honest.

"To tell the truth," Anne said, "I did not wish to marry Beynon. And he did not wish to marry me."

Glynnis gave her a dubious look even as the corner of her mouth curled in amusement. "But of course he did or you wouldn't be here now."

Anne felt compelled to correct the woman's assumption. "The circumstances are a bit difficult to explain."

"Nonsense. He compromised you, didn't he?"

Anne nodded.

"Then he made a choice. One I know he wouldn't have made lightly." The older woman paused then made a face that suggested she was slightly pained. "This is a rather awkward thing to say about one's son to his new bride, but considering the circumstances, there is something you should know about my oldest."

Anne's breath caught. "Perhaps you shouldn't..." she began carefully, thinking of Beynon's response if he knew his mother was about to tell some secret—even as she was desperate for any bit of insight to the man she'd married.

The older woman quickly waved off Anne's half-hearted protest. "Since the current earl is acknowledging his siblings, I assume you know of the circumstances surrounding Beynon's birth." Anne nodded and she continued with a soft smile. "Well, from a very young age, Beynon has been painfully aware of the consequences that can result from careless...passions. Because of that, he's always been very selective about who he's taken to bed. He's certainly never dallied with an innocent. If his actions with you went against such strictly enforced behaviors, it reveals one powerful truth."

She smiled again. "He wanted you, my dear. Badly. Do not doubt that for a second."

Anne wished the woman's words had given her some confidence, but they really only reinforced what she already knew. "From what I understand, lust can make a man do many things he otherwise wouldn't."

"True," Glynnis replied thoughtfully before narrowing her gaze a bit. "And are such passions reciprocated, my lady?"

Anne's quick blush answered the question the easily enough.

With a sigh, Beynon's mother reached for Anne's hands. Her grip was warm and gentle but no less secure. There was strength in the woman's hands, but it was a quiet, constant sort of strength.

Her dark eyes held Anne's as she said, "Many happy marriages have started with less. Miserable marriages, as well," she added bluntly. "Only time will tell what this one will prove to be."

Then she leaned toward Anne to ask intently, "Now, tell me...did you win?"

"What?" Anne blinked.

"The games? Did you win?"

"Yes, we did, actually."

Glynnis clapped her hands and a delighted little smile curved her mouth. "Of course you did."

———— ❧ ————

BEYNON CONSIDERED WAITING outside his mother's room for Anne then quickly decided against it. His mother had made it very clear she wished to have a private word with his bride. Despite a deep rebellious streak, he'd never gone against his mam's express wishes and sure as hell didn't intend to start now.

He couldn't imagine what his mother and Anne might have to speak about, but he supposed it wasn't his business. The women, despite their obvious differences, would be sharing a household and would have to sort through that fact in their own way.

So, instead of lurking in the upper story hallway, he made his way downstairs. There was a great deal to be done now that he was home again. He quickly discovered the carriage had already been unloaded and had been brought round to the barn. Aron was tending to the horses while Eirwyn had seen to refreshment for their driver.

His oldest sister was just coming from the kitchen as he reentered the house. They met in the cozy entryway between the front parlor and the study, which would always feel like his stepfather's despite the fact Beynon had been using it since the man's passing.

They paused and assessed each other in a disturbingly similar manner.

Beynon was the first to speak. "Anything I need to be aware of regarding the farm?"

The girl shrugged. "Nothing in particular. The main flock is in the northern pasture. Gilly had her foal a fortnight ago. All is in readiness for shearing at Michaelmas."

Not for the first time, Beynon considered how close in age Caillie and Eirwyn were. Only a couple years apart. Perhaps that was why he'd felt such a quick kinship with his sister in England.

When he'd first learned of his sire's other offspring, he never intended to meet any of them. The prior Earl of Wright had been a despicable, selfish man who'd spread his seed in a decade-long act of vengeance against an unfaithful wife. Beynon had absolutely no desire to connect to anyone else associated with such a man.

It had been his mother who'd finally insisted he accept the invitation from the earl's heir. Beynon had gone to London more than two years ago with the intention of never allowing his two families to meet. He saw no purpose and no good of such a thing.

But now, as he acknowledged his sister's intelligent and somewhat solemn gaze, he wondered if perhaps such a separation was unrealistic. He could suddenly imagine Caillie and Eirwyn as two sides of the same coin. One so upfront, fearless, and restless. The other so capable, confident, and far too pensive for her age.

They could be good for each other.

Or they could dislike each other immensely.

"Is there anything else, brawd?"

Beynon cleared his throat and glanced toward his stepfather's study. "No. I suppose not. I think I'll just try to get caught up on things for the rest of the night."

Eirwyn nodded. "Would you like me to arrange anything specific for dinner tonight?"

He realized then that his sister had likely taken on a lot of the duties their mother typically tended to during her illness. That in addition to his own.

"Whatever you decide for tonight is fine," he muttered. "I reckon Lady Anne will wish to be included on such discussions in future. Perhaps you and Mam—"

"I'll see to it," Eirwyn interrupted.

Beynon scowled at the unexpected note of authority in her voice. Why did it feel like she'd suddenly grown up in the months he'd been gone?

"Thank you," he muttered then watched as his sister gave a nod before walking away.

The study was little bigger than a pantry found in some of the larger London homes he'd visited of late. But the cramped little room, filled with a desk, two chairs, a bookcase lined with texts, and little else held a particular nostalgia for him.

After his mother had married Cedric Thomas and they'd moved from their tiny room at the back of the village inn to this grand old house, this was where his new stepfather had sat him down any time they needed to discuss his behavior. It was where Beynon had learned what a father's love looked like. How a man could be stern and loving at the same time. How a father could disapprove of a son's actions and mete out discipline if needed while still believing in the child's potential for better.

This was the room where, little by little, week by week, year after year, Beynon had learned to accept responsibility for his mistakes and what it meant to work hard to support a family.

Family.

Beynon tensed and his stomach knotted.

Could Lady Anne already be carrying his child? Would she know by now?

Even as he wondered, he knew he wouldn't ask her. Despite the current strain and lack of communication between them, he trusted that if she were to discover she was with child, she'd let him know.

He sure as hell couldn't allow himself to dwell on it. Because thoughts of children led to the idea of conception, which immediately reminded him that their marriage had yet to be consummated. And that was one thing he really couldn't dwell on or he'd end up doing something rash and stupid to correct the situation.

So, instead, he decided to focus intently on getting back into the rhythms and patterns he so loved about his life on the farm. No doubt his mother and Eirwyn had managed everything without issue. But he preferred to have firsthand knowledge. Perhaps he should visit the pastures. He'd count every damned sheep in the flock if it helped him keep his mind away from his reluctant bride.

He might have forced her into an unwanted marriage, but he wasn't about to force any husbandly rights when she'd made it quite clear she wanted nothing to do with him.

Perhaps in time she'd recall the passion they'd shared and she'd seek him out...

He shoved his hands into his hair and clenched his jaw.

Think of something else. Anything else.

He picked up a stack of paperwork and leaned over the desk to review every notation with focused intent.

Chapter Twenty-eight

L ady Anne's first dinner in her new home was unlike anything she'd ever experienced. The Thomas children were already seated around the table when Anne came down. The sound of their overlapping voices and boisterous laughter could be heard through much of the house. They welcomed her to the dining room with wide smiles and happy greetings. The food was already on the table, filling the room with savory scents that made Anne's mouth water. She later learned with no small bit of awe that their meal had been prepared entirely by Eirwyn.

When Anne found out Beynon would not be joining them as he'd already made himself a plate to eat in his study, she experienced a quick, sharp pang to her chest. But she refused to show her disappointment, especially once Glynnis entered the room. Though she was clearly still weak from her illness, the older woman's cheeks were a lovely color and she insisted that she needed to be up and about more often if she were to fully regain her strength.

Anne was grateful to the woman for the obvious gesture at welcoming Anne to their table and their home and made a strict point of not worrying about Beynon's choice to do the opposite.

Once she put Beynon firmly from her mind, Anne had a wonderful time. She'd never before experienced a meal where children were present. It was clear the Thomas children were all very close. So close they had absolutely no trouble teasing and taunting each other rather relentlessly. Though Glynnis expressed her apologies more than once for the somewhat disruptive atmosphere around the table, Anne honestly found it all fascinating.

And delightful.

Because although the children were often at odds with each other in some way or fashion, there was still an undeniable connection between them. And that made her wonder if the dynamic changed at all when Beynon was present. It was very difficult to imagine him interacting in the same manner—with robust laughter, ready smiles, and bold banter.

Of course, as soon as she thought of Beynon, a heaviness fell over her mood. She did her best to dispel it quickly but happened to glance toward her new mother-in-law before she'd completely managed the emotion.

Something in the older woman's gaze had her wondering if she didn't know exactly what had caused the dampening of Anne's spirits.

Placing a wide smile on her lips, Anne did her best to counter whatever might have been detected as she turned to answer Carys's very serious question as to whether Anne preferred peas or green beans with her roast lamb.

The small girl apparently abhorred both as they were both green and she absolutely didn't like eating anything green.

After dinner, Anne lingered in the parlor as long as she could manage—long after her mother-in-law offered her apologies for retiring early and Eirwyn had taken the younger children up to bed.

She wasn't specifically awaiting an appearance by Beynon, but she couldn't help but glance to the doorway every time the old house made the slightest creak.

Even so, it was still rather early when she made her way up to the bedroom she'd been given. The days of travel and the intense anticipation leading up to her arrival today had been exhausting. Gratefully, someone had seen to keeping a low fire lit and a few

candles flickered near the bed. She readied herself quickly and barely
registered tucking herself beneath the covers before she was deeply
asleep.

---⟨∾⟩---

THE NEXT MORNING, ANNE awoke with a start, feeling as
though something had drawn her sharply from slumber. But as she
blinked the sleep from her vision and glanced about the unfamiliar
room, she didn't see or hear anything that could have disturbed her.

No doubt, it was simply the discomfort of waking in a new place,
she decided as she glanced around the cozy wood-paneled room.
The windows faced the north, so the morning sunlight was soft and
indirect. The air was fresh and only a bit cool, while the bedcovers
kept her warm and contented. As she stretched her limbs and spine,
she realized that even the unused side of the large bed held a hint of
warmth.

After rising, she washed quickly and dressed in a simple day dress
before pinning her hair into a neat bun at her nape. She'd promised
to join Glynnis for breakfast and she didn't wish to be late.

As soon as she stepped into the hallway outside her bedroom,
she realized her habit of rising early was not an exception in this
household. She could hear children's shouts from somewhere below
followed by the bark of a dog and running feet. Making her way
down the corridor toward the corner room at the far end, she nearly
collided with Carys as the small girl dashed out of a room to the right
and practically flew down the stairs without ever once seeing Anne.

What on earth could have roused everyone to such a degree so
early, she wondered as she reached her mother-in-law's door. Though
it was slightly ajar, Anne still knocked respectfully.

"Come in."

Anne entered to see Beynon's mother once again seated against
the pillows in her bed. Today, she was fully dressed and sat atop

the covers, though a woven blanket had been draped over her legs. Her black hair glinting with silver had been freshly washed and was twisted into a thick chignon.

"Bore da, Lady Anne," her mother-in-law greeted warmly. "Please have a seat." She indicated one of two chairs that had been positioned at a small table pulled up beside the bed.

"Good morning, ma'am. You appear well rested this morning," Anne noted with a smile.

"I'm feeling a great deal better. Unfortunately, I still tire rather easily. I have to be honest; I haven't been ill like that since I was a child." She gave a little scowl. "I can't say I appreciate the experience."

"Which is exactly why it's time for you to work less and find some more restful hobbies to occupy your time." This was said by Eirwyn as the young woman entered the room with a large serving tray. Her tone was admonishing, but a smile tilted her mouth as she set the tray on the table.

The older woman gave a snort of derision but did not voice a contradiction to her daughter's observation.

In efficient movements, Eirwyn settled an empty tray across her mother's lap to which she transferred a steaming cup of tea and a plate of eggs and sausage. After serving her mother, the girl took the chair across the table from Anne.

"I hope you don't mind a simple breakfast, my lady. I'm afraid our stores don't currently provide options for anything elaborate."

"Everything smells wonderful." Catching the girl's eye, she added, "And please, I hope you'll call me Anne."

The girl gave a half-smile and nodded.

"Now," her mother said as she lifted her fork, "as Gwaynynog's new mistress, I imagine there's a great deal you'd like to know about the place. Where shall we start?"

"I haven't the slightest idea," Anne admitted freely. "I'm afraid my education is rather lacking in this regard."

"Of course, fy annwyl," Glynnis said with a pat on her hand. "It'll take some time to adjust, no doubt."

"For us, as well," Eirwyn noted bluntly, a hint of annoyance in her tone. "It might have been nice for Beynon to send some sort of notice regarding his nuptials."

"Everything happened rather suddenly," Anne noted in Beynon's defense, "otherwise, I'm certain Beynon would have sent word."

Eirwyn gave a soft snort of disbelief and her mother laughed.

"He might have, though he just as likely might not have," Glynnis replied. "That son of mine has always been stubborn about doing things his own way."

"Regardless of what anyone might say," Eirwyn interjected with a roll of her eyes, which incited another chuckle from her mother.

Though they were criticizing a man who wasn't even present to defend himself, Anne suspected by the warmth in their voices that it was done with love and she couldn't help adding a comment of her own. "Even if it results in getting lost in a maze until after dark."

Two pairs of dark eyes widened with surprise before Eirwyn noted with amusement, "Oh my, I imagine that got him quite heated."

"Indeed," Anne replied with a gentle grin. "But we managed to find our way out. Once he started listening to me, that is," she added pointedly.

Glynnis cleared her throat to say with a smirk, "Well, it's good to know he can be reasonable on occasion."

"It would certainly be a new trick," Eirwyn noted skeptically before turning to Anne with an earnest expression. "Please don't get me wrong. My brother can be a terrible grouch. He can be frustratingly stubborn and overly protective. But he is undeniably devoted to his family. And we are quite grateful for him."

"And now you are also part of this family," Glynnis noted as she met Anne's gaze. "I sincerely hope we don't make you rue that fact."

"Never," Anne noted quickly and honestly. She might not have the greatest hope for her relationship with Beynon, but she was optimistic when it came to the rest of the family, which she was quickly coming to adore. "Although such a full household is a very new experience for me, I'm quite prepared to love every moment of it."

Just as she finished speaking, a shrill scream sounded from downstairs. It was followed by swiftly running feet and Carys's small voice yelling, "Mam! Mam, Daryn smeared mud in my hair."

The accused boy reached the open doorway a moment before his little sister to add, "Only after *she*"—he pointed a sharp finger toward the girl who came up beside him with an undeniable streak of brown muck coating one of her braids—"put a giant frog on my pillow."

Carys's smile managed to be mischievous and innocent at once. "He just wants to be friends."

The children's mother sighed heavily as she turned a pointed gaze to Anne. "I suspect we might have to remind you of that sentiment every now and then."

"Daily, no doubt," Eirwyn offered in a dry tone as she set down her tea and rose to her feet. "I'll take care of it."

As the young woman herded the smaller children back downstairs, interrupting their impassioned pleas for justice with a firm and patient tone, a strange tension filled Anne's chest, squeezing around her heart. The Thomas household was exactly what she used to wish she'd had while growing up. Laughter, activity, companionship, loyalty, and love.

Regardless of what happened in her marriage going forward, she wanted to embrace all that it meant to feel like a part of this family. Even if she hadn't the slightest idea where to start.

"What is the matter, fy annwyl?"

Anne met her mother-in-law's compassionate gaze. There was something about the older woman—an utter lack of judgement and prejudice, perhaps—that inspired complete honesty.

Without hesitation, Anne confessed, "I imagine I'm not the kind of wife you'd have wished for Beynon but I've no intention of being a burden. I know I have a lot to learn, but I can be quite determined when I set my mind to something."

The older woman leaned forward to take one of Anne's hands in hers. "Trust me, where you come from is not nearly as important as where you hope to go. I know this firsthand. When I married Cedric, I didn't know the first thing about sheep farming. But I learned. Eventually." Then she winked. "Don't worry. We'll have you shearing the flock with the rest of us come Michaelmas."

Anne's eyes widened. Michaelmas was only weeks away. The older woman gave a husky laugh, which did not at all clarify whether her declaration had been made in jest or in all seriousness.

Chapter Twenty-nine

The woolen blanket slipped from around Anne's shoulders but she didn't bother replacing it. Unable to sleep, she'd pulled one of the armchairs over to the windows in her bedroom. Though the night air wafted freely through the open casement, it was warm and pleasant despite the fact she wore only a thin cotton nightgown.

She'd been at Gwaynynog for nearly a week now. And in that time, she'd begun to develop a true friendship with Glynnis and had learned a great deal about the village and the farm's history as they talked over tea each morning. She'd stood alongside Eirwyn in the kitchen, sharing amusing anecdotes from her London seasons while the girl walked her through basic cooking tasks. At Anne's request, the young woman had also started teaching Anne some common Welsh phrases. She'd spent a lovely afternoon with Aron and Daryn as they showed her the barn and the yards walled with stacked slate where the sheep were brought for shearing. And she'd tramped hand in hand with Edwin and Carys as the two youngest Thomas children led her around the lower pastures, which were thick with grass and wildflowers since their flocks were kept in the mountains during the warmest months.

Everyone in Beynon's family had been more welcoming and warmer than Anne could have hoped. Though they occasionally teased her for her unavoidable ignorance on some things, they never made her feel like she didn't belong. In a short time, Gwaynynog had begun to feel like more of a home than the house in which she'd grown up.

Anne was grateful. So much of her anxiety had proven to be unnecessary. Of course, life was significantly different from what she might have expected as the wife of a lord, but she couldn't help but feel this was exactly where she was supposed to be.

She felt grounded here. Connected. And though she still had so much to learn about her role and responsibilities on the farm, she believed she'd get there. If her life had taught her anything to date, it was that she knew what it took to meet a challenge. And for the first time, she felt as though she was doing it for her own satisfaction and enjoyment rather than simply because it was what was required of her.

There was only one thing keeping her from feeling utterly content with her new life.

In the six days since her arrival, she'd seen Beynon a total of five times. Briefly and at a distance. He was always gone by the time she rose in the mornings, and if he happened to be within the old stone house, he was likely to be holed up in his study.

One day, Anne had heard his voice from where she'd been helping Eirwyn prepare meat pies for their supper. By the time she'd gotten to the front hall, she noted his study door was closed—a clear indicator he was inside. Determined to see him, if for no other reason than to force him to acknowledge her presence, she'd strode toward the door, only to be brought up short by young Edwyn.

The quiet, keen-eyed boy had stepped in front of her and held his finger to his lips.

"You can't go in there."

"I only wish to say hello," she explained gently.

The six-year-old boy gave a vigorous shake of his head. "It's the only quiet room in the house and it needs to stay that way."

Anne had smiled, understanding why such a rule might have been created considering how *unquiet* the rest of the house could get with five children running about. Not wanting to undermine the sanctity of the master's study, she'd allowed Edwyn to lead her away.

She took a deep breath now as she stared out to the black night sky.

The oddest thing about the fact that she'd had no personal interactions with Beynon in so many days was that, somehow, she still felt his presence. Especially in the mornings when she first awoke. There was always this warm sense of intimacy surrounding her as she opened her eyes and stretched her body to wakefulness. A few times, she even thought she'd caught a hint of his scent and her body had reacted immediately to the suggestion of his nearness. Her belly had tightened and her core melted with a physical longing she felt she'd never shake.

She missed him.

She missed seeing him every day as she had during Lily's party. She missed the arguments and his broody, challenging manner. She missed his gravelly voice and his rough hands. She missed the way he looked at her and the way he *looked*.

If she closed her eyes, she could still see him as he'd been that morning on the lakeshore or crouching at her feet in the twilight maze or towering over her as he pinned her to the wall in the darkened hallway.

It had been less than a week since they'd arrived at his home—less than two since their wedding day, yet Anne had had plenty of time to determine this was not how she wanted to continue in their marriage. And if he wasn't going to do anything about it, then she'd have to.

She'd been reluctant to ask anyone where his room was located because it was embarrassing to admit she had no idea. The house wasn't that big, after all. The rooms were limited. Yet she hadn't managed to figure it out on her own.

But to acknowledge such an ignorance was to announce that their union was strained. And though she had no doubt everyone suspected it anyway, her pride simply wouldn't allow her to admit it out loud until she'd at least tried to resolve the situation herself.

Having come to that decision this evening, she was beset by questions on just how she was to go about such a thing.

She'd been sitting by the window for hours now. The fire in the hearth was down to the faintest glowing embers and the candles had burned out. She had no idea what time it was but the heavy silence filling the house suggested it had to be very late. Yet she wasn't the least bit tired.

She was determined. And annoyed. And perhaps a bit concerned.

She needed to seduce her own husband but hadn't the slightest idea how to go about it.

If the decision hadn't been made out of pure lonely desperation, the idea would have been as amusing as it was shocking. But she craved more with the man she'd married. She might have resigned herself to the fact that they might never develop a friendship of trust and consideration. But must that mean they could have nothing at all?

What about physical connection? What about desire? There was a longing inside her that grew stronger every day. Why should she deny it?

They'd given in to their intense passion for each other once before. Perhaps, if they embraced it more fully, there was a chance it could grow into something more. She had to believe it was possible.

At the faint sound of a footfall in the hall outside her bedroom, Anne was pulled from her heated musings and turned to look at her closed door with a faint frown.

Was it possible someone else was still awake at this hour?

She listened for another sound then stiffened as the handle of her door turned. A moment later, the door swung silently open to reveal the silhouette of a large and familiar form.

Beynon.

Anne's breath caught as she watched him enter the room with very slow, deliberate steps. He was clearly trying to be as quiet as possible and didn't seem to have noticed Anne sitting by the window as his attention was intently directed toward the bed. Then he closed the door behind him, enclosing them together in the darkened room.

Anne's heart leapt to a reckless pace but she said nothing.

Why was he here? Had he come in search of her?

She might have thought so if not for the fact that he was obviously trying very hard not to wake her.

But then, several steps into the room, he stopped. Anne watched as he turned his head to scan the room, clearly having noticed she wasn't in the bed as he expected. When he finally spied her sitting before the window, his large body tensed and a heavy sound issued from his throat.

"You're still awake." His words were gruff and almost abrasive in the night silence. There was a hint of accusation in his voice, but mostly it was surprise and what Anne suspected but could hardly believe was uncertainty.

"I am," she replied. When he didn't say anything more in response but remained standing awkwardly in the middle of the room, she decided to be bold. "Why are you here, Beynon?"

Another rough sound rolled through his throat as he glanced toward the bed, then toward the door. And in an instant, she understood.

Heat flooded her body as she realized why she caught his scent in the mornings and why the bed was always so warm—even on the empty side—and why she'd sensed his presence over these last days though she'd so rarely seen him.

"This is *your* bedroom, isn't it?"

He turned and strode to the bed. Sitting on the edge, he removed his boots. "Would you have preferred to share a room with Eirwyn and Carys?"

Anne frowned at the annoyance in his tone. But she could be annoyed, as well.

"So, this is what you've been doing each night? Waiting until I'm asleep so you can sneak in and then sneak back out again before I awake in the morning?"

He paused in the process of loosening the neck of his shirt before he gave a huff and dragged the garment up over his head.

"I didn't want to disturb you," he muttered.

As his bared torso was revealed in the faint glow from the hearth, Anne's breath stilled and her mind went momentarily blank. She suddenly wished she'd kept the fire going longer so its light might illuminate her husband's strong form more clearly. Even so, what she could see of his muscled body sent tingling thrills along her nerves.

Then he stood and walked around to the far side of the bed, and without another word, he pulled the covers back and lay down, still wearing his breeches.

Anne remained in the chair for a few long minutes as she considered the situation.

He was clearly intent upon ignoring her. She wouldn't put it past him to pretend to fall asleep in the next few minutes just to avoid further discussion. Did he really think he could just continue sleeping beside her without any acknowledgement? Was she supposed to just lie down and accept the boundaries he'd set in their marriage?

It had been too long since she'd last challenged his decisions. Decisions that affected her as much as him.

She'd decided on seduction.

No better time than the present to start.

Rising swiftly to her feet, she let the blanket fall to the chair as she strode purposefully to her side of the bed. Drawing back the covers, she slipped between the sheets. Lying on her back, she could hear the even rise and fall of his breath, but beyond that, he remained intensely still.

Rolling to her side to face him, she tucked one hand beneath her cheek and studied his profile. His eyes were closed. The covers were draped low across his body and one of his hands rested over his abdomen. His hand nearest to her was propped beneath his head.

She lay there for a long time—watching the rise and fall of his chest, breathing in his scent, soaking up the warmth of his nearness—while a myriad of emotions swirled through her. There was a breathless sort of anticipation tightening her chest and a tingling in her belly that extended to her fingers and toes. The desire to be daring and bold overwhelmed her, but a stubborn thread of fear held her back.

What if she reached across the few inches that separated them and he rejected her touch?

If he'd wanted her, surely, he'd have come to her.

She thought of the kisses they'd shared. The tenderness and the fire in his embrace. She recalled the passion and desperation in his eyes when he'd laid claim to her body—when she'd readily surrendered to the desire between them.

She wanted to feel that again.

Her hand trembled as she slid it across the smooth surface of the mattress. There was a chance he'd shrink from her touch and devastate the uncertain hope welling in her heart.

But what if he didn't?

Chapter Thirty

Holding her breath, she touched him with just her fingertips first before she lightly slid her hand across his ribs until her palm rested over the steady beat of his heart.

He didn't move beyond a subtle tensing.

Anne exhaled on a soft sigh.

She didn't for a second believe he was asleep. The air between them was too charged. He was as aware of her as she was of him. But she couldn't be sure yet if his stillness was an indication of acceptance.

Holding her lower lip between her teeth, she slowly smoothed her hand across his chest in a gentle exploration. She trailed her fingertips along the curve of his pectoral muscle then the dip of his sternum before boldly seeking the taut ridges of his abdomen.

He didn't try to halt her questing caress. Instead, his body remained perfectly unmoving.

But when her hand drifted low across his belly, his muscles there tightened beneath her touch and his breath came to a harsh stop as his hand fell heavily atop hers.

Anne bit hard to her lip as she waited for him to shove her hand away. But he didn't. The weight of his palm flattened her hand to his stomach, holding it there as his breath deepened and Anne's quickened. When the anticipation building inside her became too much, she whispered a soft plea.

"Let me touch you, Beynon. Please."

His groan was thick and rough and rumbled fiercely through his body, thrilling Anne to her marrow.

Then, with his hand still covering hers, he guided her fingers lower, over the waistband of his breeches to the hard, thick length of his erection.

Her breath left her in a puff before she sucked more air into her lungs and held it.

In a slow, deliberate motion, he moved her palm along his arousal. To the base then back to the blunt, rounded tip. On the second stroke, she felt him tense as he lifted his hips, trying to press more firmly into her hand.

It was stunning and exciting and intimately erotic to touch him such a way. To feel his hand guiding hers, squeezing her fingers tighter, as his breath became stilted and tense. But after a few more strokes, she grew unsatisfied. She wanted more. She wanted to wrap her fingers around him without the barrier of clothing. With a soft sound, she halted the movement.

He freed her immediately. She sensed the tension in him and then heard his sigh of relief as she clumsily started to release the fastening of his breeches. A moment later, the impossibly hard, hot length of him was in her hand. She hadn't expected it to feel so smooth, like satin over steel. Her fingers explored him eagerly, discovering the ridge near the top and the soft-textured veins running down to the base nestled in a crisp patch of hair. Wrapping her hand around him in a secure grip, she marveled at the way he throbbed in time to his heartbeat.

There was so much life and power in him. Pure virility. It called to her. Tugging on a thread deep inside her, unraveling her until her core became languid with need.

She didn't even realize she'd scooted closer to him and had slid her leg up over his until his hand fell to her thigh. With firm intention, he brought her knee higher, until it pressed against the base of his cock as her hand continued to slide up and down his length.

His breath came shorter now. And as she lifted her gaze, she could see the bunching and releasing of the muscles in his jaw and the way his eyes were tightly closed beneath a furrowed brow. Every now and then, he'd press his head back into the pillow as he lifted his hips to shove himself more forcefully against her palm.

It was beautiful. The way he gave himself over to the sensations. The way he silently demanded more.

She gave it willingly. Enthusiastically. She wanted him to have more. She wanted to give him everything.

His fingers tensed and flexed around her thigh as her hand moved faster up and down his erection. Brushing her thumb over the hard tip, she felt something unexpected. A drop of moisture.

Intrigued, she brushed her thumb over him again.

A guttural moan slid from his throat.

She did it again and more moisture beaded to her touch. Fascinated by the workings of his body, she smoothed the drop over the satiny crown before taking him once again in a secure grip.

This time his groan was more of a growl as he suddenly lifted his head and shoulders from the bed to loom over her. Sweeping his arm beneath her head, he held her secure as he captured her mouth with his.

The kiss was ravenous, harsh, and hot.

His breath mixed with hers in panting gasps and throaty moans as their tongues tangled. Shifting his weight further, he rolled over her until his belly pressed against hers and his hips settled between her thighs. Hooking a hand behind her knee, he pulled her leg high along his hip, opening her to him. The smooth, hard length of his erection lodged firmly against her sex and the melting heat of her core soon soaked the cotton of her nightgown.

She moaned at the feel of him so hot and heavy against her sensitive flesh.

But then he broke abruptly from the kiss and lifted himself away from her. She nearly cried out in protest but then realized he was shoving his breeches down. As soon as he kicked them free of his feet, he remained kneeling between her parted legs to grasp the hem of her nightgown and whip it up over head in one smooth, almost violent motion.

When her hands tangled in the voluminous material above her head, he paused, braced on all fours over her.

Spread out naked on the bed, Anne looked up into his shadowed face. His gaze, deep and mysterious in the darkened intimacy of the bedroom, roved over her body. He looked like a conquering warrior about to claim his prize and her heart fluttered in response. She wanted nothing more than to be consumed by the ravenous hunger he couldn't hide.

Wanting to tell him but unable to find the words, she arched her spine, lifting her breasts and rolling her hips. The action felt wanton and brazen in the best way as a low sound rolled through his chest. He tightened his hand in the material of her gown, twisting it more securely around her wrists.

Staring silently down at her, he rested his other hand at the base of her throat. His palm was warm and heavy and his fingers spanned her collarbone from shoulder to shoulder. For a second, she felt...claimed. Possessed and kept by him. It should have shocked her. It *did*, in a way, but only because of the warm rush of pleasure it roused in her blood.

Ensnared by the heat in his focus, she breathed through parted lips as he slowly smoothed his hand down to cup one breast. He completely covered her, his palm engulfing the gentle mound of flesh. But as he slid his hand lower, the pad of his middle finger found her peaked nipple and tapped it gently.

Pleasure sparked through Anne's core. Her breath quickened. She wanted to discover more of what his touch there could inspire.

But his hand continued lower still—now pressing to her belly, now spanning her hips as the tip of his pinky finger extended through the curls covering her mound.

She held her breath. And he held her gaze.

Then he slid his hand firmly between her thighs and cupped her heated, sultry sex.

She moaned. She couldn't help it.

He held her like that for a moment, with the roughened texture of his palm pressing to her sensitive folds, his other hand holding her wrists above her head, and her naked body stretched out in between. But she couldn't lie still. Her core pulsed and her heart raced and something inside her reached for more.

She instinctively arched her back as her legs shifted against his knees braced wide between them. A soft keening sound slid from her throat.

With a low huff of breath, he held her sex more securely in his hand and lowered his head to take one peaked breast into his mouth.

Wet heat surrounded her aching nipple in a soothing possession. But then he gave a hard draw of his mouth, sucking her softness deep into his mouth before releasing her just enough to tease the hardened peak with fiery flicks of his tongue.

Her gasp was sharp in the silence. Her body tensed then melted beneath the fierce attention of his lips, tongue, and teeth.

And then he added more torment.

Shifting his hold between her thighs, he dragged his fingers along her parted folds, spreading her moisture over sensitive nerves. He circled the swollen bud of her clitoris with the pad of a blunt fingertip in a slow, deliberate rhythm, building the sensations that began to swirl low in her belly. The muscles in her thighs tensed and her fingers fisted in the cotton of her nightgown.

A feeling of deep, heavy, pulsing anticipation started to twist through her and she knew the pleasure she'd experienced that night in the storage closet was upon her again.

But before the feeling inside her could release, he slid his finger lower, pressing it into her body in a smooth, purposeful invasion. The sudden, elegant pressure inside her was a relief and torment at once. She realized with a gasp that it was exactly what she'd been craving, but it also roused new sensations, new cravings. Especially when he began a gentle thrust and retreat of his finger that had her nearly whimpering for more. Yet once again, just as she felt herself beginning to tumble over that rising precipice, he withdrew his finger and returned to the now aching bud at the apex of her sex.

He continued the pattern—circling then thrusting then circling again, adding another finger after a while as the pace of his thrusts quickened.

Anne didn't even notice when he'd lifted his head from her breast and began watching the pleasure slowly unravel her. But as the mindless sensations grew, she found herself staring hard into the silent possession of his dark gaze. As his fingers worked magic with her body, she surrendered to his stare, allowing him to claim everything she was. Relinquishing her heart and her pleasure into his keeping.

And as soon as she did so, the relentlessly winding tension inside her snapped and a flood of pleasure rushed through her in a pulsing release. Her breath held and every muscle in her body tightened. Her heart raced and her teeth clenched. But her gaze remained locked by his as his fingers continued to move within her, coaxing every bit of pleasure her soul had to offer.

And finally, when her limbs began to soften then tremble and her breath eased to a quick but steady rhythm, he carefully released the tangled cotton gown from around her wrists. Easing his weight down atop hers, he braced himself on an elbow as he took himself in hand and aligned the broad, smooth tip of his heated erection to her still-pulsing sex.

But before he went further—almost as though he couldn't help himself—he claimed her mouth in another scorching kiss.

Anne reveled in the taste of him. The heaviness of his body atop hers. The smooth warmth of his back beneath her roving hands. And when he began to press into her body, she tilted her hips, easing his entrance, until his cock was lodged so deeply inside her she could feel the beat of his pulse kissing her very core.

His plunging thrusts started out long and deep as he withdrew almost completely before rocking fiercely forward once again, pressing her into the mattress with every stroke as he sucked on her tongue and bit at her lower lip.

But soon the intensity increased. His breath shortened and he ceased kissing her to lower his head beside hers. Every now and then, between panting breaths, he'd press an open-mouthed kiss to the side of her neck or the curve of her shoulder, sending delicious shivers across her skin.

As his thrusts quickened and shortened, reaching an aching sensitivity inside her, and the swift, hard rocking motion of his hips caused a wonderful friction against her sensitive clitoris, she felt the pleasure building in her blood once more. But it was deeper this time—lusher and darker and heavier. She wrapped her arms around him and held on. Turning her head, she found his mouth. Recklessly, she thrust her tongue along his as she gasped and panted. Lifting her hips and squeezing her thighs as his movements grew more frantic and demanding.

Then he tensed. His entire body hardened as he lifted his head and arched his neck. His fierce, quick strokes suddenly slowed and deepened as she felt a pulsing rush of liquid heat inside her. That was what sent her over the edge—the slow plunge of his hot flesh gliding slick along her sensitive nerves.

She arched and moaned as another burst of pleasure consumed her. Her body melted as her heart beat in time to the thundering of his. Consciousness slipped slowly from her grasp and a rich warmth wrapped around her, keeping and holding her as she drifted to sleep surrounded by him.

When she awoke again, it was to the harsh light of morning and the cooling sheets of an empty bed. With a clenching sadness, she realized he hadn't said a single thing throughout their lovemaking.

Not even low whispered words in Welsh.

Chapter Thirty-one

Anne walked through the barn, trailing her fingers along the rough wood of the low stall walls. In a few short weeks, it would be Michaelmas, a time when the sheep would be brought down from their high-level pastures to be clipped one last time before colder weather set in.

Anne was looking forward to the holiday. Not only would she finally have a chance to observe and possibly participate in one of the farm's major events, but she hoped it would require Beynon's oversight, which meant he'd actually be nearby for a change.

It had been several days since she'd woken after their night together to discover not only that her menses had arrived but also that her husband had left Gwaynynog. She'd learned of his departure from Glynnis, who hadn't bothered to hide her look of concern as she explained she wasn't sure where her son had gone or how long he'd be away.

Anne had tried not to take his sudden exodus personally. It was certainly possible he had planned the trip before she'd caught him sneaking into their bedroom...and what had come after.

But deep in her heart, she suspected otherwise. He'd left because of her.

Though a quiet sort of sadness filled her at the knowledge that no child grew in her womb, she focused instead on her anger over Beynon's sudden departure. It was the anger that kept her from hiding in her bedroom in melancholy and regret. It motivated her to redouble her efforts to learn how to cook and speak Welsh. It encouraged her to explore more of the rugged farmland with the children as her guides—a generosity she repaid by offering lessons in painting and archery. It urged her to take on more household management tasks, which led to the discovery that the farm was more profitable than she'd realized and that Beynon was in fact rather wealthy and had not been in need of her dowry at all.

Unfortunately, her quietly smoldering ire did not keep her from gazing out across rolling pastures or down the curving dirt lane, hoping for a glimpse of Beynon's return. Her relentless scanning of the horizon was becoming quite annoying. So much so that, after a week of repeating the frustrating habit, Anne decided to forgo her daily walk and chose instead to tuck herself away in the barn, where it was quiet and dim and the scent of dirt and dried hay filled the air.

As she strolled in and out of the faint shafts of sunlight that filtered between gaps in the weathered boards, she decided she rather liked the earthiness of the place. She liked the textures and colors. And on days like today, when the children were all off splashing about in a nearby creek, she liked the solitude of the empty building.

She spent a couple hours seated on a small wooden chair in the corner of the barn as she sketched images and impressions of her time in Denbighshire. Realizing it was nearly time to start preparing the midday meal, she'd just collected her things and rose to her feet when she heard someone approaching. It took only another moment to recognize Beynon's long, purposeful stride.

Holding her breath, she remained where she was, hoping it was not just her willful imagination that had Beynon suddenly appearing in the sun-drenched doorway. But he looked far too good to her starved gaze to be anything but the real thing.

She'd loved seeing him in formal wear the night of Lily's ball, his black hair combed back from his face, his boots polished to a shine.

But she loved him like this even more.

AMY SANDAS

He was dressed casually in trousers and dusty boots, with his coat removed and held in one hand, his sleeves cuffed to his elbows, and the collar of his shirt opened to reveal a light sheen of sweat at the base of his throat. Since she hadn't heard the approach of a horse, she assumed he'd walked home from wherever he'd been. His thick hair had been tousled by the wind and fell in unruly waves that made her fingers curl with the desire to run them through the satiny locks.

But the most devastating detail of all was that he'd obviously forgone his daily shave while he'd been gone. A thick beard darkened his jaw and accentuated his rugged features. He looked wild and harsh and just a bit dangerous. Anne's belly clenched and her heart thundered in a swift visceral response as longing claimed her with an almost debilitating force.

Since the interior of the barn was significantly darker than the summer day outside, it took a few moments for his eyes to adjust before he finally caught sight of her in the corner. As soon as he did, he came to a quick halt.

It was far too late for him to turn and walk away, though she could see by the sudden darkening of his expression that was exactly what he wished he could do.

Still clutching her sketchbook to her breast, Anne straightened her spine, dropped her shoulders back, and started toward him. She'd have to pass by him to exit the barn and fully intended to do so without offering the slightest acknowledgement of his presence.

Let him see how it feels to be utterly ignored.

But with every purposeful step she took, her body became more tightly wound with awareness and expectation. Her nerves leapt and danced at his nearness and her heart raced wildly. And when she risked a flickering glance at his scowling glare, her belly gave a deep and lovely twist, releasing a flood of heat through her veins.

Damn him for ruining her resolve to remain cool and emotionless. Damn him for appearing just as she managed to stop wishing for him. Damn him for staring at her now as if she were a wicked enticement he wanted to consume in one swift bite.

Recognizing the fire in his gaze for what it was, Anne's body hummed in response and her steps faltered. When she should've swept fiercely and proudly past him, she felt herself slowing.

And then, without warning, his arm swept out to curl around her waist and he pulled her roughly against him. Her sketchbook and pencil fell unheeded to the dirt as she lifted her hands to grasp his upper arms. The heat and muscled hardness beneath her palms sent tingles to her fingertips. Lifting her gaze to meet his, she struggled to claim a breath, let alone find words to question his intention.

He peered intently back at her, as though frozen in indecision. Then his gaze swept over her face to settle harshly on her mouth. The need hardening his expression was akin to fury.

She barely managed to draw in a swift breath before he was kissing her. Deeply. Hungrily. With the fervor and recklessness of a man starving. She recognized the taste of wild desperation on his tongue. She felt it too.

She wrapped her arms tight around his neck and gave as much in the kiss as she received. With a heavy sound, he hauled her up against him, taking her off her feet. Sucking on her tongue—a growl rolling through his throat—he carried her into a stall and lowered her to a mound of hay. Still kissing her as though he'd claim the very breath from her body, his movements were rough and almost frantic as he shoved her skirts up and parted her thighs with his knee.

Anne was frantic too. She sunk her teeth into his lower lip as she grasped and tugged at his shoulders, arching her spine to press her breasts to his chest. She needed more of him. The weight of his body pressing down on her and force of his desire fueling her own. The hunger arcing through her was intense and demanding. It blasted through her uncertainty and her anger.

Or maybe it simply transformed her anger into another type of fury. Furious desire.

Just as she felt she might go mad without some relief, he was there.

His heat. His hardness. Thrusting into her melting core.

The ferocity. The desperation. The heavy sound of pleasure vibrating in his chest. The texture of his beard against her sensitive skin. It unfurled something inside her. A deep, unfettered frenzy of desire and need. A primal demand.

Her hands fisted in his hair as she claimed his full bottom lip with her teeth. Tilting her pelvis, she met every merciless thrust of his hips with a silent demand for more. Harder. Faster.

Answering her plea, he lowered his chest over her, his weight crushing her in the most satisfying way, as he slid both hands beneath her buttocks and lifted her to take the full punishing rhythm of his plunging cock.

She surrendered. Giving herself over to the power in his body and the strength of their shared passion. Almost instantly, her body tightened in anticipation. Her muscles tensed and her heart seemed to stop. She gasped for breath and clung to him as the first delicate flutters began. But they did not remain delicate for long. Her next inhale caught and held as pleasure erupted with a force that nearly stole her consciousness.

Only the sound of his weighty groan and the punishing grip of his fingers on her bottom kept her tethered to earth. To him. He gave a final heartbreaking thrust then tensed and his pleasure pulsed into her—hot and slick and unrelenting.

As her body softened and his grew heavier, she held him in a sated embrace, reveling in his closeness, in the sound of his breath steadily slowing and his heart beating raggedly against hers.

But she wasn't allowed to enjoy it for long. Before she was even close to being ready to release him, he shifted and abruptly shoved himself off of her.

The scents of hay and dirt and the essence of their lovemaking drifted around her as she slowly sat up. He was already standing, facing away from her as he closed his trousers. She could see the tension in his shoulders and what she hoped to God wasn't regret bowing his head.

Ignoring the moisture seeping from her body, she roughly tossed her skirts over her legs and rather gracelessly pulled herself up to stand. Bits of hay had gotten tangled in her hair and were poking her scalp, but she ignored them. Despite the ache in her chest, she stood calm and quiet as she waited to see what he'd do.

She wasn't asleep this time. Would he say something? Or just walk away?

Neither, it seemed, as the undeniable sound of children approaching forced a sudden end to the interlude.

He stiffened and glanced over his shoulder at her. The alarm in his fierce expression shifted swiftly to concern and then resolve as he took in her undoubtedly tousled appearance.

"I'll intercept them," he said gruffly as he tucked the tails of his shirt into his trousers.

Anne wanted desperately to argue. To insist he stay with her. To force him to acknowledge what had just happened.

But he was right. Now wasn't the time.

She gave a short nod and a moment later he was gone. As she heard his low baritone addressing the children, she quickly shook out her skirts then did her best to remove the hay from her hair. After ensuring Beynon was still keeping the children occupied, she scooped up her dropped sketchbook and pencil then slipped from the barn. She skirted the yard, then reentered the house and made her way to the bedroom, where she finally released the pent-up breath that had been straining her lungs.

From the window, she watched as Beynon strolled with his brothers and youngest sister toward the creek, fishing poles in hand. Her stomach twisted as she felt the same deep sadness she'd known as a girl when her father had ordered a footman to take her fishing rather than take her himself.

———— ∿ ————

THAT EVENING, BEYNON—UNFORTUNATELY shaven once again—surprised them all by joining the family for their evening meal.

Anne wanted desperately to think it was an overture for her specifically. However, although he was pleasant and polite through the meal, most of his attention was directed toward his siblings. Only twice did Anne catch him watching her with that familiar brooding intensity. And as soon as the meal was over, he retreated to his study.

Though she tried her best to wait up for him, she fell asleep in the chair before the fire only to awaken again as he lifted her in his arms to carry her to bed. Still half-asleep, she reached for him when he would have left her there. Curling her hand around the back of his neck, she pulled him down to her and kissed him. He didn't resist, and at the first swipe of her tongue along his, he moaned roughly and settled his weight atop her.

The kisses were languid and long, keeping her in a semi-dreamlike state as his clothing seemed to melt away and her nightgown disappeared and they were suddenly, wonderfully naked. His mouth and hands seemed to be everywhere at once, igniting sparks of pleasure beneath her heating skin, teasing and tormenting with a gentleness she never would have expected from this man.

But she found she enjoyed the tenderness as much as the ferocity and she slipped easily into the pleasure he gave her. When he lifted off of her to lie on his side then pulled her back against him, she had a moment of confusion as she feared he might be ending the interlude before it had fully begun.

But then she felt his erection against her bottom as he splayed his hand low over her belly and tilted her pelvis back to receive him. He entered her from behind in a long, slow motion.

Once he was fully inside her, he curved his arm beneath her head and grasped her breast firmly in his hand. As his other hand slid between her thighs to caress the aching bud of her sex, he rocked in and out of her in short, deep thrusts that soon had her gasping and arching and shuddering in his arms.

She drifted to sleep still tucked into the curve of his body.

By morning, he was gone.

And so, a new routine began.

Though Beynon continued to occupy himself away from the house throughout the day, he did start joining the family for dinner almost every night. Anne was initially surprised by how relaxed and easy his demeanor could be when he interacted with his mother and siblings. It was a side of him she'd never seen before and it hurt to note that, in stark contrast, his manner toward her remained stoic and distanced.

Even their lovemaking—for all its passion and ferocity—seemed to be restrained within certain invisible boundaries he'd constructed, then failed to explain the rules to her.

It felt as though he was intentionally keeping as much distance between them as possible, only giving in to his lustful nature when he was overcome despite himself.

Gratefully, the man was overcome rather frequently. Any time they happened to encounter each other while alone and free of possible observation or interruption, there was potential for a fiery mating.

Over the span of several days, they made love in the tall grass that grew along the creek, against a great ancient oak in an overgrown pasture, in the hallway leading down to the kitchen late one night, and twice more in the privacy of their bed.

Beynon was utterly insatiable. And Anne suspected she might actually be even more so.

However, although it was exciting and immensely pleasurable to experience all the ways they were learning to find pleasure in each other, Anne's frustration and sadness continued to grow.

It simply wasn't enough.

She wanted more from Beynon. She wanted to walk with him over the fields and pastures. She wanted to ride side by side to the village. She wanted to talk in intimate whispers as they lay in bed together. She wanted him to share his hopes and dreams for the farm and the future. *Their* future as husband and wife.

The few times she'd tried to speak of such things, he'd quickly change the subject or make some excuse to walk away. So, she'd stopped trying in fear it would only push him further away. But, considering the virtual chasm currently between them, she was starting to feel like she truly had nothing to lose.

Chapter Thirty-two

Beynon was doing his damnedest to avoid her. To avoid the unbelievable satisfaction of having her in his home, his bedroom, his *bed*. He exhausted himself every day and locked himself in his study until the earliest hours of morning in his determination to stay away from her.

Yet with each day—and night—that passed, it was becoming more and more apparent that, when it came to Anne, he had absolutely no command of his baser needs—and the emotions that fueled them. Despite his best efforts, it took very little—a sideways glance, a light touch, a gentle smile—and an instinct to claim her as his own took over all rational thought.

And why shouldn't he take pleasure in his wife's bold caresses and deep sighs and sultry moans?

Because he feared she'd hate him for it.

He'd seen firsthand the unfairness and cruelty of a society that held women accountable for the selfish behaviors of men who betrayed them. And he'd sworn to himself he'd never treat a woman so carelessly.

He'd already failed in that with Anne when he'd made her his wife.

Though she often reached for him in their bed and uttered quiet pleading words that so easily broke his resolve, he knew she could easily come to regret her desire for him.

And he didn't think he'd be able to bear it when she eventually looked at him and saw nothing but the man who'd ruined her, trapped her into marriage, and taken her away from a life of privilege in London to one of rural domestication.

So, he stubbornly continued trying to keep his distance. And failed more frequently than he succeeded. He was starting to fear he'd never be able to stay away from her—that he didn't have the strength required to protect her from himself.

Earlier in the day, he'd caught a distant glimpse of his wife running playfully with Carys through one of the pastures near the house. Her pale hair had slipped from its pins and fell in a reckless tangle down her back. Though he couldn't see her flashing smile at such a distance, he'd heard her laughter—a sound so light and lovely it had pierced his chest like a golden-tipped arrow.

Her happiness was a pleasure and a pain at once. He was warmed by the sight of her frolicking with such a careless freedom. But he was fully aware that she'd never shown such lightness of being while in his company.

Angry with himself and frustrated by the very walls he'd forced between them, he stayed away from the house, missing dinner for the first time in several days. When he finally crept into his home, all was quiet, suggesting everyone had retired. Still, he knew he couldn't go up to bed just yet.

He feared she'd be waiting up for him as she'd been doing lately. Her stubbornness was proving to be a fair rival to his own. And if he saw her now, he wasn't entirely certain he'd be able to maintain the façade he'd been wearing for so long. His heart felt too heavy and his throat ached with so many things he'd never say.

He turned instead toward his study, fully acknowledging his cowardice.

As soon as he opened the door to his private sanctuary, he knew she was there.

Her presence overwhelmed the space. Her gentle scent. Her warmth.

His body responded instantly. Heating. Hardening. Tensing in a desperate bid to keep his emptions buried within.

She stood in front of his desk with her back to the door as her fingers trailed lightly over the ink stand. She looked so slight in her pale pink nightrobe cinched tight around her waist. Bare feet peeked from beneath the hem and her pale hair fell in soft waves down her back to lightly brush the rounded curve of her bottom.

Beynon's heart tumbled to a hard stop. His hands curled into fists. And his blood roared through his veins.

She'd come to him—sought him out in this small cave of a room. Awaited him like a sensual snare.

He should've known she'd do it eventually.

He *had* known it. It was exactly what he'd been trying to prevent.

Whether he made some sound or she simply felt his presence, she gave a subtle start and looked over her shoulder at him. Her lips were a perfect tint of rose and her eyes were rich and turbulent in the candlelight. He could see the determination in the set of her chin. The pride and the disappointment.

Whatever she'd come here to say, he wasn't ready to hear it. So, he stopped her in the only way he knew how. Closing the distance between them, he swept his arm around her middle before she managed to turn around. She melted against him. Her sigh was husky and her head fell back against his shoulder as her lashes lowered over her gaze.

She always responded so beautifully to him. Her surrender only a brief precursor to the passion and hunger that quickly followed.

Desperate to feel her skin beneath his lips, he swept her hair to the side and set his mouth to the side of her neck. He sucked her silken flesh against his teeth, drawing it in sharply enough to cause her to flinch before he laved the tender spot with his tongue.

The softness of her buttocks cradled his throbbing cock and he couldn't stop himself from rocking against her.

Her moan nearly killed him.

Tightening his arm around her, he stepped her forward, until her upper thighs bumped against the edge of his desk. Trailing his lips over her nape, he palmed one of her perfect breasts. The firm peak of her nipple burned his palm as she arched her back and pressed her bottom more firmly against him.

Any thoughts of retaining control of the need roaring through him had fled the second he'd seen her there. Nothing in the world could keep him from touching her, kissing her, consuming her.

When she tried to turn in his arms and lift her mouth to his, he stopped her with a low growling sound of denial. Then he wrapped his fingers around her wrists and pressed her hands flat to the top of the desk. She whimpered softly, but when he urged her hands farther along the desktop, forcing her to bend forward, she did not resist.

With a final biting kiss to the side of her throat, he grasped the material of her robe and nightgown and swept it up to her hips, baring her gorgeous legs and shapely arse. Holding the material there with a hand pressed to the dip of her lower spine, he dropped to his knees behind her.

As his warm, heavy breath bathed the creamy nakedness of her perfect bottom, her thighs trembled. And Beynon's stomach twisted with delicious hunger.

After ensuring her skirts would stay up and out of the way, he smoothed his hands down to the delicate bones of her ankles then back up to the crease beneath her buttocks, where his thumbs rested, holding her still as he leaned forward to press a kiss to the center of first one warm cheek then the other.

Her gasps were short, desperate sounds. He could feel the anticipation vibrating through her body. He could smell it—musky and sweet.

Reaching up, he pressed his hand to her back again, urging her to bend more fully over the desk. After just a second of hesitation, she did so. The deeper position tilted her hips and exposed the deep rose of her luscious folds.

Beynon's breath stopped and his blood thundered. With shaking hands, he urged her to widen her stance. She made a soft sound of question, but she did as he wanted.

She was gorgeous. Glistening and dusky pink.

Massaging her trembling thighs, he leaned forward to place a kiss first to the very base of her spine. Then he dipped his head and gave a suckling kiss to the soft flesh of her inner thigh. The sounds she made deep in her throat slipped through him like liquid desire—thick, sultry, and full of promise.

Unable to deny himself any longer, he grasped the full flesh of her hips in both hands and sealed his open mouth to her sex.

Her body jolted at the first feel of his tongue along her flesh. His next lick slipped deeper between the folds as he sought the source of her honeyed desire. As her knees threatened to buckle, he tightened his grip, holding her firmly against the edge of the desk, using his tongue to soften her flesh and tease her to a heightened sensitivity. Then he suckled and nipped at the satiny folds of her sex, leaving nothing untouched. He tended to her swollen little bud with teasing flicks that quickened her breath before he stiffened his tongue and thrust it into her heated core.

And finally, when her body shook and bucked with every thrust of his tongue and his cock ached with the need to be buried within her, he gave one last sucking kiss to her clit. The cry she released was thick with pleasure and it nearly broke him.

Rising to his feet, he held her in place with one hand on her low back while he opened his breeches with the other. As soon as his cock was freed, he guided it into her ready body. Her hot, wet channel gripped him, holding him as a faint fluttering began in her inner muscles.

She was going to climax. And he wasn't far behind.

He withdrew swiftly and plunged forward again. Then once more, before she gave a soft cry and tensed sharply beneath him. Slowing his thrusts to a deep, gentle rocking, he guided her through the pulsing rhythm of her release until her body softened and a deep sigh emptied her lungs. Then he pulled himself slowly free of her grasping sheath, until just the tip of him kissed her opening.

He took a breath there, trying to slow his heart rate, trying to convince himself he was still in control.

But the woman wouldn't allow it.

With a deliberate tip of her pelvis and a quick push back, she reclaimed him and he was lost. A guttural groan escaped through his clenched teeth as he plunged forward once again. The climax he'd been trying to resist tore through him like an explosion. No corner of his existence was left untouched as pleasure destroyed everything in its path as his body shuddered through the release.

When awareness finally returned, he looked down to see his hands gripping hard enough to her hips they'd likely leave bruises. Her legs shook against his thighs as she remained bent over his desk. Her hands were curled tightly around the far edge and her pale blonde hair lay in a tangle around her. He could see a fine sheen of sweat on her face and her breath came fast. Teeth marks were evident in the soft cushion of her bottom lip.

Though he would have liked to stay buried in her warmth for all eternity, he forced himself to withdraw from her body.

Her soft whimper had him cursing himself for his roughness.

If he'd hurt her in his passion, he'd never forgive himself. But as soon as he left her, she tried to push her hips back toward him again, as though she regretted his absence.

Beynon quickly pulled a handkerchief from the pocket of his coat and wiped away the moisture from between her thighs. As he tucked himself back into his breeches, she slowly straightened. But her knees wobbled and she swayed as her skirts fell to cover her legs.

Though touching her again would be a torturous test to his endurance, he took her waist in his hands anyway. Steadying her as she turned to face him. An insistent voice in his head shouted a warning not to look into her face, but he couldn't heed it.

The rich, swirling color of her bold feminine stare stopped his breath.

There was so much intensity there. So much power and certainty. And though he could see the storm building in the blue and green, could see the sparks illuminating her gaze, he didn't release her.

With her legs still shaking, she leaned her hips back against the desk and braced her hands on either side. But the angle of her chin as she looked up at him was confident and full of pride. There was also an unmistakable hint of accusation in her eyes.

"We must discuss this, Beynon."

Her voice was firm and her words instantly filled him with dread. The sensation was stark and painful after the intense pleasure he'd just experienced and everything in him rebelled.

He took a step back, lowering his hands to his sides. "It's late. We can talk tomorrow."

"No," she stated sharply as she pushed away from the desk and straightened to her full, impressive height, forcing him to take a step back. "We'll talk right now."

Squaring his shoulders, Beynon gave her a heavy scowl as he crossed his arms over his chest. "I'm in no mood to hear your grievances tonight."

Her eyes widened as she blinked hard, twice. "No mood? Grievances? Are you serious?" The incredulity in her tone was only eclipsed by the sharp wave of rising fury. "If you keep insisting on avoiding this, we're never going to make it through the rest our lives together."

Unable to remain so close to her, he turned and paced to a safer distance before turning back to face her. Her ethereal loveliness struck him silent for a moment. But it was the look of fire and determination in her stare that made his heart tumble heavily into his stomach.

His admiration for her in that moment knew no limits.

"What is there to say?" he asked harshly. The raw nature of his voice was impossible to disguise, but he was grateful as it made him sound more frustrated than terrified. "We both knew we were a wretched match. I thought you'd resigned yourself to it—that you knew what to expect in this marriage."

She licked her lips and her tongue paused over the tender spot where she'd bitten into her lower lip only moments ago while in the throes of passion. Then her eyes narrowed and she took a steadying breath.

"This is what it's to be then?" Her question was raw and abrupt. "Lust and nothing more."

Beynon's stomach gave a violent lurch. He forced himself to ignore the sharp pain angling through his chest in order to grumble a response. "What else could there possibly be?"

He barely finished speaking before she retorted sharply, "A great deal."

She stalked toward him—closing the distance he'd only just created between them. When he looked into her eyes, a sudden rush of trepidation claimed him. He hardened himself against the reaction. Against her strength. Against his own damned heart.

"But you insist on denying me," she noted in a hard tone he'd never heard from her before. It chilled him.

Her intent gaze swept over his features, then lowered to the last couple inches separating them. "So be it," she muttered. There was an odd finality to her voice. "I spent far too many years of my life accepting the paltry courtesies my father deigned to grace me with, if he thought of me at all. It took a long time for me to believe I was worthy of more." She lifted her chin with fierce pride. "I *deserve* more, Beynon."

Her words twisted through him with wrenching effect—tearing at his heart, making his throat burn. It was exactly what he'd been saying to himself from the moment he met her. And now she'd accepted it as well. And just as he'd feared, she hated him for it.

With a sad shake of her head, she stepped around him. He was unable to stop himself from watching her graceful form as she reached the door he hadn't even closed behind him upon entering. When she turned back to him then, she looked every inch the fairy queen he'd always suspected she was. Dressed in the palest pink, her starlight hair falling wild and untamed, her lips rosy and full, and her eyes so piercing they cut to his core like a dagger.

But then, suddenly and inexplicably, her eyes softened with the glisten of moisture.

"I would have given you everything," she whispered.

His body tensed to stone. It was the only way he kept himself from to charging after her as she slipped into the darkness of the hall.

It was a long time before he managed to shuffle across the room to drop heavily into his desk chair. He didn't sleep at all that night. At the first light of dawn, he went for a walk. A long walk. But the familiar hills and vales did not comfort him as they so often did.

With every footfall, his wife's parting words and the finality in her tone echoed relentlessly through his mind.

I would have given you everything.

What could she possibly have meant by that? She'd already sacrificed so much. Her dowry. Her life in London. Her expectations for the future.

I would have given you everything.

He couldn't possibly hope for anything more.

But even as he had that thought, his heart clenched with longing for the one thing he'd never given himself permission to want. And for just a moment, he gave in to that feeling. He allowed the hope and yearning free rein inside him and finally acknowledged the one thing he wanted more than anything else.

I would have given you everything.

With the sudden shock of understanding came a wave of gut-wrenching remorse for the damage he'd wrought in his ignorance and pride. But when he rushed home, desperate to confess the heavy truth of all he was feeling and beg for her understanding and forgiveness, Anne was gone.

Chapter Thirty-three

"**G**o talk to her."

Beynon looked up to see his mother standing in the study doorway. Her hands were fisted on her hips and her expression was one he remembered well from the days of his youth when he'd done something particularly disappointing.

"No," he replied solemnly as he looked back down to the ledger he was updating.

His mother made a sound of deep annoyance and stalked into the room. "Don't be an arse about this, Beynon. It's been long enough."

Seventeen days.

With as fierce a scowl as he'd ever given anyone, he met his mother's stubborn stare. "She is the one who left."

After the night in his study, once he'd worked through his devastation at learning she'd left him, he'd quickly gone in search of her, fearing she might be hurt or lost. But he'd discovered instead she was quite all right. She'd sold a couple of her finest gowns and a jeweled necklace to a peddler and used the funds to rent a cottage in the village.

"If she'd been happy here," he grumbled, "she'd have stayed."

Glynnis rolled her eyes and threw up her hands. "You're right, she was miserable here. And what do you suppose was the cause of that? I'd really hoped you'd come around on your own, but it seems you'd rather continue being an idiot."

Beynon barely resisted the urge to growl. "What do you want from me, Mam? I knew she wouldn't find happiness here. It was hopeless from the start. I did the best I could."

"Did you?" His mother's voice was curt. "What exactly did you do to help her become accustomed to life as your wife? Did you...show her around the farm? No. The boys did that. Did you explain the rhythms of our work and what was expected each day, each season, each year? No. I did that. Did you help her to find her place in the household? No. That was Eirwyn."

Beynon held his hand up. A sick feeling was churning in his stomach. "I get your point, Mam. But you don't know what her life was like—what I took her from. How could she ever find contentment as a farmer's wife?"

"I did."

"She's nothing like you."

His mother tilted her head and gave a glare. "Don't you remember what a disaster I was those first years we lived here? My father had been a butcher. The only experience I had with animals was how to handle their carcasses. I was lucky Cedric loved me as much as he did. He'd had every right to annul the marriage more than once. I was a *terrible* farmer's wife."

Beynon stared at her. Disbelief running through him.

"Without your stepfather's infinite patience and unconditional love, I never would've found my home here."

He'd had no idea. Thinking back to those early years, he realized he'd been so wrapped up in his own emotions and struggles, he'd never noticed his mother going through the same.

"I'm starting to wonder if you know your wife at all. Anne is far more capable than you might believe."

Shame rushed through him. He'd hated how others always seemed to underestimate Anne. Yet he'd done the exact same thing. And he did know better.

"Your wife was unhappy here, so she went to find her own contentment. And from what I've seen, she's turned that little cottage into a lovely home."

Beynon clenched his teeth. "You went to see her?"

"Of course. Several times, in fact, as have the children, which you'd know if you bothered to peek your head out of this room. But my point is...she deserves more. You both do."

"You don't understand," he muttered.

"Bullocks." His mother stepped around the desk and took his face in her hands. "If there's one thing I know about you," she continued forcefully, "it's when you're fighting your feelings. Your emotions have always been written all over your face. Even your darkest glowers can't hide them," she added with a flicker of a smile and brusque pat on the cheeks. "You love her. So much it hurts you. Go after her, Beynon."

He closed his eyes as an icy wash of regret flowed through him. "It doesn't matter, Mam. She's better off without me."

Releasing his face, his mother took a step back. Her hands returned to her hips. "How do you know? Have you asked her? Have you told her how *you* feel?"

He'd intended to...right before he'd discovered she'd left him. He'd never felt pain like he had when he'd realized she was gone. It had torn through him like a winter storm, chilling him to the bone.

Glynnis made another exasperated sound. "Why do you think she only went as far as the village?"

He gave a heavy shake of his head. "Her friends are probably on their way to come get her even now."

"She let the cottage for a full year, Beynon," his mother said softly.

A year? So, she wasn't intending to leave? Why?

Rising to his feet, he crossed to the window. Could there still be hope? Without turning around, he asked in a low voice, "What if she doesn't want me?"

"Then you'll do what you've always done."

He glanced over his shoulder, brows drawn in question.

His mother grinned. "You'll fight."

BEYNON DECIDED TO WALK to the village. It wasn't a short distance, but he needed the physical exertion to tame the chaotic energy inside him and the time to think through what he'd say to Anne. Even after taking a detour to pace back and forth in an open pasture, he still didn't have the right words. But as twilight started to fall and he realized he'd be walking home in full dark at this rate, he charged into the village with a stern, if not slightly terrified, determination.

His mother had told him Anne was staying in a tiny cottage set back from the main road within a cluster of ancient oaks. As he turned up the footpath and started toward the tiny stone house, he struggled to believe this was where Anne had been staying for the last three weeks.

It was little more than a hut.

The roof needed rethatching before winter and most of the shutters were warped, loose, or missing altogether. Vines grew up the walls and chimney and the old picket fence barely held back the riot of flowers overflowing the front path.

It was a far cry from the grand estates she was used to.

She'd been comfortable enough at Gwaynynog.

Comfortable but unhappy.

Because of you!

He was still struggling to reconcile everything his mother had said. The hope that had taken root inside him warred with the fear that it might be far too late.

But he was here now. Standing in front of her door. If he left...he'd never know if there was anything to hope for.

Reaching the cottage door, he gave a solid knock that seemed to echo in the silent approach of night.

When there was no answer and no suggestion of movement within, he knocked again.

Silence.

As concern started to overcome his nerves, he glanced around. The cottage was quite a distance from any neighbors. If anything had happened to Anne, no one would know.

Gripped by a sudden fear, he pounded more forcefully on the door.

"Back here," Anne called out. The words coming from behind the house.

Hearing her voice after so long sent an immediate rush of warmth and tension through Beynon's body. His relief that she was all right was quickly overcome by the acknowledgement that he still hadn't the slightest idea what to say to her.

Another glance around revealed a stone footpath nearly completely covered by moss. As he started around the house, he noticed a large patch of upright Amaranthus just off the path. On impulse, he gathered a handful of the deep red flowers in a makeshift bouquet.

His stomach in knots, he continued along the path. The back garden was just as riotous as the front. Flowers growing in no particular plan, falling over each other and keeping Anne from view until he was almost upon her.

When he did finally see her, his feet and his heart stopped at once.

She sat partially turned away from him on a blanket spread over a tiny patch of grass. She wore a shawl around her shoulders and her hair was styled in a simple chignon at the back of her head with gentle wisps brushing her cheeks. The quickly fading light of day reached her on a low slant, giving an almost unnatural glow to her skin. Her paint box and a small easel were set up beside her as she gazed toward a mixed bed of aster and salvia. She was clearly very focused on the stunning watercolor she was creating and didn't turn around to greet him right away.

Beynon was grateful as it gave him a moment to soak in the sight of her and calm his riotous emotions. It was only another moment, however, before she glanced over her shoulder with a questioning lift of her brows.

Her eyes widened. "Beynon."

His name was a sigh and a question at once. The sound of it made his hands fist and nearly destroy the flowers he held as an achy heaviness settled behind his sternum. He couldn't bring himself to walk toward her—not trusting his ability to resist the fierce urge to haul her in against him. But when she started to rise, he shook his head. "No need," he muttered.

She hesitated a moment, a slight frown tugging at her brows, but she settled back on the grass, her paintbrush still held tightly in her fingers.

He couldn't approach her but he couldn't stand still either. So, he turned and started forging a gentle path through the shrubs and bushes and plots of randomly mixed flowers. He could feel her watching him, focused and slightly wary.

She didn't seem angry to see him. But she wasn't elated, either.

It became clear that she wasn't going to speak first, so when he reached a dead end at a trellis covered in climbing honeysuckle, he turned around.

His mouth went dry and his heart raced as he tucked the handful of Amaranthus behind his back.

Don't muck this up.

Caillie's words remembered from weeks ago were not exactly the vote of confidence he would have preferred at that moment, but at least they managed to loosen his heavy tongue.

"You look well," he muttered.

She stared at him silently for a moment, then gave a light sigh before replying, "As do you. You grew a beard again."

He lifted a hand to self-consciously brush his knuckles along his jaw. "I did."

Her reply was barely above a whisper. "I like it."

The small talk was unbearable. He wanted to rush toward her and drop to his knees and pull her into his arms. He wanted to fill his lungs with her scent and steal her taste with his tongue.

Instead, he scowled.

And she scowled back. "Why are you here, Beynon?"

His throat closed as he looked at her—really looked at her.

She was so beautiful. So confident and strong and proud.

The overgrown garden surrounding an aging but quaint cottage suited her. The sunset and the soft grass and the light breeze that teased the pale wisps of hair falling against her cheeks suited her. The quiet yet undeniable self-assurance in her expression and the glint of challenge in her eyes also suited her.

But damnit, his kisses suited her, too. As much as the soft, pleading sighs she issued while in his arms and the husky little moans that told him she was close. And her smiles when she frolicked with Carys or spoke in animated conversation with Eirwyn. And her laughter when the boys competed with each other to impress her.

"Are you going to stand there and glare at me all evening, Beynon, or do you have something to say?"

He couldn't tell for certain, but he thought he detected a hint of amusement threading through the annoyance in her tone.

He met her steady gaze. What he wanted to say was, *Come home with me.* But he changed his mind at the last moment to ask instead, "Are you happy here?"

She blinked as she tended to do when surprised—a habit that had always charmed him. "You want to know if I'm happy?" He nodded. "*Here* at the cottage?" she asked. "Or *here* in Wales?"

Beynon wasn't sure. His heart thundered heavily against his ribs and his hands clenched into fists. He wanted to pace again and could feel his brows drawing lower as his frown deepened.

Yet she remained calmly seated on the blanket, looking up at him with a quiet but insistent expectancy.

Fuck.

He had to stop being such a coward.

He took a step toward her and she gave a subtle flinch. He stopped, scowled, and took one more step. She was still well out of his reach, but now he could see the swirl of green and blue in her eyes.

"Are you happy...as my wife?"

The words sounded rough and ragged as they forced their way past a tight throat. He held his breath, waiting for her answer.

It came quickly. Immediately, in fact.

"No."

Beynon's heart plummeted.

For a moment, he couldn't speak as a wave of pain and anger and fear overwhelmed him. When his temper rose in such a way—when his emotions grew too intense for him to manage—he'd learned to clench his teeth and walk away or risk losing control.

Every muscle in his body tensed as his brain directed it to turn and leave her there in the twilight glow of the garden. To accept her rejection silently—regardless of the pain tearing through him—and acknowledge that he'd been right all along. They didn't belong together.

But as he prepared himself to do all that, he recalled his mother's words.

He had to fight.

Not with fists or fury. But with the truth.

As he looked into his wife's eyes, he understood. The fight he had to wage was against his pride. And his assumptions and prejudices and his own damned fears of never being good enough.

Stepping forward, he extended his fist holding the Amaranthus. "For you."

Her eyes widened again as she reached up to take his impulsive gift. But then she brought the flowers in against her chest and lowered her chin and he could no longer read her expression. His voice was heavy and raw. "Come back with me."

She took a visible breath, the inhale lifting and lowering her shoulders. Then she turned to set her paintbrush and the handful of flowers atop her box and gracefully rose to her feet. Brushing the wrinkles from her skirts, she squared herself to face him. "Why should I?"

The woman never made anything easy for him. He furrowed his brow. "It's where you belong."

She seemed to stiffen. Her gaze dropped for a second before she forced it up again with a strong, jutting chin. "Is it, though? By what evidence? Was it the many nights I fell asleep alone in our marriage bed? Or was it how my husband made it abundantly clear he had no wish to welcome me into his life? Perhaps it was the regret I saw in your eyes whenever your desire was sated."

Beynon's heart felt like a stone in his chest. He wanted to dispute her words, but he couldn't force any sound around the lump filling his throat as she asked in a choked whisper, "Is there something so very wrong with me?"

A bone-deep anguish unlike anything he'd ever known before gripped him. "No. You're perfect."

The words were barely audible and all he could manage.

Her eyes brightened with a suspicious glimmer. "Then why am I always so easily forsaken? Why did my father see me as so unworthy of his time and...affection that he did all he could to forget I existed? And why, no matter how hard and how long I've loved you, have I failed so miserably to earn your love in return?"

As the last words left her lips, a tear slid down her cheek. And though she wrapped her arms around her middle and frantically shook her head to keep him away, Beynon pulled her against him. With an arm strong around her back and one hand palming her head, he tucked her into his warmth and pressed his lips to her temple. Though her sobs were silent, her body shuddered with a sadness and loneliness *he* had caused.

Never again. From this moment forward, he'd demonstrate his love for her at every opportunity so she'd never doubt it or him again.

When her trembling ceased and her breath slowed, he carefully loosened his arms. Lifting his hands to frame her face, he tipped her head back so he could meet the brilliance and depth of her gaze. A truth he should have uttered ages ago tumbled roughly from his lips, "You are perfect in every way imaginable. I bloody love you. I adore you. I admire and revere you." His lips tilted awkwardly. "I might even be a little afraid of you. But only because I value your regard so deeply and I'm terrified of how short I must fall. It's *I* who is lacking. I've never been good enough for you and I knew it from the second I saw you. Everything about you was an enticement I couldn't allow myself to crave. I constantly reminded myself of the great chasm between your existence and mine so I wouldn't be tempted by false hope." He paused to scowl. "I may have done too good a job of it. But the truth is...the message in the flowers I chose that day were more honest than I was. Already, I'd developed a secret affection for my partner. One that's true and constant."

She tensed, her gorgeous eyes blinking rapidly. "You discovered the meaning of the flowers?"

He nodded and her attention instantly shifted to where the Amaranthus lay on her paint box.

"Unfading love," he muttered, "for you. Forever. If you'll allow me another chance. I can be boorish and coarse. I'm no good at social niceties and I honestly don't enjoy the company of most people. But I work hard for my family and I'll work thrice as hard to make you happy at Gwaynynog."

As she slipped her slim arms around his waist, he dared to release some of the tension in his spine. Yet her gaze was serious as it held his.

"I love you, Beynon, with all my heart. But I'll not be shoved aside and ignored. Never again."

His arms tightened around her. "You've no idea how sorry I am. I thought I was protecting you, but I was really just guarding myself. I was certain you'd come to hate me. I couldn't imagine you'd ever truly want me. Not in the way I wanted you."

She sighed and lifted her arms to loop them around his neck. "I want you, Beynon. I want to share a life with you. I want to talk about things—the important and the mundane. I want to go on walks together and share our dreams for the future." Her cheeks pinkened and her lashes fluttered. But she held his gaze. "A few words of love every now and then might also be quite nice."

He groaned roughly as he looped one arm around her waist and brought his other hand to warmly squeeze her nape. Lowering his head until his lips hovered just over hers, he murmured every phrase of love, devotion, and desire he knew.

In Welsh. In English. In a mixture of them both.

Until her gaze sparkled then darkened with passion. Until her warm sigh bathed his lips before she stopped his words with the firm press of her mouth to his.

The kiss was instantly heated. They'd been so long apart and the passion between had only grown in the separation. Within moments, they were tumbling back down to the blanket, frantic in their efforts to remove each other's clothing. He succeeded first and immediately became mesmerized by the glow of the rising moon on her skin and the way the awakening stars reflected so brightly in her eyes.

He was awed and frightened.

He didn't want to muck this up. He *couldn't*. Losing her was simply not an option.

"Beynon."

His name on her lips was a plea and sigh. A sound of contentment and need.

Suddenly frantic once again, he shoved away the rest of his clothing. But before he could lower himself between her thighs, she pressed her hand firmly to his chest. With anticipation glinting sharply in her eyes and a smile that could entice the surliest of devils, she urged him to lie back on the ground as she rose up to straddle his hips.

With a shock of pleasure so deep and moving it stopped his breath, he realized her intent. Though he grabbed her hips firmly in his large hands, she had all the power and control as she lowered herself along his aching length. Once in possession of him, she began to move. The sight of her atop him was enchanting and magnificent. Her pale hair slipped free of its pins to tumble in moon-kissed waves over her shoulders while she made love to him with slow undulations that rolled through her body like a dance.

Emotion surged through him, making his teeth ache and his chest feel full to bursting as he became fully entranced by her deep and turbulent gaze, willingly surrendering to all the magic of her.

Chapter Thirty-four

The days leading up to Michaelmas were a flurry of activity.

All around Denbighshire, people gathered to help their neighbors and friends with their final harvests of the year. Flocks were brought down from the mountains to lower pastures where they'd be sheared one last time before colder weather set in, grains and produce were gathered, and the last blackberries of the season were baked into pies.

In the first couple days after Anne returned to Gwaynynog with Beynon, they were essentially inseparable. He took her around to his favorite places on the farm and talked hesitantly at first about how difficult it had initially been for him to accept the new life he was expected to live when his mother married Cedric Thomas and moved them from the village to the farm.

Anne could hear the respect and near reverence in his tone as he spoke of the man who'd seen more in him than he'd ever seen in himself. The man who'd trusted him with his legacy. She could also hear the grief and Beynon's firm determination to make his stepfather proud by continuing to improve and grow their flock so it could one day be passed on to the next generation.

The thought of having Beynon's children filled Anne with an instant wealth of warmth and tenderness. A feeling that multiplied when Beynon turned to her with a heavy scowl.

"Though I want nothing more than to father countless children with you, there are things we can do to prevent conception if that's your wish." His voice lowered to a rough murmur. "I'll never again take away your ability to choose the path of your own life as I did with our marriage. I wish to be an equal partner to you, blodyn, in all things."

Overwhelmed, Anne had thrown herself into his embrace, wrapping her arms around his neck as she tucked her face into that enticing hollow beneath his jaw. Pressing her lips to his pulse, she whispered, "I'd love to have your children."

The sound he made in response had been deep and primitive and visceral. Then he'd kissed her until the world spun around them.

But those two days of blissful connection were short-lived as Beynon gave her a deep kiss one morning before taking his brothers with him to assist their neighbors in the late summer harvest. Carys cried about being left behind until he promised she'd be able to join them when she was a bit older and a bit stronger. While he was gone, Glynnis, Eirwyn, and Anne dove into preparations for the Michaelmas celebration which was to take place at Gwaynynog once the season's labor was finished.

There were giant loaves of bread to bake, and pies, and shearing cakes known as Cacen Gneifo. And it couldn't be a Michaelmas feast without a fatted goose or two or three. Anne was surprised by how much she enjoyed the seemingly never-ending kitchen work. Especially once she discovered the delightfully bawdy comradery that developed amongst women when they gathered around a large worktable in a room heated by a constantly glowing oven and kneaded dough until their muscles ached.

On the morning of the fourth day after Beynon left, a cacophony of sound interrupted the women as they set another batch of bread to rise. Anne had never heard such a clatter and couldn't imagine what the cause of the noise could be.

Eirwyn, however, grinned with delight as she hastily wiped her hands in her apron. "They're back!"

Anne's heart leapt as she glanced to Glynnis. With a warm smile, the older woman waved Anne away. "Go on and welcome your man home. I'll finish up here."

"Thank you," Anne breathed as she flew from the kitchen close on Eirwyn's heels.

Stopping beside the girl, she raised her hand to shield her eyes from the shining sun and watched in awe as a river of thick, wool-covered sheep poured down the mountain pass into the valley. She could see Aron, Daryn, and Edwyn leading the charge toward the shearing yards as dogs circled the flock to keep it contained. Half a dozen men walked with the livestock. Their shouts and laughter could be heard even above the sound of bleating sheep and countless hooves clattering on the rocky hillside.

Where was Beynon?

Anne's chest began to ache, telling her she'd been holding her breath. Forcing herself to exhale, she scanned the men again.

And then she saw him.

Walking at the rear of the flock, he carried a large sheep across his shoulders. Just as the other men, he wore no coat due to the warmth of the day and his shirtsleeves were rolled to his elbows. Even at the distance, Anne could see the flash of his grin standing out within his dark beard.

A thrill swept through her to settle with a fierce flutter in her low belly.

He was devastating.

Not only because his masculine strength and rugged handsomeness were so strikingly apparent in that moment, but also because Anne could see the pride in his stride and the depth of his happiness. She couldn't help but grin widely in response.

And it was then that his gaze found her.

Her body tingled with sparks and her heart gave a mad leap. Even though his expression shifted swiftly from easy joy to something dark and anticipatory, Anne's happiness didn't waver. Because as his piercing gaze held hers, she felt something flowing right through her very soul. So deep it felt intrinsic to her very existence.

Heart-stirring, sizzling-hot connection.

Though Eirwyn rushed forward to meet them all at the yards, the weight of emotion claiming Anne in that moment kept her rooted in place. There was simply too much to process.

As though sensing her disquiet, Beynon quickly lowered his burden to the ground, then skirted around the remaining flock to head toward her in ground-eating strides.

Each step he took shortened her breath and fired her blood.

By the time he reached her, she'd gotten herself worked up to a state of near madness. As he swooped her up into his arms, she grasped his broad, beautiful face in her hands and pressed her mouth to his in a gloriously wanton display of possession and desire.

A heavy groan vibrated his chest as he tilted his head to thrust his tongue demandingly past her lips. The taste of him was heady and rich, but the sound of whistles and laughter soon had her recalling that they weren't exactly alone. He ended the kiss with obvious reluctance but didn't set her away from him.

His black eyes glittered dangerously. "Later, blodyn, I'll demonstrate how much I've missed you. But there's still a great deal of work to be done before the sun sets."

Anne blushed as she lowered her hands to his shoulders. "Of course. I'm sorry..."

He growled deep and tightened his arms around her. "Never apologize for welcoming me home in such a way." He swallowed hard before grinning with another flash of teeth. "No doubt I'll set a new shearing record knowing you'll be awaiting me at the finish."

THE MICHAELMAS FEAST at Gwaynynog drew folks from all parts of Denbighshire. It was an event most people looked forward to all summer when the bounty of their various labors over the last several months was laid out in a feast to be enjoyed by all. It was a day of pride and appreciation. A time to honor the ending of one season and the start of another as the rhythms of life shifted from the fields to the hearth. The tradition to have the annual celebration at Gwaynynog versus the village had started with Cedric Thomas decades ago and no one really seemed to remember exactly why the decision had been made. But it was one of many things Beynon hoped to continue from his stepfather's legacy.

Standing in the doorway of the barn, Beynon took a moment to gaze out over the gathering.

A long table had been set in the yard and nearly overflowed with delectable foods of all sorts. Folks gathered in small groups on picnic blankets or perched along the slate walls. His mother was seated on the grass beside his oldest sister near the games, cheering on the younger Thomas children as they competed for a coveted bag of sweets. Glynnis had finally fully recovered from her illness and appeared as robust and hearty as ever. Beynon smiled as he witnessed Aron stopping in the midst of a footrace to help Carys back to her feet after the small girl took a tumble in her efforts to keep up with the older children. Carys's tears turned quickly to laughter when her brother hoisted her onto his back so they could finish the race in tandem.

It was a good day. The harvest had proven fruitful, and with the help of nearly a dozen others, the shearing yesterday had, in fact, been completed in record time. Beynon managing a personal best.

Not particularly surprising since every time he glanced up from the sheering bench, he caught sight of Anne watching him with her lips parted and her gaze sparkling with pride and admiration.

He'd have sheared the entire flock himself if it could've ensured she'd always look at him with such a dreamy, desirous look in her eyes.

As soon as the last shorn sheep had been rinsed in the creek and set out to pasture, Beynon hadn't cared who'd watched him as he swept his wife up into his arms and stalked into the house. Though he'd have taken her straight to bed, she had a steamy bath set up for him and insisted on taking the time to wash him from head to toe as he soaked away the aches of his labor.

The bath proved to be as much of a pleasure as what came after.

Beynon had watched with heavy-lidded eyes as Anne lovingly soaped and massaged his shoulders, back, and chest. By the time her hands dipped below the surface of the water, they were both breathless with anticipation. Her touch instantly dispelled any remaining physical tension or exhaustion. When he rose swiftly from the tub and tossed her onto the bed, her laughter slid swiftly into a low hum of appreciation as he lowered his wet body to cover hers.

Though he'd intended to shave before taking her, judging by her swift gasps and honeyed moans, she seemed to enjoy the texture of his beard as he nuzzled her neck, breasts, and inner thighs.

Just thinking of his homecoming last night had Beynon scanning the yard for his wife. He'd seen her only in brief glimpses throughout the day. Helping his mother and Eirwyn set out the feast, laughing over something Daryn said as he dangled from the branches of the apple tree, and striding alongside Carys as the girl skipped to the small pen where the youngest lambs were being kept.

Where was she now?

As his brows furrowed with an intense need to lay eyes on the woman who'd laid total claim on his heart and soul, he heard a loud whoop go up from a group of young men gathered off to one side. It took a moment for Beynon to see that they'd set up a makeshift archery target.

Beynon couldn't see through the small crowd to confirm who was shooting, but when he saw the next arrow fly to meet the first in the center of the target, he had a pretty good idea who it was.

When the third arrow joined the other two, there was another round of excited shouts and cheers. And as the group of men started to shift and Beynon caught sight of Anne glowing with unfiltered happiness, he feared his heart might beat right out of his chest.

How could he have gotten so damned lucky?

How could he possibly deserve a woman so perfect?

An old fear stabbed sharply through him. Maybe he wasn't worthy. Maybe this was nothing but a dream.

But then his wife's lovely gaze fell on him as he stood in the shadows of the barn. Her smile softened into something quiet meant only for him. Without a word, she handed her bow to the man beside her and started across the yard to Beynon. Her steps were long and graceful. Her bearing as elegant as ever. But there was also something undeniably new in her manner.

She seemed to move with an air of confidence and ease he hadn't witnessed in her before. In a simple dress of pale green and her fair hair twisted into a loose chignon, she embodied everything he could have hoped for in a wife.

His fairy queen.

His partner.

His love forever.

When she joined him in the shadows, he brought her into a snug embrace, loving the way she fit against him and how she tipped her head back to meet his dark stare. When her attention drifted down to his lips, a jolt of heat shot through his body at the smoldering hunger he saw in her eyes.

"How much longer until we can sneak away?" she murmured softly.

Beynon offered a grin. "I'm glad you asked." Taking her hand in his, he led her back through the barn and out to a side yard where a small wagon had been hitched to a horse. Grasping her waist in his hands, he lifted her up to the seat then hopped up beside her.

"What are you doing?" she asked with a short laugh of surprise.

Taking up the reins, Beynon gave a flick of his wrists and they started off. "I'm taking you away."

"What? Where?"

He slid her a heated sideways glance. "Our cottage."

"The cottage in the village? But I canceled my lease as soon as I left."

"And I renewed it." When she blinked in stunned confusion, he explained, "I thought it'd be nice to have a place we could go every now and then...just the two of us. Consider this a honeymoon of sorts."

Her eyes were wide. "But there will be so much to do after the celebration."

Beynon laughed. "I've already talked to Mam. She and the children will manage. The next several days are ours. No sheep, no children, no chores." The dark, heated look he gave her brought an instant flare of desire to her gaze. "Just us. Just pleasure."

Her reply was husky and breathless. "That sounds nice."

"Nice?" Beynon grunted. Dropping the reins, he scooped Anne up from her seat and lifted her onto his lap.

"Beynon, the horse!"

"Knows the way," he finished gruffly. Dragging her skirts up to her lap, he palmed the back of her thigh and gave a rough squeeze. "You, however, seem to have forgotten something. My love for you is infinite. My devotion, unquestionable." His voice dropped to a possessive growl. "But there is nothing even remotely *nice* about my passion for you."

Her lashes fluttered as her breath left her lips in a sigh. But when he slid his hand between her thighs to palm her heated core, the sigh turned swiftly to a weighted moan. With a roll of her hips, she pressed herself more firmly to his hand. Then she leaned toward him to press a trail of sweet kisses in the hollow beneath his jaw.

"You're right, husband. I might be in need of a steady dose of reminders."

Her tongue flicked against his pulse and a gravelly groan rose from his throat. He lifted a hand to cup her nape, tilting her face to his. The swirl of love and desire in her gorgeous gaze made his chest tighten with wonder and emotion.

"I'm yours, blodyn," he murmured thickly. "Have been from the moment I first saw you."

Looking deeply into his eyes, she whispered in perfect Welsh, "Dwi'n caru ti."

Contentment flowed through every vein as he brushed his lips over hers. "And I love you."

Epilogue

Four years later

F *our years later*
"I swear on me life, this is the dullest fucking party ye lot have dragged me to yet."

Beynon gave his half brother Max one of his darkest glares. "Watch your language. This isn't St. Giles."

"No shite," Max replied with a flashing grin before he downed what was left of the high-end brandy in his crystal snifter. "If it were, those two fine doves over there would be dancin' on the tables by now, their skirts flyin' about their ears, and I'd have a bottle of gin in me hand instead of this tiny glass—which is woefully empty, by the way."

"A moment ago, that tiny glass held some of the finest French brandy to be had," Roderick noted as he settled into the empty leather chair opposite Beynon. "And this party is for our sister's benefit, not yours."

"No doubt Caillie would agree with me," Max replied without an ounce of contrition.

Roderick turned toward Beynon, lifting his brow in question.

Beynon's response was a dark look which basically said Max was being as Max tended to be.

Difficult.

All of the prior Earl of Wright's children—legitimate and illegitimate—had gathered at the Wright family estate in Kent for a week-long party in celebration of Caillie's seventeenth birthday.

It was the first time in almost two years since Beynon and Anne had been back in England, and with the recent discovery that Anne was expecting their second child, it was likely they wouldn't be back again for some time. He'd hoped to make the most of this visit by really getting to know the brother who'd grown up in such a different world than himself.

But after several days in the young man's company, Beynon was forced to come to terms with the fact that Max—for all his ribald humor and brazen attitude—maintained a foot-thick stone wall between his half siblings and the more personal aspects of his life.

Though Roderick and Colin both had made significant efforts at bringing Max Owen more closely within the folds of their makeshift family, the mercurial young man continued to do only and exactly as he pleased, which seemed to change drastically depending on his mood at the moment.

Beynon scowled, noting how his younger brother's irreverent cockney thickened as he called out to a footman and gestured for more brandy. Max could easily disguise the rougher patterns of his speech when it suited it him. Apparently, it didn't suit him tonight.

Several hours later, as he and Anne lay snuggled in bed together after settling their daughter down to sleep in the room next door, Beynon contemplated the challenge that was Max Owen.

No doubt sensing the disquiet in him, Anne lifted to her elbow so she could look down into his face. As her gaze roamed over his features, a frown tugged at her brows before she gave a soft smile and leaned forward to kiss his lips.

As always, her taste and scent instantly triggered a rush of desire, but he didn't act on it just yet.

Leaning back again, she asked, "What has you worried?"

Beynon smoothed his large hand along her thigh and up over her hip to flatten against the small of her back and pull her a bit closer. As she lifted her bent knee until it rested against his groin, he struggled to put his concern into words.

"Roderick and Colin are optimistic, but I fear Max might be too entrenched in his life as a criminal."

His wife sighed as her expression turned thoughtful. "You might be right. But the fact that he's here at all still says something. I think he's trying."

"But to what end?"

Her eyes widened briefly, understanding his concern. "You don't trust him?"

Beynon made a gruff noise. "I don't know. He is a dangerous man who's likely done things in his life none of us could imagine. We can't just ignore that."

"Do your brothers have the same concerns?"

"Roderick might, but he's not saying anything outright. And I think Colin is so determined to win him over, he might overlook any signs of risk."

"And what does Caillie think?"

"She adores the man," Beynon muttered with obvious frustration. "Illicit lifestyle and all."

As his doubts swirled chaotically through his mind, Beynon forced them away. His wife's slim hand had started making lazy circles over his chest and the sensation was awakening other parts of his body.

Worries about Max could wait until morning. Right now, he had a warm and loving woman deserving of his attention. A low growl rumbled through his chest as he hauled her over on top of him. Her pale hair fell around them as she parted her thighs over his hips and stared into his eyes.

"Any tenderness I need to know about?" he asked as he began to knead the fullness of her bottom. Her prior pregnancy had come with an array of physical discomforts and he hated the thought of aggravating them even on accident.

Her smile was slow and sensual. "Nothing yet," she murmured huskily as she lowered her mouth back to his. "No need to hold back, husband. I want you to give me everything."

"Always, blodyn," he answered in a rough tone before cupping the back of her head and taking her mouth in a kiss of wicked passion and utter devotion.

HELLO READER,

I hope you liked Beynon and Anne's story as much I do! Continue reading for an excerpt from the next book in the series, Seducing the Knave, which is available for pre-order now.

All the Best,

Amy

Seducing the Knave

Book Three in the Wright Bastards series

Available for Pre-order Now!

https://buy.bookfunnel.com/mm4bhosp4d

Chapter One

March 1824
The Rose and Swan Inn
Northern Hampshire, England

Lady Elvina Fowler sat in the corner of the inn's common room. The table she'd chosen was near the window where she could watch the comings and goings of other travelers, which were few and far between. The deep hood of her cloak shadowed her face, but she still received an array of glances ranging from openly curious to somewhat discomfiting.

She ignored them all. There wasn't much she could do about the fact that she appeared distinctly out of place at the rural inn. Not that it was unheard of for wealthy travelers to pass through on their way to London, but certainly never a wealthy young lady *alone* and at such an ungodly early hour.

If she'd had a bit of forethought, she'd have switched out her rich velvet cloak for something a bit more common. But her departure had been rather sudden and quite desperate, considering she'd just been told by her wretched excuse for a guardian that she was to become his bride whether she wanted him or not.

She absolutely did *not* want him. And he'd known it well since she'd shouted exactly that right into the man's flushed and furious face a moment before he'd struck her hard enough to send her to the floor. As she'd looked up at him with shock and anger, she'd seen the pure contempt in his eyes and knew exactly what marriage to him would be like.

Unacceptable in every way.

Jasper Reed, her father's distant cousin who'd inherited the title and holdings entailed to the Marquess of Ilworth upon her parents' sudden deaths two years ago, was morally bankrupt in ways she hadn't known was possible.

She'd first met her cousin nearly two months after her beloved mother and father had been put to rest. Apparently, it had taken the estate solicitors some time to find the man and inform him of his sudden good fortune. From what she'd gathered, Mr. Reed had been discovered deep in his cups in a Parisian brothel.

That should have been the first clue to his dissolute nature, but she had been naïve back then. Barely eighteen, she'd lived a relatively charmed and sheltered life. Born into wealth and privilege, she'd also been an only child who'd been doted on by her loving parents. She couldn't recall a single day of her life that had been touched by adversity until her entire world had crashed around her when she received the news that a horrid accident had taken both parents from her in an instant.

Overwhelmed with grief, she'd barely taken note of her cousin's brief visit and awkwardly uttered condolences. What did she care for his discomfort when she was in pieces?

After only a few days at the Ilworth family seat in Hampshire, the new marquess who had also become her legal guardian had left her to her mourning, deciding he preferred to set up permanent residence in London rather than the country.

She'd been grateful at the time, needing the solitude and comforts of the home she'd grown up in to come to terms with her loss and the significant changes to her future. But soon, rumors and whispers had started to reach her in Surrey. The reprobate swiftly became infamous for his extravagant spending and endless debauchery and gossip on the new Lord Ilworth's wastrel behaviors soon seemed to be everywhere.

At first, Elle couldn't have cared less how the man preferred to comport himself. But the consequences of Jasper's recklessness effected more than his reputation as word of the many Ilworth properties and holdings falling to ruin and disrepair also became common knowledge.

In barely any time at all, the man had practically destroyed his entire inheritance along with the good-name her father and his father before him had built.

And now Jasper expected to gain access to her dowry by forcing her to marry him.

Utterly unacceptable. She would not abide by it. She'd been raised to expect so much more.

Thankfully, there were still servants in the home where she'd grown up who were loyal to the prior Marquess of Ilworth's daughter and though Jasper had locked her in her bedroom, he obviously hadn't considered she might heft herself over the balcony railing, leap to the branches of a nearby tree, and scurry through the garden in the middle of the night.

She might never have thought herself capable of such a feat either, but desperation bred a particular kind of courage in Lady Elvina Fowler and she'd never been more desperate than she was to escape the fate her guardian intended for her.

After walking for hours across the countryside under a moonless sky, convinced that every sound was an indication that her flight had been discovered, she finally reached the nearby village in the foggy hour before dawn. The first part of her impulsive escape had been accomplished but she was far from free just yet.

She needed to get to London, where she hoped to take refuge with her mother's long-time friend, Lady Gilchrist, until she could determine a proper course of action.

From what she knew of Jasper's habits, the man would likely be abed until mid-day, which gave her a head start of several hours, but it wasn't nearly enough. On a fast horse, he could catch up to her easily.

She had to continue her journey as quickly as possible.

Unfortunately, not a single traveler had arrived at the inn in the last hour. Everyone she'd seen had been a local farmer or villager and even they had been few and far between.

What if she failed to find someone heading to London? She could be stuck here all day. If Jasper found her...

As soon as the desperate thoughts started to crowd her mind, she shut them down.

She wouldn't give up so easily. She'd only just begun.

Taking a quick glance about the room, she wondered if one of the current patrons breaking their fast might be convinced to take her at least as far as the next village. Surely, someone could be convinced.

The sound of carriage wheels on cobblestone suddenly drew her attention back to the window just as an elegant private carriage rolled to a stop in the small courtyard. It was painted a bold green and black and the crest on the door looked slightly familiar, though she couldn't quite place it.

Holding her breath, she stared intently through the murky dawn as the carriage door opened before the liveried groom even had a chance to assist. A gentleman wearing a greatcoat and top hat emerged, stepping to the cobblestone in swift, efficient movements. He paused briefly to look around—first one way, then the other—as though assessing his surroundings. Then he said something aside to the groom before giving a short laugh and clapping the man on the back.

Elvina had never seen a gentleman act in such a way toward a servant—with such a familiar manner. And his stride as he headed toward the door of the inn was far too long and easy to be that of a true gentleman. Where were the stiff, straight shoulders? The measured steps? The arrogant head tilt?

The newcomer sauntered into the common room with the same bold nonchalance she'd witnessed through the window. More than curiosity and her pressing incentive to find someone willing to take her to London had her studying the gentleman rather intently. She couldn't help but sense something strangely...*strange* about him.

He was young—mid-twenties, she'd guess, which was still a number of years older than her own twenty years—and unexpectedly handsome in a careless sort of way with caramel-colored hair that fell in a haphazard fashion over a sturdy brow. His jaw was strong and square and he possessed deep-set eyes beneath slashing brows that angled slightly upward toward his temples. Beneath his black greatcoat, his eveningwear denoted wealth and refinement and was unexpectedly formal.

Despite the early morning hour, it was obvious that he'd left an important party of some sort when he began his journey. That he hadn't taken the time to change into something more appropriate for travel suggested he might be in a bit of a hurry.

When he paused in the entryway to remove his hat and scan the room just as he had the courtyard outside, Elvina got the impression he saw far more than most with that single sweeping glance. There was an odd sort of calculation in the otherwise careless action. As though he were instantly assessing everyone in the room. And just when she believed she passed beneath his notice, his gaze flickered sharply back to her location as she sat alone by the window.

A chill slid down her spine and she tensed before remembering she was safely concealed by her cloak. Though there was no way he could see her face as shadowed as it was beneath her hood and she kept her head turned slightly away from him so he wouldn't guess she was watching him...she still felt as though he peered right into her soul.

Despite his oddly casual demeanor, his gaze was that of a man who held total dominion over himself and his world. A man who answered to no one but himself. A king. A czar.

She just barely resisted the urge to shiver when his eyelids lowered to half-mast over his stare and a smirk curled one corner of his mouth.

She was tempted to be insulted by the man's reaction until she realized the futility of it. What did she care what the stranger thought of her cloaked and solitary form?

She continued to watch him as he turned toward an empty table not far from her own. Striding through the room, he seemed to both ignore and take note of every person he passed. Anyone he happened to make eye contact with quickly lowered their gaze or turned their attention elsewhere. Without saying a word or doing anything overt at all, he seemed to have taken command of the entire room.

Reaching the empty table, he tossed his hat to its surface and lowered himself to the chair tucked into the corner where he had a full view of the room. Within seconds, a buxom barmaid nearly tripped over herself to reach his side.

"Good mornin', sir, er, m' lord?" The serving girl stammered her way through the greeting, obviously flustered by his air of power. And his somewhat sculpted handsomeness, no doubt.

The gentleman gave a teeth-flashing grin as he leaned toward her to murmur something to the maid that had her blushing furiously as she glanced around in a furtive manner.

Elvina rolled her eyes. She'd heard of men like him. A rake. Unconscionable, obviously.

Making a clear effort to collect herself, the serving woman noted in a flirty tone, "Can I fetch ye something to break yer fast? We've a hearty sausage pie if you've a good appetite."

Another flash of teeth. "I do love warm pie."

He kept his voice low and the tone was sort of smoky and dark. For some reason, his reply caused the maid to giggle furiously behind her hand.

Elvina couldn't comprehend what was so amusing, but her curiosity was sharply piqued by the odd intonation of the man's speech. He did not speak like a member of the peerage. In fact, he sounded a lot like one of their old grooms who'd grown up in London's rough East End. Certainly not how she'd expect a man to sound when he dressed with such sophistication and traveled in a liveried and crested carriage.

How odd.

Doing her best not to appear to be eavesdropping, she had to strain her ears as the barmaid lowered her voice to a rather intimate, hopeful tone, "And will ye be stayin' with us a while?"

"Afraid not, luv. I've got to be getting back to London and just stopped in for fresh horses and the pleasure of a hot meal."

Elvina failed to hear the maid's reply as her heart started thundering in her ears.

Was this her opportunity? This irreverent rogue?

Could she really going to consider putting herself in this man's company for the remainder of her journey to London? He was an utter stranger who was clearly not at all what he appeared to be.

But if she didn't seize this chance to continue her journey, there was no guarantee she'd get another. And every minute mattered if she were to successfully reach London where she might have a chance of staying out of Jasper's reach until she determine a more permanent solution.

Maybe she wouldn't have to endure the man's company. Perhaps she could convince him to let her purchase the use of his carriage, leaving him behind to continue some other way?

As soon as the maid sauntered away from the gentleman's table with a deep swing of her generous hips, Elvina stood. Giving a tug on the hood of her cloak to ensure it stayed in place, she stepped forward in a focused stride. A stride that threatened to falter when the gentleman casually tilted his head to watch her approach with those intent and piercing eyes.

She suddenly felt utterly conspicuous. Naked and vulnerable despite her voluminous cover. Some urging inside her screamed to stop. To turn back and consider another option. But Elvina was nothing if not determined and she forcefully ignored the warning.

"Good morning," she said courteously as she reached the gentleman's table.

He leaned back in his chair and crossed an ankle over the opposite knee as he looked up at her with a smirk of arrogant amusement.

"That didn't take long." The tone was insolent.

Elvina lifted her chin to an imperious angle, though much of the effect was likely ruined by her concealing hood. "I beg your pardon?"

"Ye've been staring at me since I walked through the doors." His lips curled. "Did ye think I wouldn't notice?"

She ignored the way his overbold gaze and arrogant tone made her want to slap the taunting smirk from his handsome face. "I've a proposition for you," she noted coolly.

His grin widened as he splayed his hands atop hard muscled thighs. "Of course ye do. State yer business, luv. I haven't got all night."

Put off by his brusque and crude demeanor, Elvina straightened her spine and narrowed her gaze. Just because her current circumstances required this man's assistance didn't mean she had to sacrifice her dignity by accepting his utter lack of manners. "May I sit?"

A dark brow arched over his deep-set eyes, which she could now see were a dark gray color, not unlike unpolished antique pewter. Then he gave a short laugh and a dismissive wave of his hand as he used a booted foot to kick a chair out from under the table. "Suit yerself, princess."

She had to clench her teeth to stop herself from taking issue with his mocking attitude, but as she lowered herself into the chair, the odious man actually chuckled.

What in hell did he find so amusing?

"Look," she began haughtily, "I know you are traveling to London and intend to continue on after your breakfast. I am also heading to town, but find myself without a way to get there. I—"

"A mail coach should be along soon enough."

She ground her teeth at the interruption. But forced herself to reply. "The mail coach won't pass by until this afternoon. I cannot wait."

One slashing brow twitched upward. "Why?"

"The reason for my haste is my business."

"And what'll I get for the trouble of taking on unwanted company?"

"I'd actually prefer to purchase the *sole* use of your carriage."

His laugh then was brusque and humorless. "Not a chance."

Elvina tensed. Faced with a choice between having to wait for the mail coach or continuing her journey this morning—with this man—she truly had no choice. She just didn't like it very much.

"Fine," she retorted. "As an additional passenger, then. I'll pay you. Handsomely," she added, thinking of the near fortune in jewelry she'd managed to stash on her person before leaping from her bedroom terrace.

He spread his arms and flashed a grin. "Do I look like I need blunt?"

He didn't. Now that she was closer, she could see exactly how fine his attire was. Made of the best materials with expert stitching, he clearly had his share of wealth if not refinement. Yet, as she looked into his eyes, she sensed something there. Something acquisitive and calculating. Almost...predatory.

A wolf in sheep's clothing.

"No," she answered, "but you do look like a man who wouldn't turn down a worthy reward so easily earned."

His lips curled in an interesting fashion, forming something that was more of a snarl than a smirk. Her stomach twisted uneasily at the sight as a strange prickling teased her nape.

His words were low and weighted when he finally replied. "Very perceptive, princess. But I haven't made up me mind yet if ye're as *easy* as ye claim."

Elvina tensed her spine and lowered her chin. His tone was blatantly suggestive. Surely, he didn't dare to think...

"I offer payment in jewels, sir," she noted firmly. "Nothing more."

With another chuckle, he leaned forward and rested his forearms on the table. His eyes were sharp and steely as he responded in a throaty whisper. "Don't worry, luv. I don't fuck no-one 'til they're begging me for it."

His crude words caused a swift flare of alarm through her blood. Gasping despite her fierce desire to appear in control and unperturbed by this man, Elvina had to force herself not to flee his presence right then and there. Gentlemen simply didn't speak that way in the company of ladies. It was unsettling in the most intimate way but she couldn't decide if it was triggered by shock or fear or something else she couldn't quite name.

Be brave. You can do this. You have to do this.

"Then this remains a very simple transaction," she noted firmly. "I provide payment. You take me to London."

His gray eyes flickered.

There was a long pause. A heavy sigh. Then he leaned back again in his chair and offered a smile. "No."

Elvina opened her mouth to argue, but her words were stopped short by the sound of the inn door opening and multiple pairs of boots stomping across the worn wood floor. She turned to see three men standing at the entrance to the common room. Pure panic hit her in the chest with the force of a cannonball.

She swiftly looked back to the table, her chin tucked and her hands twisting in her lap.

He'd come for her!

Not Jasper specifically since he'd never do for himself what he could have someone do for him. But she easily recognized the men as his personal guard.

How had her absence been discovered so quickly?

Any minute now they could spy her across the room and force her to return with them.

She couldn't allow it.

Her frantic gaze darted to the man seated across from her. Despite obviously having noticed her distress at the new arrivals, his expression was one of dispassionate curiosity.

He had no intention of helping her.

She had to change his mind.

Reaching into the hidden pocket of her gown, she withdrew a priceless broach and set it in the center of the table.

"Get me out of here," she demanded in a low whisper. "Now."

Elvina held her breath as his pewter eyes spared just a flickering glance at the gleaming ruby surrounded by an array of tiny diamonds set in gold filigree.

And then it was too late.

She'd been so focused on the man across from her, she'd failed to notice her guardian's men approaching their table. All of a sudden, their large forms were there, looming over her. Her heart dropped and her stomach twisted.

"'Ello, mates," the man across from her drawled, a total lack of concern in his voice.

Before the guardsmen could reply, the one closest to her companion suddenly flipped from his feet to his back, landing hard on the floor with a loud crack, as though his legs had been swept from under him. She barely managed to register what was happening before the stranger stood and the second guard fell back against the table behind him, propelled by a fist to the face so swift and powerful she barely saw it executed. The last guard managed to swing a meaty fist toward his opponent, but it never connected. A sharp jab to the stomach had him doubling over before an elbow to the back sent him face first to the floor.

It all happened in the blink of an eye as Elvina sat frozen in shock.

As the guards groaned in pain, one of them struggling to drag himself off the floor, the stranger swept his top hat onto his head and held a hand to her.

"Right then. Let's go."

Still totally stunned, she glanced to the ring, but it was gone. She'd never even seen him reach for it.

"*Now*," he said as he sent a knee into the ribs of the guard who'd nearly reached his feet, sending him toppling toward another one.

She placed her white kid gloved hand into his black leather clad one and he roughly tugged her from her chair. His grip was tight as he took off toward a narrow hall at the back of the room. Lifting her skirts, she rushed to keep up with his long stride.

Dashing through the kitchen, he flashed a grin to the serving maid who stared at their sudden passing with wide eyes. "Change of plans, luv." He tossed a small sack of coins into her hand. "Anything ye can do to slow the brutes down would be appreciated," he noted with a wink before striding to the back door of the kitchen, pulling Elvina along behind.

Pre-order Seducing the Knave Now!

https://buy.bookfunnel.com/mm4bhosp4d

Follow me on Book Bub for notifications of sales and new releases!
https://www.bookbub.com/profile/amy-sandas?follow=true

Or sign up for my newsletter to receive regular updates on what I'm up to.
https://www.amysandas.com/contactus

Don't miss out!

Visit the website below and you can sign up to receive emails whenever Amy Sandas publishes a new book. There's no charge and no obligation.

https://books2read.com/r/B-A-PMBH-GAVUB

BOOKS 2 READ

Connecting independent readers to independent writers.

Also by Amy Sandas

Regency Rogues Box Set

Wright Bastards
Tempting the Earl
Enticing the Devil
Seducing the Knave
Charming the Rogue

Standalone
Kiss Me, Macrae

Watch for more at amysandas.com.

About the Author

Amy grew up in a small dairy town in northern Wisconsin and after earning a Liberal Arts degree from the University of Minnesota – Twin Cities, she eventually made her way back to Wisconsin (though to a slightly larger town) and lives there with her husband and three children.

She writes Regency and Western Historical Romance about dashing and sometimes dangerous men who know just how to get what they want and women who may be reckless, bold, and unconventional, but who always have the courage to embrace all that life and love have to offer. The rest of her time is spent trying to keep up with the kids and squeeze in some stolen moments with her husband.

Read more at amysandas.com.

Ingram Content Group UK Ltd.
Milton Keynes UK
UKHW010739150523
421757UK00001B/100

9 798201 275587